ESCORTING THE ROYAL

THE ESCORT COLLECTION, BOOK FIVE

LEIGH JAMES

Copyright © 2021 by Leigh James

All rights reserved.

No part of this book may be reproduced in any form or by any electronic or mechanical means, including information storage and retrieval systems, without written permission from the author, except for the use of brief quotations in a book review.
v.print.6.21.2021

Cover Design © 2021 by Cormar Covers.

Sign up for Leigh's mailing list at http://www.leighjamesauthor.com/subscribe.

CLIVE

I READ the text from my friend again. *I have the perfect solution.*

There is no such thing, I texted back. *This is the wedding from hell. There's no 'perfect' in hell!*

Chase immediately responded. *You might as well have fun while you burn.* Shrugging emoji.

The sound of heavy breathing interrupted my conversation; bloody Herbert was still chasing me. I tucked the phone into my pocket as he advanced. The steward was short, his stubby legs buckling beneath his round belly as he attempted to power-walk toward me across the South Lawn.

"Your Highness." Herbert sounded desperate and perhaps as though he might cry.

"I'm still ignoring you." I headed toward the palace, and the little shit struggled to keep up.

"Your Highness, *please*. The King said that you *must* give a response—"

"Tell him my response is that he should stuff it." I grinned, picturing a red-faced Herbert relaying my message to the King. "Tell him I'm tired of his commands and that I've gone rogue."

"Oh...dear. Oh my." The steward fretted as he chased after me. "What about Princess Isabelle? What shall I tell *her*?"

I stopped walking and faced him. Herbert, my father's top steward, was one of my least favorite people at the palace. He'd been tattling on me since I was a little boy. "Tell her I said *congratulations*, you imbecile."

He opened his mouth as if to speak. Then, after a moment, in which he looked pretty confused, he closed it.

I took that as my cue to escape—I turned on my heel and fled. This time Herbert didn't follow me.

Maybe, after all these years, he was finally smartening up.

* * *

The respite didn't last long. My younger sister, Izzie, threw open the door to my study. "What do you *mean*—congratulations? You already *said* congratulations! I don't need your bloody congratulations—I need your cooperation!"

I arched an eyebrow as she slammed the door behind her, dramatically collapsing into the armchair across from me. My sister glared. Her chocolate eyes narrowed as she looked me up and down. Her dark-brown curls tumbled over her riding jacket. She smelled like fresh air, but her expression was dark, like a basement—or perhaps a tomb, where she might very much like to bury me.

"Hello, Izzie." My feet were up on my desk; I didn't bother to take them down.

"Don't you dare *hello* me!" Her eyes flashed. "Father said you were making idle threats."

"I'm not sure I would characterize them as idle." I smiled at her without warmth. "What can I do for you?"

Izzie groaned. She'd lost weight for the wedding, and her cheeks looked hollowed out. I'd feel sorry for her if she wasn't my nemesis—and also, our father's little puppet.

She sat forward. "Will you *please* come to the wedding? *Please?* I am literally begging you."

I could tell she meant it; Izzie never begged. "I told you I would come to the wedding," I said. "But on my terms, not yours."

She lifted her chin. "I don't think it's too much to ask you to find a proper date."

"You're right. It's not." When she looked relieved, I quickly added, "That is, if I *had* a proper date. But I don't. I'm not seeing anyone, and I won't do it just for the press. I told you, I'm done playing the game."

"D'you think—for *once*—that you could put our family first?" Izzie's voice shook.

"I've been putting our family first since the day I was born." As heir to the throne, it wasn't as if I had much choice. "Whether I like it or not."

"This isn't about you, Clive." She shook her head. "It's about the biggest day of *my* life. I don't ask you for much—"

"All everyone does around here is ask—"

"*I* don't ever ask you for anything. Not anymore." Izzie's cheeks turned pink. "I gave up a long time ago. But I'm asking you for this: please come to the wedding and bring a date. That's all the reporters have been hounding me for. They don't even care about my *dress*. All they want to know is who Prince Clive is bringing. You know how unrelenting they can be—it's been impossible."

"Then it's time we stop giving *in* to them." My temper rose. Over the past fifteen years, the press's obsession with our family had become unbearable.

When I'd been growing up, the constant public scrutiny had been a nuisance; with the internet, it had become an all-consuming pain in the ass, one requiring continuous care and feeding.

"I understand how you feel, but the situation is what it is," Izzie said, her voice firm. "You can't hide from this by going off and digging a ditch in some remote village."

"That's hardly fair." Even though I'd vastly prefer to flee to a remote village and dig a ditch.

Izzie sighed. "My wedding's in three weeks. We can't change the world in three weeks. Everyone wants to see the prince with a date—it's been years since you've been linked to anyone. They have a *right* to be curious. Whoever you marry will be queen someday..."

"I disagree." My shoulders tensed. "Just because I'm a prince doesn't mean my personal life is for public consumption."

"You're a public *figure*. You're the heir to the throne. That makes it the public's business." Izzie frowned. "Hey... What about Freya Wilson? She's already invited. I know she'd love to hear from you."

Freya Wilson was a reed-thin, auburn-haired socialite who'd been circling me like a shark for years. My cousin, the Duke of Clifton, had asked her out several times. Finally, she'd flatly refused, informing him that a duke held no interest for her; she wanted a prince. "I'll pass."

"Fine." Izzie jumped up from her seat. "I don't care *who* you bring. Just find someone acceptable. Figure it out soon—she needs to be vetted. I promise I won't ask you for anything ever again."

I snorted.

"You really are a prat, you know that?" Izzie hustled to the door, giving me one backward glance. It was the most honest expression I'd seen on her face in years: a mixture of hurt and hatred.

"If you don't come up with someone by the end of the day, I'm calling Freya." She slammed the door for dramatic effect.

Fuck. Izzie drove me crazy. She was both my father's puppet—always conspiring with him—and also the press's darling. Izzie always played the game. I don't know how she had the stomach for it, but she did. She was even marrying the most boring man on the planet, George Smith—even his name was boring!—because my father had arranged the match.

I, on the other hand, had lost my taste for conformity. Like in a fairytale, I'd consumed a drop of poison and would never be the same.

I'd had a girlfriend, once. I'd met her at university. She was Lithuanian, from a working-class family, and was attending uni on scholarship. She'd been so loyal and sweet—that is, until my father paid her to break things off with me.

Much to my surprise, she took the money and ran.

In her defense, it was an *awful* lot of money. But that experience took away all my illusions that I would ever lead a normal, happy life. Who was I ever going to be able to trust? My father believed he was in control of my life and that it was his duty to make choices for me.

What I wanted didn't matter. What mattered was being a royal—our image, our lineage, our removed and superior position with the people of our tiny country.

Everything was a duty. Even my sister's wedding.

But I was heir to the throne. So one day, I would be King. And no matter my mixed emotions about my family, I truly loved my country. So, therefore, I would do my best to serve the people of Astos.

My sister was right. I needed to go to her wedding, and I needed a proper date because it was customary. I sighed and took out my phone, re-reading Chase Layne's text. *You might as well have fun while you burn.*

You know, he might be on to something.

Send me the number for the agency, I wrote.

My sister wanted me to bring a date. So…what if I hired one?

Chase sent me the contact information immediately.

I'd been friends with the American quarterback for years; we'd met ages ago at Wimbledon. I'd never met his second wife, but I'd heard she was lovely and that they were incredibly happy.

I'd also heard she'd been his escort.

I wasn't looking for a wife—I was looking for a date. I was *also* looking to point a big middle finger right at my father's face, even if he never knew the truth…

I took a deep breath. And then I called AccommoDating.

"We will test her for sexually transmitted diseases," the Madame purred. "I guarantee clean girls who follow strict birth-control protocols. You can relax about being intimate with her and enjoy yourself."

I groaned. I hadn't been with anyone in a long time, but I would *not* have sex with the escort. Paying women for sex was human trafficking in my book. I wouldn't take part in something like that—I wouldn't support it.

But would I pay for her to pretend to be my date? *Hell yes.* Anything was better than being trapped with Freya Wilson!

"I don't plan on using that particular set of services," I said quickly. "But thanks for letting me know."

"Really?" The Madame, Elena, surprised me by not sounding at all surprised. "Well—please remember that you have the option. You might change your mind when you meet her. My agency employs some of the most gorgeous women in the world."

"I just need someone who can behave in a civilized manner. No binge-drinking, no drugs, nothing inappropriate." My cousin, the Duke of Clifton, had once brought a young woman to one of our parties. She'd had too much champagne and attempted to swing from the chandelier. They had banned the Duke from the palace for a month after that…

"I think I have *just* the girl. She's young, early twenties. Is that acceptable?"

"Yes."

"And she's blond—platinum blond. Long, thick hair, athletic, gorgeous skin…she's quite stunning."

My cock was stirring. *Fuck.* I was a sucker for long, platinum hair—the Madame had done her research.

"She sounds perfect. And although your fee is exorbitant, I've heard good things about your services. This has to remain *completely private*. I'll take care of the details on our end, but you need to make sure the woman you send to Astos is clear on these terms. I'm paying her a lot of money, but it's a onetime deal. If she comes back at some point, looking for more or threatening to sell her story to the press, she will be *very* sorry. Are we clear?"

"Crystal, Your Highness." Elena sighed, a happy sound. "I am *so* glad you chose AccommoDating. Trust me. You won't be disappointed."

"You'd better be right about that." I hung up before she could tell me more about the hot escort.

I needed a proper date. I needed no strings. I did *not* need to be fantasizing about having sex with a hooker. The very last thing I needed was a messy entanglement, or worse, setting myself up for being blackmailed.

Hiring an escort for my sister's wedding was bad enough.

And "bad enough" was…good enough for now.

TARRYN

My client wriggled his pale, hairy ass in the air. Then he waited.

I sighed. I would never get used to this. No matter what the Madame said, *no*. Just…no.

My client popped the pacifier out of his mouth. "Tell me I'm a bad boy!"

I gritted my teeth. "You're a bad boy." *The worst.* Honestly, this guy was a *freak*. He was wearing a freaking bonnet!

Being an escort meant you shouldn't judge—it was part of the code. Our clients had their hang-ups. There were always reasons for it, reasons best left alone. But the internet had just made everything worse because now there were chat rooms. Chat rooms gave people

Ideas. Bad Ideas. Like…bonnets. And pacifiers. And being spanked by an escort.

"Aren't you going to spank the bad boy?" My client sounded gleefully hopeful.

I sighed again. "Of course I will—you *bad* boy."

He was paying me two thousand dollars! It was the least I could do.

I CALLED Elena on my way to the T. "Do not *ever* give that John to me again. He made me spoon-feed him applesauce!"

"Honey, they are *all* babies." The Madame sighed. "You already know that. Plus, he pays cash."

"I don't care. He gives me the creeps."

"They all give you the creeps," she said, which was true.

"If you want to keep working for my service," Elena continued, "you're going to have to toughen up. My daughters said they want to take horseback riding lessons. Do you know how much private riding lessons cost?"

"No, Elena, I don't." Horseback riding was decidedly outside my budget.

"Of course, I understand, I understand." But Elena

seemed distracted. "Listen, can you come into the office later? I might have an assignment for you—a lucrative one."

That got my attention—I stopped walking. "How lucrative?"

"Private-horseback-lessons lucrative," she purred. "It's a top job. I've narrowed it down between you and one other girl. Blond versus brunette. Come in, and we'll see, okay? You might want to adjust your attitude—this could be your big break." She hung up before I could ask more.

I hustled to the T. Sometimes AccommoDating, the escort service where I'd recently begun working, got seriously rich clients. There were rumors that some of the girls had earned up to a million dollars *for one assignment*. I would spoon-feed a *baboon* for a million dollars!

I took the train home, standing with my back against the wall, paying close attention to my surroundings. I never scrolled on my phone while on the train. I never read a book. Instead, I stayed alert, making sure no one got too close to me and that no one was watching.

The T reached my stop, and I climbed the stairs from the platform carefully, confirming that I was alone. I checked the street before I went up the stairs to my apartment, the third floor of a tri-level with a sagging porch. *All clear.*

I always paid close attention, and I constantly scrutinized my surroundings. I had to.

"Mom?" I turned the key and went inside, deadbolting the door. "Mmm, it smells so good in here." My mother had made lasagna, one of my favorites.

My mother came around the corner, drying her hands with a dishtowel. She looked like she always did—fabulous. My mom was blond, pretty, and forty. People often thought she was my sister. Since she'd had me at sixteen, it made sense.

"Hi, honey." She smiled at me.

I peered past her. "Where's Ellie?"

"Shh, she's still down for her nap."

"Oh." I fought the urge to pout. "Will she be up soon? I have an appointment."

"Don't worry about it—she knows how much you love her." My mom patted my arm. "I took her to the swings this morning, and I think they tired her out."

My heart twisted. "She loves the swings." I didn't want to think about what *I'd* been doing while sweet Ellie was at the playground...

My mother narrowed her eyes at me. "You okay?"

"I'm fine," I said, brushing the question off. "I'm going to go take a shower, okay?"

"Sure, honey." God bless my mother. She didn't pry,

and she didn't judge. What she specialized in was *worrying*. And cooking.

Mom disappeared back to the kitchen, which she commanded with fierce intensity. The way my mother showed love was through food. Good thing I had a fast metabolism because she loved me a *lot*.

I peered into Ellie's darkened room as I headed for the shower. She was in her little toddler bed, on her side, her chest rising and falling. Her blond hair fanned out over her pillow. She looked like an angel, a gift from God. Which, I supposed, she was.

She was *my* angel. She was also my secret.

ACCOMMODATING, Inc. was located in Boston's trendy South End, a far cry from my apartment in a run-down section of Dorchester. The office was airy and elegant, but I still hated it.

I hated it because I loathed what I did for a living. But have you ever tried to pay over three-hundred-thousand dollars' worth of medical bills with waitressing tips? Good luck with *that*! Someday I'd go back to school and get my degree. Someday I'd have a proper job, and I wouldn't have to spank men with hairy asses for a living. Someday.

But as I checked in at the front desk of Accommo-Dating, I knew today was not that day.

"Hello, Tarryn." Elena came out from her office, a broad smile on her face. "Thanks for coming in."

"Sure thing."

Elena, the Madame, was tall and imposing. With her black spiked heels, she stood well over six feet. Today she wore an onyx pantsuit, square-framed glasses, and her signature maroon lipstick. Her short hair was pushed off her face. I wasn't sure how old Elena was. Her daughters were in high school; that was the only detail about her private life she'd ever shared with me.

None of the other girls knew how Elena had gotten into the business. It was a bit of a mystery.

"Come on. I need to discuss a few things with you." We headed into the back room, where we kept racks of clothes, shoes, and accessories. One of the perks of working at AccommoDating was the clothes. Elena shopped for us constantly so that her employees had stylish, expensive outfits to wear on assignment. She wanted us to look good, and to fulfill an expectation: a beautiful, perfect woman, the best that money could buy.

Business was booming. Clients paid a lot of money to spend time with one of AccomoDating's escorts.

"So." Elena's heels clicked as she turned to me. "Elisabeth is going to arrive in a few minutes. But I wanted you here, first."

"Okay...?" Elisabeth was the agency's top escort. Like Elena, she was tall and imposing. Her long chestnut hair cascaded over her shoulders. Elisabeth had a body that wouldn't quit—she was so beautiful, it was hard not to stare.

"You know I don't like to play favorites," Elena continued, "but Elisabeth has worked for me for a long time. She's very professional. She's earned my trust."

I had a feeling I knew what was coming next.

"*You*, on the other hand, have been giving me some trouble. What's with all the complaints? The client I sent you today is a repeat customer. He always pays cash, he tips generously, and he never even asks for penetration." Elena frowned at me. "So *what* is the problem?"

"As relieved as I was that the client didn't ask for penetration..." My cheeks burned as I cleared my throat. "I still found his requests off-putting."

"The spanking?" Elena threw up her hands. "Is spanking some sort of a big deal for you?"

"No. It's just the..." I fidgeted. "It's just the *yuck* factor. Like, what is *wrong* with these men? Who wants to suck on a binky and get spanked when you're forty?"

"Lots of people." Elena looked incredulous. "You

haven't been doing this for very long, so maybe kink is a little new to you. But our clients use our service because they want to express their preferences freely and without fear of judgment. Do you understand that?"

I nodded. But understanding it and having to deal with it were two very different things…

"Part of the reason I asked you here is *because* you're new. I think a fresh face is better suited for this client. Elisabeth is fabulous, but she's been doing this for a long time."

"Who is the client?" I was dying to know.

"I can't tell you that. Not yet." Elena pursed her lips. "This is a very delicate assignment, Tarryn. It's extremely prestigious—there's a *ton* of money on the line. So I need a complete professional. There is zero room for errors."

At the mention of a ton of money, my heart rate kicked up. "I'll do a good job, Elena. You won't be sorry if you pick me for this."

Elena's gaze raked over me. "You've got the right look. But I need the right *attitude*."

I licked my lips. "I can have the right attitude—I promise I'll do better. The client today didn't know I thought he was weird," I said quickly. "I'm good at hiding my emotions. I'm *definitely* interested in the assignment."

"Who wouldn't be?" Elena grabbed a tablet from a nearby table and started tapping on it. "I've been running the numbers. If we meet the client's parameters, this job will earn the agency an *insane* amount of money. And the girl who completes the job will earn seven-hundred-thousand dollars."

I felt faint. "Seven hundred…?"

"That's right. Seven-hundred *thousand* dollars."

My heart thundered in my chest. "I'll take it! I'll do anything!"

"You might have to." Elena pulled her glasses down on her nose. "If *this* client wants you to spank him, or spoon-feed him, or play with his balls, you better freaking spank him and spoon-feed him—*while* you play with his balls—and act like you *like* it! I'm not kidding."

"*I'm* not kidding! I'll be freaking flawless for seven-hundred-thous—"

Just as I was blurting out the number—the incredible, impossible, life-changing number—Elisabeth strutted in, her chestnut hair bouncing in waves against her ample chest. She eyed us with interest.

Not on my watch, bitch. That money was *mine*.

"Please," I said to Elena, keeping my voice low. "I *need* this. I can't even tell you how much. I *promise* you I'll do everything that he asks, and I'll smile while I do it. *Please.*"

My palms were sweating. This assignment would change my life—and Ellie's life. And my mother's.

"Fine." Elena's tone was calm. "But you are going to owe me for this one. Are we clear?"

I nodded. "Crystal."

"You fly out on Friday. We have a lot of work to do between now and then. So sit tight while I deal with Elisabeth." Elena clicked off toward the other escort.

Fly out? I wondered where I was going…and then I remembered I didn't care. All that mattered was the money. So. Much. Money. *Holy crap.*

I heard Elena and Elisabeth talking. "I'm so glad you came in—I have a top assignment for you," the Madame purred. "It's a gentleman coming to town from Manhattan. He's a *billionaire*. He's looking for a date for the weekend."

Elisabeth tilted her chin. "How much?"

Elena beamed at her. "Seventy-five thousand for two nights."

"Not bad." Elisabeth tossed her hair. "I'll take it."

As recently as one hour ago, I would've done just about anything for seventy-five-thousand dollars. But *that* would only be a drop in the bucket of what I owed. For years, our three-hundred-thousand-dollar debt loomed over us like a volcano, always about to erupt if I missed another payment. It was an *impossible* sum. It might as well have been three million, three billion. I could *never* get ahead.

But now, this was a chance of a lifetime…

I sat and silently prayed while I waited for Elena. *Thank you, God.*

Maybe sometimes, even sinners caught a break.

TARRYN

"Unfreakingbelievable!" Vivian slid into the open spot next to me. Her toned legs flashed against her navy minidress. "You're rich!"

"*Shh!*" I nudged her. "And no, I'm not. Not exactly."

My friend shook her head, her long, silky black hair flying. "Are *so*. I always knew you were going to make it."

"Don't tell any of the other girls about the money, okay?" I looked around, making sure that no one could overhear us. "Elena would have my head. This whole assignment's confidential."

"I know—I've got you, T. Don't worry." Viv winked at me, her big mink lash extension somehow making it look pretty.

Vivian was the one friend I'd made at AccommoDating. At twenty-five, she was a year older than me and much more worldly. Vivian was drop-dead gorgeous. Her mother was Indian, and her father was Korean; she had lustrous, caramel-colored skin, jet black hair, dark, sparkling eyes, and a wicked grin. Viv was petite, a fact which she offset daily with five-inch platforms—which she wore even to the grocery store.

Even though she was tiny, her nickname at the agency was The Dominator.

"Guess who *I* get to go spank while you're jetting off on your mystery assignment?" Viv cracked her knuckles. "Binky, your client from earlier this week."

Vivian always had nicknames for the clients. Most of them were pretty lewd.

"Binky?" I frowned at her. "His butt is white and hairy, just FYI."

She sighed. "Oh, I know all about it. I've had him before. He couldn't handle me, so he asked for someone more gentle. But now he's begging for the master again." She waggled her eyebrows. "I'll whip him into shape. I'm bringing my paddleboard. I might even bring a strap-on!"

I almost choked, and she laughed. "You're going to have to chill, girlfriend. What if your mystery date wants you to peg *him*?"

Good thing I was coughing; I couldn't begin to answer that.

"For an escort, you really are a prude—you know that?" Vivian inspected her freshly manicured nails, which were a bright, sparkly blue. "I can't believe you're going away for ten days. It's going to be boring around here. I'm going to miss you! It's just going to be Binky and me."

"I'll miss you, too." I meant it. Vivian made me laugh; plus, she was the only person I could be mostly honest with. "We'll have to text every day, okay?"

"Of course." Viv patted my arm. "I can't believe Elena *still* hasn't told you anything about this assignment—sheesh. It's *really* top secret, huh?"

I shrugged. "I guess so."

Vivian nodded towards my bags, which were neatly packed for the airport. "Show me the dress again. It's, like, *unbelievable*."

"Again?" But I hopped up and eagerly grabbed the garment bag. This was the third time I'd shown Vivian the dress, but she clearly loved it as much as I did. I unzipped the bag and carefully pulled it out.

The gown was pale lavender, with white-lace overlay, long and fitted. I'd seen the price tag: a whopping nine-thousand dollars.

"Oooh. It's the prettiest dress I've ever seen. It's

so *demure*." Vivian's eyes looked dreamy as she stared at it. "You're going to look like a princess in that."

"Yeah. *Ha*." But I reverently fingered the delicate lace. I'd never seen such a beautiful piece of clothing. When I'd tried it on for Elena, she'd clapped a hand over her heart and declared me "a vision in lavender."

As though I'd conjured her with my thoughts, the Madame hustled into the room. "Tarryn, there you are. We need to get going to the airport. Are you ready?" Her gaze flicked over me.

I smiled, hoping to mask my nerves. "I'm good to go." I'd worn the outfit she'd picked out for me: slim black pants, a black blazer, a fitted white tee, and an enormous, gauzy gray scarf. I also had a brand-new designer bag and sunglasses. The faux-casual outfit cost over three thousand dollars; I'd cut the tags off myself.

This was some rich client. Even my travel ensemble had to be on-point.

Elena seemed pleased. "You look good."

"*Good?*" Vivian snapped her gum. "She looks perfect, like a freaking actress!"

"True." Elena scowled at my friend. "How many times do I have to tell you not to chew gum in the office, Vivian?"

Vivian blew a bubble. When it popped, she said, "A few."

The Madame rolled her eyes and turned her attention back to me. "Do you have your passport?"

"Yes."

"Your wallet and the cash I gave you?"

I nodded. My heart started thudding. This was really happening.

"Your birth-control pills?"

I rolled my eyes. "Of *course*."

"Jesus Elena, she's not some hack!" Vivian complained.

"I have to check," Elena reminded us. "Fine. I'll have the bags brought out to the car. Then, I'll accompany you to the airport."

I looked at her, surprised. Elena rarely left the office.

"I need to tell you more about the assignment." Elena gave Vivian a quick look. "In *private*."

Vivian snapped her gum again. "Don't mind me, I'm just going to get ready to whack Binky's white ass." She hopped up and pulled me in for a surprisingly strong hug. "Have fun. Be safe. Text me *every* day. And remember, this John's lucky to have you, okay? He's the luckiest bastard alive."

I squeezed her back. She smelled like bubblegum and some sort of essential oil, spicy and sexy. "I'll miss you, Viv."

She wiped at her eyes when she pulled back.

"Do *not* make me run my makeup. See ya." She sniffled as she sashayed away, minidress swishing.

"I just have to wrap a few things up—I'll see you out front." Elena turned on her heel and clicked off.

Dismissed, I headed outside to the waiting Town Car. The driver opened the door for me. As I slid inside the cool interior, my nerves finally got the better of me. I glanced at my phone. My mom had sent a picture of Ellie, her blond curls tumbling over her shoulders, a smile on her face as she waved at the camera. I was blessed that my mother could take care of my daughter for the next ten days while I was on assignment; still, my heart twisted as I looked at the image. I'd never been away from Ellie for this long.

Then I reminded myself that I was doing this for *her*. For us.

Before I was ready, Elena joined me. Then the driver sped off toward Logan Airport.

"Are you ready?" she asked.

"Yes." *No.*

"Buckle up," the Madame said, "because this is about to get *really* interesting."

Elena put up the privacy screen, then turned to inspect me. "You look wonderful, Tarryn. I truly believe you're perfect for this assignment. Vivian was right when she said you looked like an actress. You're stunning."

"Thank you." I swallowed hard. "Are you going to tell me more about the client, now? And maybe where I'm flying to?"

"Open your phone's settings, please." Elena nodded as I took it out. "I need you to turn your location services *off*. I also need you to promise me that the confidentiality contract you signed earlier means something to you. You can't even tell your family where you're headed. You can't tell Vivian, either. Not yet."

"Okay…" I did what she asked with my settings and then frowned at her. "Is this job for the secret service or something?" I was only half-kidding.

"You *will* have security once you're on site, but the client is taking care of that." Elena pursed her maroon lips as she rifled through her bag. She pulled out her phone and started tapping on it. "I just texted you your plane ticket—it's for a round-trip first-class flight to Astos."

My brow furrowed. That name was familiar, but I couldn't quite place it… "Is that in Europe? I'm sorry, Elena, I haven't traveled much."

She nodded. "It's a tiny little country—you never would have had heard of it, except for the royal family. They're quite famous."

"Oh—of course—Princess Izzie!" I'd forgotten the name of the country, but even *I* didn't live under that much of a rock. The royals were famous, with all sorts of buzz about Princess Izzie's upcoming wedding.

"Isn't she marrying a banker or something?" Unfortunately, I couldn't remember much about the groom. He seemed bland compared to the gorgeous, dazzling princess with the chestnut curls and the mega-watt smile.

"Correct. Princess Isabelle is marrying an investment banker. Her wedding is next week." Elena watched me carefully.

"Right. I read about it—it's going to be the wedding of the century."

"So." Elena tilted her head. "You're flying to Astos."

I nodded. "You said that."

"You're flying to Astos *because*…" The Madame lifted her eyebrows as if waiting for something to click for me.

When I said nothing, she sighed. "You're going to be a guest at the royal wedding. That's what the lavender dress is for."

I couldn't help it: I laughed. "Elena, *stop*. Just tell me who my date is already!"

"It's Prince Clive. Princess Izzie's older brother—heir to the throne of Astos."

"Elena." I laughed so hard I snorted. "I didn't know you had a sense of humor!"

"And *I* didn't realize that you were as dumb as a brick."

That made me stop laughing. We stared at each other.

My stare turned into a gape. "You're not kidding."

She shook her head almost imperceptibly. "No, I'm not. Although the fact that you just snorted has me almost wishing I was."

Prince Clive. He was on the cover of a magazine I'd seen recently—The Sexiest Man Alive!

"How…?" Stunned, I couldn't get more words out.

"His Highness is friends with a former client of mine—one of my most successful matches." The glimmer of a smile lit Elena's face. "The prince needs a date for his sister's wedding. He's not interested in any sort of personal entanglement. He wanted someone beautiful and smart, with no strings attached. I happen to know from doing some digging that he prefers his female companions blond and charming. You fit the bill, Tarryn."

"But I'm a…*you know*." I blinked at her. "And he's a *prince*."

Elena slid her glasses down. "He's the one who hired

you. So if it's not a problem for him, it's not a problem. Period."

"Right—I understand that. I guess what I meant was, is his *family* okay with this arrangement? Princess Izzie doesn't mind that an escort's coming to her wedding?"

"Their security team will vet you, which will assure them you're not a security threat," Elena said. "Prince Clive's already begun the process."

That was a non-answer, but my mind started racing so fast I couldn't focus. I was going to the wedding of the century. Thousands—*millions?*—of people would watch Princess Izzie's ceremony on television. People might see me.

He might see me... Oh my god. This could be bad.

"Is everything all right?" Elena inspected me.

"Of course." I smiled to mask my mounting panic. *Don't think about it.* "It's just a lot to take in."

"You got a little pale there, for a second." She sounded concerned.

Worrying about the past wouldn't help me with the present. "I'm fine." I forced a smile. "So... How are we going to pull this off?"

"This isn't the agency's first high-profile client. We've done this many times before—although perhaps not on this scale. I have it handled." Elena tapped on her phone again. "I just texted you a link to a secure site.

Read everything in the file—you'll find exactly what you need: your backstory, information about His Highness and the family, details about the wedding."

My phone buzzed, and I opened the email she'd sent me.

Then I started reading about my new John: Prince Charming himself.

TARRYN

"Read it now—it's brief. Then we can talk about it," Elena said. "The link will delete itself in thirty minutes. So we aren't leaving any trace of this assignment."

I felt a little like Jason Bourne. *The link would delete itself in thirty minutes?* What on *earth*? But I didn't have time to think about it—I got busy reading the file as the Town Car snaked through the downtown traffic.

Name: Tarryn Christine Clayton
Occupation: Graduate Student at Boston University
Family: Father deceased, mother lives in Massachusetts, no siblings
Program: Computer Information Systems

I looked up. "Elena—this isn't going to work. I don't know the first thing about computers."

"No one does. That's exactly the point!" She waved me off. "No one is going to ask you about your studies because no one even knows what that major *is*. Their eyes will glaze over at the very mention of it. Keep reading."

Client: Prince Clive Harrison Wesley Richard Thomas

My head was spinning. "Is Thomas his *last* name?"

Elena shrugged. "Don't worry about it. You will refer to him as *Your Highness* or *Prince Clive* unless he instructs you otherwise."

How You Met Prince Clive: At a bar on his last trip to America, in October.

"At a *bar?*" I wrinkled my nose. "You really think the royal family is going to approve of *that?*"

"How else is a foreign prince supposed to meet an American graduate student?" Elena shrugged. "It was two-dollar margarita night. The prince was enjoying himself. You were the prettiest young woman there. You got to talking about American football, and you hit it off."

I frowned and went back to reading. I wasn't sure what was less believable—the idea that I'd met the prince at a bar or that we'd been talking about *football*. I'd never watched a football game in my life! Although, of course, like every person in Boston—except for those who felt betrayed by him—I loved former Patriots quarterback Tom Brady. I mean, who wouldn't? He had that smile, the gorgeous wife, he doted on his kids...

I shook my head and kept reading.

Relationship Status Pre-Wedding: Casual. New. The Prince is reluctant to introduce you to the public. Still, he wanted to bring someone he likes and cares about to the royal wedding.

Relationship Status Post-Wedding: Broken up. After the wedding bonanza, you realized that living in the spotlight wasn't for you. The split is amicable.

"So that's it?" I asked. "I go for the next ten days, attend the wedding, and come home?"

"Everyone will believe it was a brief relationship, one that didn't work out." Elena nodded. "His staff will issue an official statement. After that, you won't have to worry about a thing."

"Huh. It almost sounds too easy."

"Speaking of being too easy." Elena pursed her lips.

"His Highness made it very clear to me: he's not interested in having sexual relations with you."

I blinked at the Madame. "What?"

"You heard me." She arched an eyebrow. "Prince Clive is not the sort of man who pays for sex. This is strictly a business arrangement."

"So why were you asking me whether I was taking my birth control pills?"

"Because I think when he takes one look at you, he's going to change his mind," Elena said smoothly. "But I wanted you to be prepared. He might not initiate any physical contact with you."

"Fine with me." Although Prince Clive was hot and I *was* an escort, I didn't exactly enjoy having sex with strangers. So ten days in Astos, sex-free, sounded just fine to me!

I tapped through the rest of the file, committing it to memory, and then closed the link. "I have more questions."

"I'd be worried if you didn't," the Madame quipped.

"First of all, you said I'd be vetted. Don't you think the royal staff will figure out that I'm not really a graduate student?"

Again, a smile ghosted her face. "This is where it gets sort of fun. The prince has resources we can only dream about. He was able to make a few calls—they officially enrolled you in this program at BU. They have a transcript for you and everything. You made the Dean's list last semester, by the way."

"Woah." I licked my lips. "But what about my name? It's my legal name, Elena. They'll be able to dig something up on me, eventually."

I held my breath. It *was* my legal name. But it wasn't the name I used growing up. Would his security team be able to figure that out? What would they find if they did?

Elena looked thoughtful. "You know, it's interesting—I had my tech gal do a deep dive on you. You aren't anywhere on the internet."

I nodded. "I told you that when you hired me—I don't do social media. Never have."

She scrutinized me. "It's the rare person you can't find *anything* on. Not an address, not one trace of an online footprint."

I shrugged, keeping my expression neutral. "That's good, right? That way, clients like Binky can't stalk me, and the Prince doesn't have to worry about the press digging things up. So it's win-win, don't you think?"

"I truly hope so." Elena's voice was deadly serious. "Don't fuck this up for any of us, Tarryn. My girls really want those riding lessons."

I raised my right hand. "I swear to you I'll follow the

contract to the letter. Whatever Prince Clive wants, Prince Clive gets." Elena's girls might yearn for private lessons, but my daughter *needed* a fresh start.

I was going to do a flawless job with this assignment. And then my daughter—my precious, miracle, angel of a daughter—was going to get a future I'd never even allowed myself to dream about.

Safe. Healthy. Debt-free. After paying the surgery bills, I could even buy a small condo for us in a decent neighborhood, one with good schools…

I looked the Madame in the eye. "I promise you won't be sorry you gave me this assignment."

"I believe you." She patted my hand. "You haven't been in the business long. But I can tell you understand—this is the sort of opportunity that only comes around once in a lifetime."

～

"Woah." I gaped as the flight attendant showed me to my first-class "suite." It was like a little cubicle, with a big cushy chair, a ledge to put my feet up, a large flatscreen television, and a privacy wall. I would be very comfortable for my seven-hour flight to Astos.

I'd never flown first-class in my life. Thank goodness I had the benefit of the agency's clothes and accessories.

I clutched my Louis Vuitton tote like it was some sort of talisman, warding off inquiries about whether I belonged with the other rich people on the direct international flight. I was glad for the privacy wall; no one could see me in my little cubby, gaping at all the luxury.

Elena had been crafty when she packed my carry-on —she'd included multiple magazines that featured the royals. So I was free to ogle Prince Clive in the glossy pictures without making anyone suspicious.

And ogle I did. *Holy hell*—the prince was hot! He'd *earned* that Sexiest Man Alive title! Prince Clive was six-foot-three, with broad shoulders, a square chin, and dark-brown eyes. He also had a well-trimmed beard, which somehow made him even more attractive.

No matter what he turned out to be like, he was already better than Binky.

From everything I'd read, the prince was the strong, silent type. He didn't give interviews. He was rarely photographed smiling. Instead, he seemed to keep to himself, working in his official capacity as a goodwill ambassador in the tiny, rural counties that comprised most of Astos. There were pictures of him digging a well in an isolated village and touring a factory. The one photo that caught him smiling was when he'd visited a rural school. The young children surrounded him, cheering; a gorgeous smile lit his face as he beamed down at them.

I was curious about the prince. What was he like? Why didn't he smile much? Why would the Sexiest Man Alive need to hire a fake date?

My curiosity increased as I read articles about Princess Isabelle's wedding. The ceremony would take place at a pristine, ancient chapel. Three hundred guests would attend. There was speculation that the Princess would have a minimum of nine bridesmaids. One article suggested her gown was custom couture and had cost over thirty-thousand dollars.

I gaped at Princess Izzie, too. Like her brother, she was tall with brown eyes. Her famous chestnut curls tumbled over her shoulders. But, unlike Clive, she smiled non-stop and often gave interviews. She gushed about her fiancé, the wedding, and the royal family. There was a sparkle in her eyes that made her seem every inch a fairytale princess, one deserving of her happily ever-after.

I was nervous about going to Astos. It petrified me to meet the prince and to interact with the *freaking royal family*. But part of me—albeit a tiny part—was *thrilled*. I'd never expected to have an adventure like this in my life!

The flight attendant came to take my order, breaking

my reverie. I frowned at the menu. There were things I'd never tried before—duck *confit* and a lettuce soba noodle salad. Was that made from lettuce or noodles? Or lettuce noodles…? *Huh?*

"I'll have the buttermilk fried chicken and a Caesar salad."

The flight attendant smiled. "Excellent choice. Champagne?"

"I'll just have water, thanks." Alcohol would help with my nerves, but I didn't want to be puffy when I met the prince.

"Perfect—excuse me." The attendant hustled down the aisle. Someone a few rows behind was ringing their bell repeatedly.

"Is it possible to get some *normal* food around here? And I want more free champagne!" The female passenger's voice was nasal and a bit shrill.

I sank back against my seat, feeling sorry for the flight attendant. I had some experience dealing with demanding customers, too. Which made me wonder again… What *would* His Highness be like? Would he be nice? Would he want to talk to me, or would he be super aloof? Would he be rude, yelling at his staff to bring more champagne?

Elena had taught us it was best to mirror our client's behavior: if they were chatty, we were supposed to smile and engage with them. If they were quiet, only speak when spoken to. So what would Prince Clive be like? From the magazines, he seemed reserved. What on earth was he going to act like with his paid fake date?

Good thing it was a long flight. I had a lot to think about.

"Hey—can I borrow that?" It was the same nasal voice from a few rows back. A woman stuck her face into my cubby and pointed at my stack of magazines. Heavy perfume rolled off of her, engulfing me and making my eyes water. Short and curvy, she appeared to be in her late forties. She had frosted-blond curls, a large nose, and wore hot-pink lipstick that matched her velour jumpsuit.

She jabbed a manicured finger at the pile. Her pink nail polish matched the jumpsuit, too. "The top one."

"Sure." I handed it to her quickly.

"Thanks." She immediately began leafing through it. "Thank *god* for you—I was late to the airport and didn't have time to pick anything up. All they freaking have in my cubby is *Architectural Compendium* and some other crap. A girl needs her gossip rags!" She laughed, a loud honking sound that actually startled me.

"I'm Mindy, by the way. Mindy Fitz." She grabbed my hand for a firm handshake.

"I'm Tarryn. Nice to meet you."

Mindy winked at me. "You're a pretty girl, Tarryn. I hope you have fun on your trip. Thanks for the magazine." She sashayed away, velour swishing between her thighs.

About an hour later, as I was finishing my excellent buttermilk fried chicken, I heard Mindy asking the harried flight attendant for more free champagne.

The rest of the flight passed quickly. I read a few more articles, took a nap, and then refreshed my makeup. I disliked travel most of the time, but my cubicle was way more comfortable than even my crappy futon back home. First-class did not suck!

Before I was ready, the pilot announced we were landing. Grateful for the privacy wall, I closed my eyes and crossed myself as we touched down. *Please let me do a good job.* That was literally what I prayed for. *Let the prince like me. Let me not screw this up, god. Amen.*

I touched up my lip gloss again, shook out my hair, and, taking a deep breath, headed into the terminal. I didn't know what to expect. But there was a man there with a sign: *Clayton.* Clutching my tote, I headed toward him.

But Mindy Fitz—all five-foot-two of her—was suddenly beside me. She'd refreshed her lipstick and fluffed her hair. She gently elbowed my side. "You have a driver?"

"Um...yep." My cheeks heated.

"*Nice*. And he's not too bad to look at, is he?"

We both glanced at the man—beneath his impeccable dark suit, he was tall and muscular, maybe in his fifties, with thick hair pushed off his face. He saw us staring and smiled.

Mindy stuck out her velour-encrusted chest at him. "I like Astos already. You have fun, Tarryn. Be good—but not *too* good, you know what I mean?" Then, with a wink, she disappeared into the crowd, perfume trailing in her wake.

I finally reached the man, and he lowered the sign. "Ms. Clayton, it's an honor. My name's Stellan, and I'll be your driver during your stay with us." He bowed. "My associate will collect your luggage. Please, follow me to the car."

Stellan wove through the crowd, and I followed, both let down and relieved that Prince Clive hadn't greeted me at the airport. But of *course*, he wasn't here—the press watched his every move. I would do well to remember that his circumstances were very different from anything I'd encountered before. The normal rules would not apply while I was in Astos.

Stellan led me outside. The sun was shining, and the warm, humid weather was a far cry from the sterilized, freezing atmosphere of the air-conditioned terminal. I'd read that the climate in Astos was milder than New England; their winters didn't include heavy snowfalls, and spring came to the tiny country about a month earlier than it did back home.

I smiled as I followed the driver to a large black SUV waiting at the curb. I loved the warmer weather. This past winter in Boston had been brutal, with weeks of freezing rain and temperatures hovering around ten degrees.

I was still smiling as Stellan held the door open for me. I climbed inside the SUV's cool interior, relaxing against the buttery leather seat.

"Ah—there you are." Much to my surprise, Prince Clive himself leaned forward, an apparition appearing out of the darkness.

"Oh!"

Time seemed to stop. I had a funny feeling in my head, almost as if I was spinning. I gripped the seat, holding on for dear life. The prince was even more handsome in person—it almost hurt to look at him. He wore a navy suit with a pressed white shirt, open at the throat. I glimpsed his chest, tanned skin peeking through. His dark eyes were intense as he looked me over.

He was, unequivocally, the most gorgeous man I'd ever seen.

He raised his eyebrows, waiting for me to speak.

"H-Hi, Prince Clive." Oh my God, he was so handsome he made me stutter!

"Hi yourself, Tarryn Clayton." He assessed me coolly. "Welcome to Astos."

CLIVE

❧

"Welcome to Astos." I heard my words, aloof and self-assured, as though somebody else had spoken them. Somebody who had their shit together. Somebody who didn't feel as though someone had punched them in the gut.

My escort was the most gorgeous woman I'd ever seen.

I couldn't help but stare. It was as though nature itself had designed for me—she pressed every single one of my buttons. Long, white-blond hair. *Check.* Bright blue eyes. *Check.* Porcelain skin, lush lips, and perfect round breasts. And she was mine. For ten glorious days, she was all mine.

And I'd vowed not to sleep with her. *Fuck!*

The Madame's words rang in my head: *"You can relax*

about being intimate with her and enjoy yourself." That fucking Madame knew what she was doing…

Besides being beautiful, the young woman was dressed perfectly. Her outfit was precisely the sort of thing my sister would wear on a flight, understated, expensive and elegant. She looked more like a celebrity than a graduate student, which was the backstory I'd agreed on with the Madame.

I shouldn't be surprised. All told, this fake date was costing me over one-point-five million USD. So she'd *better* be perfect.

"Thank you for agreeing to come." I nodded at her, trying to be cool.

"It's my pleasure." She smiled at me, and my heart stopped.

What the fuck? Was I a high-school *boy*?

Note to self: don't be celibate for too long. It makes you a lunatic… I cleared my throat. "Have you been to Astos before?"

"Never." She peered past me out the window. "I've looked at pictures, though. It's beautiful."

"Yes…quite beautiful." But I was staring at *her*. I adjusted the collar of my shirt. Was it getting hot in here? "But we can certainly do better than pictures."

I leaned forward, desperate to occupy myself with

something besides gaping at her. "Stellan? Take the scenic route to the palace, please. Ms. Clayton should see some of the country before it becomes impossible to venture out."

When she looked confused, I explained, "The press will hound us as soon as they learn you're here. We probably won't be able to leave the grounds for the next ten days."

Tarryn nodded. "I understand if we can't leave the palace. I'm sure it's difficult to have any sort of privacy in your position—I can't imagine."

"It comes with the territory." I felt uncomfortable talking about my life with this stranger—this gorgeous, paid stranger I was thrusting into a complicated situation. She had no idea what she was getting into…

I pointed out the window. "That's an Astos landmark—the Gray Tower. It was originally used as a place of worship, and later, as a lookout for enemies." The Tower jutted into the sky; it was a formidable building of smooth gray stone, stunning to look at.

"Wow." Tarryn leaned closer as she peered through the window. She was so close I could smell her shampoo—for some strange reason, it made my mouth water. "That's amazing."

Tarryn sat back, and I caught another whiff of her shampoo. *Unf.* Seriously, what was my fucking problem?

It's not like she was the first gorgeous woman I'd had in the back of my SUV!

"Astos is small, but our biggest industry is tourism," I explained, trying to act like a normal human being. "People come for the beaches, the mild weather, the architecture, and of course, the royals."

Tarryn nodded. "The wedding's been all over the news. People are really excited about it."

The entire world seemed to be fascinated by my family. I didn't understand the obsession, but my father and sister did an excellent job playing the press, making sure that our pictures were constantly circulating. The royal family had a very active social media presence—but I took no part in it. I had little desire for my image to be commented upon and scrutinized by millions of strangers all over the world. It happened anyway, of course. Anyone with a cell phone could take my picture and post it online. It made me feel exposed and vulnerable, two things that I loathed.

My father argued our fame was good for business. Many of our subject's livelihoods depended upon Astos's popularity with international tourists. So the king had his reasons to lead such a public life, but then again, there was a trade-off. We couldn't leave the palace without being chased by the press. There was a lot of pressure to always appear perfect, to always be smiling.

My mother, in particular, had a tough time with the constant scrutiny. Over the years, she had shrunk into herself, avoiding contact with the outside world. She rarely left the palace grounds.

"Your Highness." Stellan glanced in the rearview mirror. "It appears we have company. Shall I return home?"

"Yes, of course." I nodded and immediately closed the SUV's tinted window.

"What's wrong?" Tarryn asked.

"It's nothing—just the press. My security detail is also following us, so they'll handle it." A dull headache formed in the back of my head. My American escort hadn't even been in the country for an hour—and already, they were chasing us.

Stellan turned down the road that led to the royal compound, beautiful Astos passing by in a blur.

I glanced at Tarryn. The press was terrible; my family was even worse. I hoped she would forgive me for what I was about to put her through.

∼

SECURITY OPENED the gate to the private entrance. We pulled onto the property, and Tarryn's blue eyes grew huge in her face. "Oh, my goodness…" Her voice trailed off as she gaped. "I've seen pictures, but in person—wow. It's *so* beautiful. It doesn't even look real!"

I tried to see my home through her eyes. The long drive stretched ahead of us, bordered by rolling green lawns and perfectly positioned, well-tended shrubs. Ancient statues dotted the grounds. The palace rose majestically in the distance, a beacon of elegance. It was a unique structure, with a yellow facade and a central copper spire that had long since turned a pleasant, seafoam green. Hundreds of steps led to the palace entrance, and terraced gardens flanked them on either side.

Tarryn's mouth was hanging open by the time Stellan parked at the foot of the stairs. "Here we are," I said gently.

"What?" She tore her eyes away from the palace in surprise. "Oh—of course." She laughed. "We need to go *in* there."

"The first thing we'll do is have you meet my security team. They'll review your file with you—and you'll have to sign some forms. I promise it won't take too long." I took a deep breath. "Then I'll show you to your room. Your attendants can unpack your things while you rest for a bit. Unfortunately, there's a cocktail party tonight. We're expected to be in attendance."

She looked surprised. "I'm going to meet your family *tonight*?"

I checked my watch. "Actually, in about three hours. So we don't have long. You have an appropriate dress, I'm guessing?"

A little line formed between her eyes. "How formal is the party?"

"Quite." My sister lived to overdress for any occasion, as did her friends. "My staff can fetch you something if you need—"

"No—no, I have the perfect dress." Her voice sounded more assured. "Elena made sure to pack everything I might need. So you don't have to worry." She waited until Stellan was out of the car before she continued, "I have something appropriate—I know I do. I promise I won't embarrass you."

I raised my eyebrows. "For over a million dollars, I wouldn't expect you to."

Tarryn's face fell for a moment, then she quickly composed her features. "Of course, Your Highness."

I'd meant it as a joke, but the words had come out sharper than I'd intended. *Way to remind her she's on the payroll, you prat!*

We looked at each other uncomfortably for a beat. The awkward silence stretched out.

"Well then." I motioned to Stellan, who was waiting outside by the car door. "We should get on with it."

Tarryn nodded. Was it my imagination, or did she seem relieved to get out of the car and get away from me?

It's not as though I could blame her. Sighing, I watched my gorgeous hired date climb down from the car. Of course, her ass was perfect, too, round and athletic. *Fuuuck.*

I'd vowed not to touch her in private. But, in public, we were going to have to pretend that not only were we happy, but that we were close—on the verge of a serious relationship.

In front of my family. In front of the world. For ten days.

And during our first meeting, I'd already managed to insult her.

What the bloody hell had I gotten myself into?

TARRYN

PRINCE CLIVE WAS HANDSOME, all right. And tall. And a little intense. And he had that beard thing going for him. But after our brief encounter, I was pretty sure he was no Prince Charming. His words rang in my ears. *"For over a million dollars, I wouldn't expect you to."*

His tone had been sharp—intended to put me in my place.

I hear you loud and clear, Your Highness.

He had high expectations, which was reasonable. He was paying me enough that embarrassing him was not an option.

I thought of Ellie, the only motivation I would ever need. Of course, I wouldn't embarrass the prince. I would wear the perfect dress to the cocktail party. I would be *flawless* for him. In real life, I hardly had my act together. But this was pretend, and there was a lot of money on the line. I could pretend to be anything—even perfect—for ten days.

Multiple staff members bustled out, bowing to us before gathering my luggage. They kept their distance, and they were discreet—no one so much as looked at me twice. For his part, Stellan bowed before getting back inside the car. "It was a pleasure to meet you, Ms. Clayton."

"You too, Stellan." I smiled as I waved goodbye, then joined the prince at the base of the massive stairs. I stared up at the palace, taking a deep breath.

"Are you ready?" he asked.

"Of course." My upbeat tone masked my nerves: I felt like we were about to walk the Royal Plank.

His Highness and I climbed side-by-side up the steps to the entrance. It was a long-ass set of stairs, which I was grateful for. Hopefully, I'd have time to get my wits together.

I tried not to pay attention to how tall he was, or how his broad shoulders filled out his suit, or that his large hands hung awkwardly at his sides. These last few moments climbing the stairs to the palace were Before. After we went inside, everything would be different: I would have to play the part of his new, loving girlfriend. And would have to play it flawlessly.

But... Should we hold hands as we ascended the palace stairs? Were people—his family, the staff—already watching us with interest?

I remembered to follow my client's lead. He didn't reach for me, so I didn't reach for him. But I kept stealing glances. Why was I staring at his big hands? *Get a grip, Tarryn!* But of course, that only made me think of what it would be like to have his enormous hands grip *me*—oh boy!

I fought back nervous laughter. I shouldn't be crushing on my client, especially when he seemed stand-offish, and *especially* especially when Elena had been clear that he wasn't planning on using my full range of services.

I forced myself to focus on my surroundings. The palace spread out before us. I had never, in all my life, seen something so stunning. The facade was a cheerful yellow and had a central, green spire. The building stretched out on either side, its entire front face comprised of floor-to-ceiling windows. The terraced gardens that bordered the stairs were equally impressive. A riot of carefully planted flowers bloomed in tiers, cascading down like a waterfall.

A piazza beckoned halfway up the stairs. "You should check out the view." Prince Clive smiled at me, then turned around to face the grounds.

I sucked in a deep breath as I followed his lead. "Oh…wow."

The grounds spread out below us, as far as the eye could see, acre after acre of perfectly manicured grass. I felt like I could dive in. "It looks like the ocean!"

To my surprise, His Highness laughed. "I never thought of it that way, but…it does."

He turned to me, the ghost of a smile still on his face. "Are you ready for this?"

"Of course." I smiled. Despite Elena's instructions—acting totally on my gut instinct—I reached for his hand, lacing my fingers through his.

He squeezed my hand and leaned closer, a twinkle in his idea. "Smart idea. They're watching us, of course."

"Thanks." But what I was really thinking was *woah*. When his big hand squeezed me like that, other things were squeezing inside of me. *Holy shit!* He tugged me a little closer, and my stomach flip-flopped. From the simple act of holding his hand, I could feel how strong he was, how powerful. And I was close enough to smell his cologne—something earthy and *unf*-y.

I didn't dare look at him and his sexy beard. Instead, I stared straight ahead, trying not to break into a cold sweat as we reached the top of the stairs. My insides felt all jiggly and tingly.

A short butler with a rounded belly opened the door,

immaculate in his tuxedo. "Your Highness. Ms. Clayton." He swept into a deep bow. "We've been expecting your arrival—your father sent me to fetch you."

The prince scowled at him. "Back off, Herbert. Ms. Clayton's only just landed."

Herbert choked, quickly disguising it as a cough. "Of course, Your Highness."

"Tell my father Ms. Clayton will meet him this evening—she's tired from her flight." There was an undertone of menace in Prince Clive's words.

"As you wish," the butler sniffed. "The King will be more than happy to meet Ms. Clayton this evening."

"Perfect, because that's his only option. Now, if you will excuse us." Clive hustled me past the butler, a sour look on his handsome face.

I leaned closer to the prince. "Herbert's not your favorite guy, huh?"

"What gave it away?" he practically snarled.

I filed the information away for later. I had a feeling that the prince was a bit like a puzzle, one I was going to have to put together piece by piece.

Clive dragged me down the hall, not giving me much time to gape at the opulent surroundings. Gorgeous, multi-colored Oriental carpets lined the floor. Crystal chandeliers glittered from above, reflecting the sunlight flooding through the windows. It was overwhelming; I felt like I should tiptoe through the gilded space. I could only imagine Ellie in the palace, running around, accidentally smashing priceless artifacts while she played...

"I promise to give you a proper tour later—we'll have plenty of time." The prince interrupted my thoughts, which I appreciated. Thinking about Ellie sprinting through the palace was going to give me hives!

"Here we are—Royal Security." His Highness stopped outside what appeared to be an office. There were several men and women inside, all wearing dark uniforms. "They're going to ask you some standard questions, just to make sure we have everything in your file prepared for release. We don't want the press surprising us with something."

"Release?" I asked. "What do you mean?"

"The palace liaison will release a bio about you to the press," the prince said. "That way, they can start running stories with information that *we've* provided to them—it's a way to maintain some control."

"So... They're going to do a story on me." It was a statement, not a question. I swallowed hard. I'd imagined that there would be snippets of text and perhaps a photo or two. Still, I didn't realize the royal family would issue the equivalent of a *press release* about me.

"The press will do *lots* of stories about us—your job is not to read them and not to think about them. We can talk about it more later." The prince's voice softened. "Okay?"

I nodded. "Of course."

A uniformed guard came out. He was tall, with dark skin, huge shoulders, and inquisitive eyes. "Ms. Clayton? I'm Phillip, Chief of Royal Security. Won't you come with me?"

Prince Clive nodded, and almost as an afterthought, released my hand.

I left him behind, following the Chief through the busy office into a private room in the back. He motioned for me to sit as he closed the door and slid behind the desk. When he opened a file and started flipping through it, my mouth went dry.

What exactly did Royal Security know about me?

"First off, I have to say thank you." The Chief glanced up from the paperwork. "You made an impossible job possible."

I blinked at him. "You're…welcome?"

He cracked a smile that immediately put me at ease. "Your online footprint is non existent. Do you know how rare that is these days? Mostly when the royals make a new acquaintance, we have a ton of scrubbing to do. But I didn't find one thing about you online, not even on the Dark Web. You're a unicorn, Ms. Clayton."

"Thank you."

He flipped over some papers. "Your tax returns are in order, as is your credit report. I had them sealed so that no one can access your files going forward. Everything else looks good, too. Birth certificate, license, passport, and your daughter's birth certificate."

I almost choked.

"It's okay." His voice was gentle. "We've had *all* the records sealed. That's the beauty of working for the royals—we do things regular people can't. And it's why we did this legwork upfront—so that the press wouldn't be able to dig anything up on you. If you'd had any sort of social media presence, this wouldn't have been possible. That's the *only* reason our office cooperated with His Highness to bring you here. When he first came to me with this, I didn't think we could support him. But the agency you work for really knows its stuff—everything on their end looks legitimate."

He continued, "And because you've been scrupulous about staying off the internet, we were able to start fresh. You have an Instagram profile now—set to private. No one can get on there, but it establishes some credibility."

I sat very still, taking the information in. I'd never told anyone at work about Ellie, not even Vivian or Elena. "So…does the prince know about my daughter?"

"No." The Chief shook his head. "No one but me

and one other member of our team, our General Counsel, knows about her. And we're the only two besides His Highness who know what you do for work."

He sighed. "You'll have to sign a release form before you leave this office. It states that, should the truth about your identity come out, you will accept *full* responsibility for the fabrication. Furthermore, you release all claims against His Highness and the royal family."

I nodded.

"The attorney put in some language that says any litigation would have to take place in Astos, so you know… It's a one-sided contract." He frowned. "But you have to sign it if you want to stay."

"I understand," I said immediately. "I appreciate you being forthcoming with me."

"Of course," the Chief said. "The rest of the royal family will *not* be privy to any information about you. They think you're a graduate student, just like it says in the file."

"Thank you." That was a relief.

"Sure—but it's self-serving. The smaller the circle, the tighter the control. What you choose to share with His Highness about your background is up to you. But be mindful that the more you tell him, the more he has to cover up. It's my job to protect him. Now that you're working with us, that's your job, too."

I nodded, my heart thudding in my chest. This was way more complicated than I'd ever considered…

Chief Phillip closed the file. "While I'm thrilled that you've stayed so scrupulously offline, it of course raises some questions."

He tilted his chin and inspected me. "Who are you hiding from, Ms. Clayton?"

Now my heart thudded in my ears. "No one."

He waited, not saying anything for a moment. "I've been doing this for thirty years. You might as well tell me now."

I swallowed over a lump in my throat.

"It's safe for you to tell me," the Chief said softly. "All I'm going to do with the information is protect you."

"I don't… I don't talk about it." I took a deep breath. "The smaller the circle, you know?"

He nodded, sympathy lighting his eyes. "Is he your daughter's father?"

I nodded once.

"Abusive?"

Another nod.

"I take it he doesn't know about her?"

I started shivering. "N-No. He can't ever find out."

Chief Phillip nodded. "When was your last contact?"

"Four years ago. As soon as I found out I was pregnant, I ran." I struggled to calm the violent shivers that wracked my body. I did yoga breathing: in through my nose, out through my mouth.

Once I calmed down enough to talk, I said, "I'm sure that sounds terrible, but I knew if I stayed, he was going to kill me."

The Chief winced. "I'm so sorry. Ms. Clayton."

I straightened my spine and looked him in the eye. As always, it was my daughter that gave me courage. "I refused to bring my child into a world like that. She deserves better."

"Of course she does—and so do you." The Chief's tone was matter-of-fact. "Thank you for telling me the truth. If you write down his name and last known address, I'll make sure that he's put on a watch list."

I nodded, accepting the blank piece of paper he slid across the desk. I scribbled Robbie's name and address down, which almost made me vomit.

"I know that's a lot to ask." Chief Phillip sighed. "Thank you. You'll be safe here. I can promise you that."

I liked the Chief, and I believed him. The *problem* was that Chief Phillip and his large entourage of armed, trained security personnel wouldn't be protecting me back in Boston when I got home. I could only pray that Robbie didn't watch the news. Or that maybe he'd move on, although I couldn't begin to wish him on another woman.

"Maybe the asshole's dead." The Chief smiled at me hopefully. "We can dream, right?"

∽

My conversation with the Chief had drained me. By the time the General Counsel came in, attractive and crisp in black-framed glasses and a pantsuit, I could barely listen to her. She explained the release forms—which were, in fact, entirely one-sided—and I dutifully signed them. What else was I going to do?

I might not understand legalese, but I still understood the deal. If the truth came out that I was an escort, I had to say I'd lied to the prince about it. The blame would be on *me*—because I'd tricked him. Even though in the real world, he'd been the one to hire me.

And if I changed my mind and tried to tell the truth —that Prince Clive had called AcommoDating, that he'd known exactly who and what I was—the royal family would sue me for defamation. And all litigation would have to take place in Astos.

I understood the gist of the contracts, all right: I was no match for the royals. If I didn't keep my mouth shut, I'd face financial ruin. *Check.*

Head spinning, I barely registered the interior of the opulent palace as I met Prince Clive again. He brought me to my room. "I had your maids unpack your gowns. You should be quite comfortable in your suite." He hesitated as we stood outside the door. "Is everything all right?"

"Yes." I forced a smile. "I think I'm a little jet-lagged, is all. What time is the party, again?"

He checked his watch. "At eight. Are you still up to it?"

"Absolutely," I said. "I'll rest for a while, and then I'll get ready."

"Your maid will assist you with your hair and makeup."

That perked me up. I'd never had my hair and makeup done. "Really?"

The prince nodded, looking a bit sheepish. "That's one benefit of staying at the palace. My sister insists upon it for all of our female guests. She wants everyone to feel special and, of course, to look smashing."

I smiled again, even though after talking to the Chief about my past, hair and makeup seemed silly. "That's really nice."

He watched me carefully. "Are you sure you're all right?"

"Yes, Your Highness." I nodded. "And I *will* be ready for tonight. So you don't have to worry."

"Then I'll see you soon." With a bow, Prince Clive left me.

I entered my gorgeous room, barely seeing it, not knowing whether to laugh or cry. Finally, I closed the door and sighed. It had already been an unbelievable day.

The handsome prince...

The background check...

The truth about my past...

Chief Phillip was the first person I had ever confided in. Only my mother knew the truth about Ellie's dad.

Suddenly, anger swept through me. This was my *shot*. Like Elena said, opportunities like this assignment only came around once in a lifetime.

I needed to keep my eye on the ball. I'd taken this job for a reason—the money. I couldn't let fucking *Robbie* come out of the fog of my past like some zombie and rob Ellie of her future.

Not on my watch, you fucker.

Lifting my chin, I vowed not to think about it for the next ten days. I was done with the past. He couldn't hurt me anymore.

It was more than time to move forward.

CLIVE

I PACED THE HALL, waiting for Tarryn. The attendant came out and said she'd be ready in a minute. I wished we could get this over with—I was dreading the evening ahead. My family would be discreet about it, but they would circle Tarryn like jungle cats eyeing a wounded wildebeest.

Any sign of weakness would be an excuse to pounce.

For my part, I was anxious about being reunited with my beautiful fake date. And it wasn't just because I felt terrible about the fact that I was about to throw her to the lions. I hadn't been able to stop thinking about her. Tarryn intrigued me. It was as simple, and as complicated, as that.

She was beautiful, of course. Stunning. But she also seemed quite normal, which was outside my expectations. It was a cliche, but I kept wondering…what was a nice girl like her doing working as an escort?

I was curious about her family, her background. But the Chief had been adamant that I wasn't to have access to her file. He'd sealed it, and after meeting with her today, would destroy it. "It's for your protection," he reminded me.

I was tired of everyone always trying to protect me. It was bloody *emasculating*. It made me want to punch something. But then again, I often felt that way when I had to suffer through one of my family's parties…

"Hey." Tarryn emerged from her room, and my heart stopped.

Chase's words came back to me again: *Might as well have fun while you burn.* "Good evening." I grimaced as I bowed to her. I was in hell, all right…

Tarryn wore a floor-length, black, form-fitting dress. It hugged her curves but had a modest neckline, all the better to make me yearn to get a closer look. The gown was beaded, yet simple, the perfect choice for the evening. Her hair cascaded in loose waves over her shoulders, and her makeup was understated and flawless, highlighting her natural good looks. She was so pretty, it almost hurt to look at her.

She twisted her hands together nervously. "Is this dress all right? The maids said they thought it was—"

"It's perfect. You look…perfect." The hallway felt uncomfortably hot; I tugged at the collar of my suit.

She smiled in pleasure. "Oh, good. Thanks."

I held out my hand to her. "Shall we?"

Her smile widened as she took it. "We shall."

I clasped her hand, resisting the urge to tug her close against my side. I would do it later, when I had a reason to, when we were in front of everyone. Hmm…a legitimate excuse to get close to her. *Maybe tonight won't be as bad as I thought.*

"So," I said as we headed down the hall, "did everything go okay with the Chief this afternoon? I didn't want to push it, but you seemed upset afterward."

"It was fine. I like him—I think he's good at his job."

"He is." I nodded. "He's been with us a long time. I trust him with my life."

Music and laughter drifted down the hall; the party was already in full swing. Tarryn straightened beside me. "Are you ready for this? Are you clear on our backstory?"

"You mean, the dive bar where we met—the one on Commonwealth Avenue?" I grinned at her. "I *do* love a two-dollar margarita."

She laughed. "Do you really think your family will believe it?"

"They know I was in America last fall doing work on

behalf of my charity. So they won't be surprised that I took advantage of being free from the press. And the fact that I met a beautiful young woman? That will probably please them."

That little line formed between Tarryn's brows again. "Has it been a long time since you've dated someone?"

"It's been a very long time," I admitted, "but that's a story for another day." *Like never.* I refused to speak about my father's interference with my affairs; I felt like that gave him power, which was the last thing I wanted.

Someday when—*if*—I decided to marry, I would keep it to myself. Yes, my wife would one day be Queen. It was still none of his damn business.

Before I was ready, the formal parlor came into sight. Guards in ceremonial uniforms were lined up on either side of the entrance. "Here we are."

"I'm nervous, but..." She squeezed my hand and looked me in the eye. "We can do this, Your Highness."

"Of course we can. Stay by my side, and let's just relax."

Tarryn blew out a deep breath. "We should try to have fun."

"Yes. You can meet my cousin, the Duke of Clifton. He's fun. Just don't let him try to steal you away from me."

"Ha, okay." She seemed to relax a little. "I can handle him."

"Speaking of handling things…" I took a deep breath. I needed to warn her that she was about to walk into a pit filled with royal vipers. "It's my family. I need to warn you: they can be very tough. My sister is a fake. She's all smiles and bouncy hair, but you can't trust her. Her fiancé is about as interesting as wet paint. My mother is a sweetheart, but she's on all sorts of medication for her nerves, and she drinks too much. And my father is the *real* villain—stay away from him."

"Oh…okay." Tarryn's jaw dropped. "A *villain*?"

"I might be being a bit dramatic, but that's probably the best word for him." It felt good to get it off my chest, but I was a little worried she might run. "Fancy a drink?" I asked hopefully.

Tarryn nodded. "After that speech? I think it's a must."

"Absolutely." Taking a deep breath, I led her inside.

The party was already packed. Of course, the space looked incredible—my sister had questionable ethics but impeccable taste. The lighting was soft, vases were bursting with pink roses, and a table laden with hors d'oeuvres. The men wore tuxedos, the women, elegant floor-length gowns. I immediately spotted my sister and her fiancé, surrounded by a group of their friends.

Everyone was drinking, laughing, and talking. Electricity buzzed in the air; the guests were genuinely excited for the wedding of the century.

Not to mention eager to see my date.

My family and our society friends were very well-practiced in the art of snooping without looking like they were snooping. When we entered the parlor, there was the briefest of pauses; then the guests returned to their drinks and conversation, acting as though our entrance barely registered. But of course, that was a lie.

Tarryn Clayton was the first woman I'd brought home. *Ever.*

Of *course*, everyone was snooping. They'd been waiting for this my whole life!

A server appeared at our side and bowed. "Your Highness. Ms. Clayton. May I bring you a drink?"

"Bourbon," I said immediately, "a large one."

"And for the lady?"

Tarryn glanced around the room, seeming to take stock of what the other women were drinking. "I'll have champagne. Thank you."

When he bowed again and disappeared, she sighed. "This is *so* glamorous. And overwhelming." Her gaze wandered around the parlor again, taking in the crystal vases, the liveried servers, and the bejeweled guests, many of whom wore crowns. "Who *are* all these people?"

"We have a large family, and they'd never miss an invitation like this—the women love wearing their tiaras." I stood close to her, relishing the proximity not only because she was gorgeous but also because she was an ally. Usually, the Duke of Clifton served that purpose, but Tarryn was much more attractive…

I motioned toward the left side of the room, where two fashionable young women were pretending to ignore us. "Those are my second cousins, Sofia and Milana. They're in their early twenties, and they're making quite a splash on the social scene. And there," I turned slightly to the right, "is their mother, the Countess. She's my father's cousin. Terrible gossip."

The server returned with our drinks, and I raised my tumbler to Tarryn. "Cheers. To us."

She raised her champagne. "To us."

"Is that your mother?" Tarryn asked, peering over her glass.

I glanced over my shoulder. My mother wore a proper navy gown, her hair pulled up into an elegant bun beneath her crown. Unlike my sister and me, she had fair hair. She was beautiful, but her looks had faded along with her spark. Her years at the palace had been hard on her.

"Yes, that's the Queen." It always made me feel sad to see my mother at social events. She sat in a corner with her one close friend, the Duchess of Idrid. Mother would stay for a socially acceptable amount of time, and then she'd disappear to her room with her drink. "I'd like to introduce you, although I expect Izzie will intercept us first."

The words had barely left my mouth when my sister trilled, "Ah Clive, there you are!" She tripped over toward us, her fitted, pale-pink gown constricting her stride. My sister's famous curls were pulled back beneath her crown; her dark eyes glittered with curiosity as she approached.

"You must be Tarryn." She clutched my date with both arms, still holding tight to her champagne, and aggressively air-kissed her on both cheeks. "This is *such* a pleasure. You have *no* idea!" The intensity with which Izzie grasped Tarryn made me want to pry her off.

"It's an honor." Tarryn gazed at my sister, her eyes huge in her face. "I'm so happy for you. Congratulations on your wedding."

"Congratulations to *you*." Izzie's smile was so dazzling it almost made *me* dizzy. "You've done what no other woman in Astos has managed to accomplish: you've landed the prince!"

Izzie leaned closer. "Every woman here is jealous of you. How did you do it, may I dare ask? As early as last week, His Highness told me he wasn't seeing anyone special!"

I grimaced, but Tarryn smiled gamely at my sister. "I was as surprised as you that Prince Clive called. It's like a dream come true, you know? A fairytale. And now I'm here, at *your wedding*!"

"It *is* astounding, isn't it? A graduate student from America." I didn't know if Tarryn caught it, but there was steel beneath my sister's white, white smile. "No one can believe it."

"Like I said," Tarryn's voice was dreamy, "me either. What an honor!"

Isabelle released her and turned to me. "You're not wearing your crown, Clive. Are you planning on abdicating the throne and running off with Ms. Clayton?"

At that, I cradled my arm around Tarryn and pulled her close. "What an enchanting idea. Oh, wait—is that Old George over there, choking? He looks like he needs some help."

George Smith, Izzie's financier fiancé, *was*, in fact, choking. He was red-faced and spluttering as my cousin, the Duke of Clifton, whacked him hard on the back. They were causing quite a scene.

"Oh, dear—how embarrassing. I *told* him to stay

away from the parmesan sticks! I'll be back." Izzie glanced over her shoulder. "Don't *move*!"

"Christ, let's get out of here." I pulled Tarryn toward my mother's corner, where we might find refuge for a minute until they pried the parmesan stick from George's throat.

"She's nice," Tarryn whispered.

"Who?"

"Your *sister*."

"Don't kid yourself," I whispered back. "She's like a Hollywood actress. As soon as the cameras are off, she's another person altogether."

Tarryn nodded slowly. "I'll keep that in mind."

"You better, because she's already obsessed with you." When Tarryn looked a little scared, I said, "Don't worry. It's just that anyone who dates me is under intense scrutiny. Whoever I marry will be Queen someday. Izzie's got a vested interest in that."

She nodded. "I get it—it's a big deal. Your life is complicated, huh?"

I shrugged as we reached my mother. "It has its moments."

Sarah, The Duchess of Idrid, rose as we approached and bowed. "Prince Clive—it has been too long."

"Hello, Duchess." I'd always liked my mother's gentle friend, who was from my father's side of the family.

"Hello, Mother." I bent down and kissed her cool cheeks. "May I introduce my friend? This is Ms. Tarryn Clayton from America."

Tarryn bowed her head to the Duchess and then surprised me by dropping into a proper curtsy for my mother. "Good evening. It's my pleasure to meet you both."

The Duchess smiled, impressed; even my mother seemed to perk up a bit. They both examined Tarryn with open interest.

"Lovely to meet you, Tarryn." My mother sounded old beyond her years, her voice frail. "Where are you from in America, exactly?"

"Boston. I'm in school there."

"For what?" asked the Duchess.

"Computer Information Systems." Tarryn smiled at them.

"Mmm, you don't say." Both the Duchess and my mother had a sip of their drinks to mask the awkward silence.

"Have you visited Astos before?" The Queen asked.

"Never," Tarryn said. "It's so beautiful. Thank you for having me at the palace—I feel incredibly lucky."

I snaked my arm around Tarryn's waist. "*We* are lucky to have *you*."

The Queen and the Duchess stole a look at each other.

When my mother turned back to us, her faded eyes had brightened a bit. "Yes, I expect we *are* the lucky ones—it's quite nice that Clive has finally brought a young lady home."

"Mother—"

"Do not use that fresh tone with the Queen," a voice boomed from behind me. "Don't you know I could have your head on a spike for that? That law's actually still on the books."

I groaned, pulling Tarryn closer against me as a tall, immaculate, scowling figure joined our circle. *Here we go.*

The biggest blowhard of them all had arrived.

"Hello, Father."

TARRYN

⤳

"You don't just say *hello*," the man wearing the crown said, "you *bow*."

He smiled, waiting, as an awkward silence settled over our little group. The King was tall and handsome, like his son. But his hairline had receded, and his face had thinned out, making his features hawkish. His Highness had a distinct air of superiority about him, his nose tilted into the air, his shoulders thrust back beneath his tuxedo, his stance proud as a peacock. In addition to his crown, he wore some sort of medal adorned to his lapel, all the better to announce just precisely who and what he was.

"Of course, *Your Highness*." Clive swept into a deep, perhaps exaggerated, bow.

When he rose, he reached for my hand and raised it,

presenting me to his father. "This is my friend, Tarryn Clayton. Tarryn, this is my father, King Wesley, Ruler of Astos."

"Your Highness." I immediately dropped into a low curtsy. Good thing Elena had made me practice!

"You may rise, Tarryn Clayton from America." The King sounded pleased, as if he'd been looking forward to this.

I drew myself back up, the smile still plastered to my face. The King smiled back, his shrewd gaze raking over me, then his son, then our proximity to each other.

"It's about time my son brought a proper woman home." His voice boomed as though he wanted to be sure everyone at the party was listening, even if he wasn't addressing them directly.

The Queen winced, the Duchess had a long sip of her drink, and Prince Clive said nothing. But as he stood stiffly beside me, I could feel him souring. Apparently, the King had that effect on people.

"Ms. Clayton—please tell us more about yourself." The King's dark eyes zeroed in on me. "I understand that you're a student?"

"Yes, Your Highness. A graduate student at Boston University."

"How impressive." I couldn't tell if he meant that. "And you are studying…economics? History? Law?"

"Computers."

"Ah. I know nothing about them, unfortunately. I have a new one I can't quite figure out—perhaps you could help me while you're staying here?"

"It would be my pleasure." Actually, even though I'd only just met the King, I wanted nothing to do with him or his computer.

He had a sip of his drink, which looked like water. His Highness wanted to stay on his royal game. "I'm assuming your accommodations are acceptable?"

I'd met men like him before—he was looking to be complimented, to have his ego stroked. *Ew.* "The palace is stunning, Your Highness. My suite is incredible."

"Well, we hope you enjoy your stay." The King's dark eyes took on a hard glint. "It's the least we can do for our son. He's hard to please, Ms. Clayton! Although I expect you already know that since you're *such* good friends."

There was something about his tone that made me uncomfortable. Was I being paranoid, or did he know that Clive and I weren't real?

I took a step closer to the Prince and gently slid my hand into his. "I don't find him *that* difficult."

"Ah, but you have your ways of charming him, I'm sure." His Highness's tone was salacious.

Clive gripped my hand. "Father—"

"You know, I'm coming down with a terrible

headache," the Queen suddenly said. "I need to excuse myself, I'm afraid. But, darling, will you take me?" She smiled at her husband.

A funny look crossed his face, but a smooth mask of superiority quickly replaced it. "I'll have one of the servants bring you up, darling. We mustn't disappoint our guests."

She smiled at him expectantly. "I think they would be more disappointed if they heard you didn't have a minute for your queen."

They stared at each other for a moment. The Queen's faded blue eyes blazed brighter as they fixed on her husband as if she were daring him to say no.

After a moment, the King said, "Of course, my Queen. Son, Tarryn, Duchess—if you will excuse us. My wife is ill once again."

The King stiffly offered her his arm, and she took it despite his tone.

She must have been quite used to it.

Prince Clive emptied his drink and was motioning for another as the Duchess came closer to me. Sarah appeared to be in her early fifties and had caramel-colored skin and highlighted hair; she was beautiful in her pale-green gown.

She patted my arm. "At least one of them has decided to favor you."

I raised my eyebrows.

"The Queen," she continued, keeping her voice low. "The last time she asked the King for anything, she got pregnant with Isabelle. So trust me when I say that whatever passes between them in the hall right now will be the longest conversation they've had in twenty years."

When my eyes widened, she chuckled. "Don't be scandalized, my dear. Life with the palace is very different from the outside world. It's vastly different from America, where everyone is so focused on their feelings and happiness."

I blinked at her. "What are you focused on in Astos?"

"Duty, of course." She smiled as the Prince turned back to join us, holding a fresh bourbon and another flute of champagne for me.

As my glass was still full, the Duchess helped herself to it. "Thank you, darling. Being around the King *does* drive one to drink."

Clive wearily raised his tumbler. "Cheers to that." He finished his bourbon in one gulp. *Oh boy.*

I took his hand. "Your Highness, there's a man across the room who keeps staring at you and trying to wave. Isn't that the Duke of Clifton?" When he'd spoken of his cousin earlier, it seemed like he liked him. Finding a non-toxic family member seemed like a good idea, especially before His Highness got his hands on another drink.

"Ah, your partner in crime." Duchess Sarah winked at him. "Have fun. I'll intercept your father when he returns, and then you will—"

"Owe you once again." The Prince grinned at her, then bowed. "It's always a pleasure, Duchess."

Her eyes sparkled. "The pleasure is all mine. Lovely to meet you, Tarryn. Welcome to the family. Now, *smile*, you two! Everyone will be watching!"

Heeding her advice, we both plastered grins on our faces. Clive put his arm firmly around my waist and steered me through the crowd. It felt like everyone was staring. Every time I tried to make eye contact, the well-bred guests looked away—pretending as though they hadn't been gawking. But, damn, they were good!

"Are you all right?" I asked the Prince, keeping my voice low.

"I'm fine—mostly. My father always manages to get under my skin." His big hand palmed my waist. "I didn't like his tone with you."

"Trust me, I can handle him." The good thing about being an escort was that you met all sorts of men, many of whom were assholes. While that might not *sound* positive, it had helped me develop a pretty thick skin.

"Your mother seems nice," I offered. "It was impressive how she handled your father back there—she didn't back down even when he gave her a hard time."

Clive winced. "I'm sure she'll pay for it. He'll see to that."

"I hope not. It was kind of her to intercept him." I looked up at him. "And the Duchess seems pretty great."

"The Duchess has been a loyal friend to my mother from the beginning, for which she has my eternal gratitude." The Prince nodded. "She's on our side."

I frowned. "Which side is that?"

He leaned closer, putting his mouth close to my ear. His scent washed over me, masculine and seductive, and my knees almost buckled. "Whatever side my father isn't on."

"Ah, *there* you two are—I've been trying to get your attention all night!" Another tall, fit, handsome man in a tuxedo landed beside us. He stuck out his hand for me to shake. He was ginger-haired, with a closely trimmed beard, a big grin, and green eyes. "I'm Cliff, the Duke of Clifton—and no, I'm not kidding, my parents have a terrible sense of humor. You must be Tarryn, right? My cousin's hot new American girlfriend."

"Ha! Hi, it's nice to meet you, Sir."

"Oh, the pleasure is *mine*. Why does Clive get all the

pretty girls? Ah, it must be the title." He winked at Clive. "How are you, cousin?"

"I'm good. I'll be better if you never touch Tarryn again or refer to her as 'hot' though." His tone was chiding, with a side of menace.

The Duke laughed and raised his hands. "I won't touch her again. I remember how your right hook feels."

"I'll forget about that night, if you will," Clive said.

"Done." But the Duke rubbed his jaw as if he still remembered it clearly. "So Tarryn, how has your stay in Astos been so far? You arrived today, so I heard?"

I nodded. "It's so beautiful, but I haven't really had a chance to explore much."

"His Highness will show you around the grounds tomorrow, I'm sure. Wait until you see it—it's breathtaking. The lake's my favorite. Make the prince pack you a picnic lunch and escape the palace for a while. It's gorgeous out there. You'll love it." He grinned at me, his enthusiasm infectious.

"That sounds lovely."

"I was *planning* on taking her," the Prince said defensively.

"All right, cousin. I'm not trying to steal your thunder." The Duke laughed. "Actually, I was hoping you two could help me. I know it's last minute, but I still haven't found a date for the wedding. Any ideas?"

"Freya Wilson?" the Prince asked. "Izzie was trying to pawn her off on me once again."

Cliff snorted. "I haven't bothered with Freya since she turned me down, claiming a Duke wasn't good enough for her. I heard she's coming to the wedding, though." He scanned the room. "Think I should give it another go?"

Prince Clive raised his eyebrow. "I think you should find a *nice* girl—not Freya—and settle down, once and for all."

Cliff turned back to him and grinned, taking in the Prince's arm around my waist. "Like you, eh?"

"Maybe." His Highness motioned for another drink. "More champagne, love?" he asked me.

Again, my knees almost buckled. "I'm fine, thanks."

"I'll have a water," the Duke said.

"Absolutely." Clive nodded at him. "You're doing so great."

"Three years sober." He winked at us. "Never felt better."

"Congratulations." I loved a man who could be honest and open about something difficult.

"Stop trying to steal my girl," the Prince growled.

"Ha, okay." But the Duke's countenance darkened. "Oh, boy—here comes Izzie. Party's over."

Princess Isabelle sashayed over toward us again, her

signature huge grin glinting in the light from the crystal chandeliers. I didn't understand Prince Clive's feelings toward her. To me, she appeared every inch the perfect Princess—beautiful, glowing, and utterly disarming.

"Good news: George made it. We got the parmesan crisp out." She grinned at us, then reached over and air-kissed Cliff on each cheek. "Thank you for performing the Heimlich on him, Cousin. Did you find a date in the past five minutes?"

His shoulders slumped. "No. I was hoping Ms. Clayton had a lovely American friend for me, but no one's turned up yet."

"Another American—*yes*—the more, the merrier." Isabelle's tone turned serious, and her eyes widened further. "The whole world loves American culture. I've already had a thousand inquiries about Ms. Clayton!"

"I hope you told them nothing." Clive had another long sip from his fresh drink. "She's none of their damn business, Izzie."

"I beg to differ." She put her hands on her hips and turned to me, a beseeching look on her face. "This is an old argument between my brother and me, I'm afraid. He insists we cover ourselves up and hide from the press; I prefer to keep the lines of communication open. But, of course, it helps to be friendly, doesn't it? People are nice when you're nice to them, I always say."

"How nice has the press been to Mom?" The Prince's voice was bitter—and, I noticed, becoming thicker due to his three consecutive double bourbons.

"Brother, *please*. This is hardly the place and time. Have another drink, okay? Spend time with your new friend. *Relax*, for once in your life." Izzie clutched me in another hug, careful not to muss either of our hair. "You must come for a walk with me tomorrow," she insisted. "We need to get to know one another better!"

"I'm taking her out tomorrow," Clive said quickly.

"You mustn't hog her the entire time!" She frowned at him, but quickly flipped it to a smile as she turned back to me. "There's a dinner tomorrow night—I'll seat you beside me. Big brother can't hoard you forever!" Then, with a wink and several more air kisses, the Princess was gone, swallowed up by another crowd of tiara'd admirers.

"She seems in good spirits," the Duke said.

"I'm not sure why," the Prince quipped. "She's marrying a houseplant."

That made the Duke laugh hard enough that he spilled his water on his jacket. He excused himself, promising to come and find us later.

"Hopefully, we won't be here later." Clive finished his drink.

As he was about to motion for another, he hesitated.

"Would you like to get out of here before I get piss drunk?"

"If you think we can make a graceful exit, I'm all for it."

He sighed, setting his empty glass down. Then he held out his arm for me. "Then let us be graceful."

He swept me toward the exit. Once again, all eyes were surreptitiously on us. I raised my chin and smiled. I was on the arm of the handsome, reclusive Prince Clive. And he hadn't gotten piss drunk. And he smelled *divine*. And that *beard*. There was *every* reason to smile!

"Ah, there's my steward—wait one moment, I need to tell him something." The Prince deposited me by the door and hustled to his attendant.

I wasn't alone for long. "Leaving so early?" a vaguely familiar, slightly oily voice asked. The King suddenly appeared from around the corner. He slunk to my side, just out of view of his son.

"Your Highness—you startled me." I curtsied quickly.

"No need to be on edge." He grinned as he looked me up and down, and my stomach twisted.

I didn't like men who snuck up on you, and I *really* didn't like men who smiled at you like that when you were on a date with their *son*. Double *ew*.

He leaned closer. "I'll send you a note about my computer. I would appreciate your assistance."

"Oh, of course." I acted as though I'd forgotten all about it. "But I'm afraid I have plans with the Prince tomorrow. He's taking me to the lake," I babbled.

"I'm sure you can find some time for me soon—and although I assume your expertise is quite expensive, I can make it worth your while." Then, with a nod of his head, he slithered out of sight right before Clive returned.

"Are you ready?" The handsome Prince smiled at me.

"Absolutely."

I was ready for the Prince.

The King was another matter altogether.

CLIVE

It was a relief to get away from the party and from the temptation of drowning my familial grudges in bourbon. But being alone with Tarryn brought a temptation all its own.

I didn't let go of her hand as we wandered down the hallway, away from the parlor. There was no one watching anymore, except for the few guards we passed. Still, I held on tight. I'd had just enough to drink to be calculatedly reckless. "You should sleep in my room tonight," I suggested.

To her credit, she only looked surprised for a moment. "Of course, Your Highness."

"Not like *that*." I squeezed her hand. "What I meant was, the staff and my family will *expect* us to spend the night together after being apart for so many months.

Don't worry, you can have the bed. My couch is quite comfortable."

That tiny line between her brows surfaced again as she nodded. "However you think it makes the most sense for us to act—I'll follow your lead. You know what's best."

"Great. We can stop by your room to collect your things."

She arched an eyebrow. "If we were in such a rush to leave the party, don't you think we'd be headed straight to your room? I'm sure you have a T-shirt I can sleep in. And an extra toothbrush, Your Highness?"

Was I imagining it, or was her underlying tone bloody *naughty*? Or maybe it was just imagining her in one of my shirts, with nothing on underneath it…

"Of course. Great idea." I coughed to hide the fact that I was choking.

I'd asked her to sleep over so that my family and the palace staff would believe in our relationship—no questions asked. But I'd *also* asked her to stay because…

Because…

"Here we are." There were two guards outside my room, which was the standard practice when we had a social event at the palace. Security was our first priority. Although my father didn't treat me with much care to my face, he was conscientious in protecting his heir.

Tarryn's eyes widened at the guards, but they didn't return her look as they bowed, letting us pass. "Good night, gentlemen."

They nodded in response. "They're the strong silent types," I joked once we got inside.

But she looked concerned. "Do you always have guards outside your room?"

"Only when we have guests on the premises—you needn't worry, it's only a precaution." I started undoing my tie.

"I'm not worried for *me*. I was just curious if that's what your normal life's like." She turned around, eyes still wide as she took in my room. "Speaking of what your life's like—this is *nice*, huh?"

I laughed. "It *is* rather nice." My suite was enormous, with a wall of windows and a balcony facing the interior grounds. You couldn't see the lawn at night or the bubbling fountain, but the lights from the rest of the palace were visible, including the parlor where the party continued.

Tarryn went to the windows and stared out. "This is so pretty," she said. "I can see the moon! I can't wait to see the grounds in the morning."

"They really are amazing—our staff does an incredible job keeping them up. They're lovely this time of year." I dug through my chest of drawers, locating a white T-shirt and a pair of sweat shorts that would be enormous on her but were still at least something. "I'll put these in the bathroom for you, and I'll find you a toothbrush."

She glanced back at me and smiled, and I noticed for the first time that she had a tiny dimple in her left cheek. "Thanks."

"It's no problem." I hustled away, internally cursing myself as I passed my immense bed. Why the devil had I asked her here? But in my bathroom, I found an answer: my butler had already set out toiletries that were obviously intended for an overnight female guest—including a new, pink toothbrush. *See?* I chided myself. *Everyone expects the hot American to sleep in your room.*

And so she was. Still, I didn't know whether to laugh or cry.

I changed out of my tux and into a pair of sweats and a T-shirt. When I returned to my room, Tarryn looked me up and down in surprise. "You own sweatpants?"

I laughed. "Of course. Doesn't everyone?"

"I didn't think a prince would wear them—I expected you in silk pajamas and a dressing gown!"

"Are you serious?"

"Yes." She laughed. "Sorry, but I mean, you *do* have a crystal chandelier in your room. And two armed guards outside in starchy-looking uniforms."

"I don't own a dressing gown." I smirked. "I'm not even sure what that is!"

"I really am sorry." She laughed again. "I guess I'm thinking about rich people in the movies. I don't have any actual real-life experience." She stopped laughing, and it got awkward fast.

"Your things are waiting in the bathroom." I smiled. "I'll set myself up on the couch. Would you like anything—water or a snack? The kitchen would be happy to send something up. Come to think of it, we didn't eat, did we?"

Tarryn shook her head. "I think we forgot."

"I'd love to have a late dinner—but I know it's been a long day."

"I'm hungry," she admitted immediately. "Actually, I'm *starving*."

"Me too. I'll order something—do you have any allergies? Are you a vegetarian?"

"No and no." She hesitated before heading into the bathroom. "And I'm not a *picky* eater, but I am pretty basic. I don't eat fish, either."

"Basic, got it—and no seafood. No worries. Our kitchen can do anything."

I got on the phone with Chef. "What can we do that's American-friendly and basic?"

"*Basic?*" Chef was French and a bit abrasive. "Je ne fais *pas* de base!"

I cleared my throat. Chef actually intimidated me a little, especially when she went all *fais pas* on me. But I was going to get Tarryn something she liked. "Cheeseburgers," I snapped. "And French fries. You should be good at that."

I actually laughed a little when I hung up. I never talked back to Chef—I liked her food too much. But hopefully, she'd locate a sense of humor and help a guy out!

Tarryn came out a few minutes later in my shirt—much to my disappointment, she'd kept her bra on. She wore my shorts, which were huge on her, rolled over several times. Her long, bare legs stretched out. She'd washed her makeup off, which made her look even younger.

My dick twitched just from looking at her. With no makeup and my clothes thrown on, she looked even more beautiful than she had in her gown. *TF?*

"Hey." She smiled at me and perched at the edge of the bed.

"Hey." My voice was hoarse, dammit. "I ordered us some food—it should be here in a minute."

"Thanks. This is like living in a hotel! Oh my goodness, I would order food all the time."

Her culinary enthusiasm sparked my curiosity. "What's your favorite restaurant back in Boston?"

"I don't actually go out to eat that much…but *ooh*, there's this little takeout burrito place in the South End." Tarryn's eyes lit up. "My friend Vivian and I go there once a week—their homemade guacamole is *banging*! They put fresh lime juice in it and something else… jalapeños? It's delicious."

"Sounds it." Actually, I was staring at her lips, wondering what they would taste like if I got closer and put my mouth on hers…

I cleared my throat again. "I had a great meal in Boston once."

"At the Ritz?" She laughed.

"No, it was this little dive bar… Some dark place on a corner. But they had an enchilada with fruit salsa that was *banging*, as you say." I laughed.

"*You* like dive bars?"

"Tarryn." I sat up straight. "You sound like you'd expect to see me eating at the Ritz in my *dressing gown*. I'm a normal guy, you know? I like dive bars. And enchiladas. And *banging* guacamole."

"Then you should come with me to the burrito place someday," she said mildly.

"And you should come with me to the dive bar."

"It's a date." She fluttered her eyelashes at me.

There was a knock on the door. "Your Highness?" the guard called. "Your meal is here."

"Bring it in."

Two maids dressed in full uniform came in, wheeling a tray. They presented several dishes, all on good silver, and I could see it in Tarryn's face: I should be wearing a dressing gown.

She looked pretty interested in the cheeseburgers, though.

"Your Highness. Ms. Clayton." The maids bowed and quickly disappeared, leaving us to inspect our meals.

"This looks delicious! I love cheeseburgers." Tarryn didn't wait for me, which I loved. Instead, she eagerly sat down and grabbed her plate.

"I was hoping you'd say that." To her credit, Chef had made us what appeared to be proper American cheeseburgers. They were large, served on grilled brioche buns, and had crispy fried pickles on top of them. *Yum.*

The French fries looked hand-cut and well done, just the way I liked them. A small, paper French flag adhered to a toothpick sprang out from the top of our servings. Maybe Chef was finally developing a sense of humor.

"Oh my goodness," Tarryn moaned. "This is the best French fry *ever*. It's sprinkled with herbs, *mmm*."

"I'll pass along your compliments to the chef."

"Please do." She had a bite of her cheeseburger and moaned again.

I laughed. "Let me guess—it's banging?"

"Try yours." Tarryn gripped *hers* as though she was afraid I might try to take a bite.

I did as I was told—and then I moaned, too. The burger was juicy and delicious. Something about the crunchiness of the fried pickles on top made it even more scrumptious. "This is frickin' delicious."

Tarryn laughed again. "I didn't think that princes said 'frickin.'"

"I'm going rogue." I waggled my eyebrows. "No dressing gown, eating an American cheeseburger in my *sweats*. It's frickin' awesome."

We both laughed, and I felt something unfurl inside my chest.

That was when I realized I might be in trouble.

TARRYN

OUR BURGERS WERE AMAZING. What was even more astounding?

The prince was actually a nice guy—not as prickly as I'd initially thought. He even made me laugh.

I *tried* not to let my gaze travel down his shoulders or over the outline of his chest beneath his loose-fitting T-shirt. But I was human—I couldn't help myself! His enormous biceps bulged out, pale and swoon-worthy, mesmerizing me with their massiveness. Prince Clive looked as though he knew his way around a bench press. Maybe I could join him in the royal gym one of these days and just sit and watch as he lifted weights...

My mouth watered, and it had nothing to do with the delicious food. *Get a grip, Tarryn!*

But there was that word again...grip. *Stop it, FFS!*

We finished eating, and I excused myself to brush my teeth. Once I was alone in the bathroom, my nerves started rattling. He'd *said* he'd be sleeping on the couch. But then again, he'd been the one to suggest I come to his room.

I understood he wanted his family to believe this arrangement was real. That made sense. But what were his plans for behind closed doors?

He'd told Elena he didn't want to have sex with me. But why not? What was his deal, anyway? I was his escort. I was his hired plaything for the next ten days. Clive didn't strike me as someone who was shy. I could tell he was attracted to me, at least a little. So…?

What *did* His Highness want?

I hesitated before heading back to the room. I wasn't sure if I was ready to find out.

He was paying me a ton of money to be here. That meant I didn't get to hide. I took a deep breath and joined him.

To my surprise—*disappointment?*—he'd kept his word. He was on his couch, snuggled beneath a comforter. He grinned at me. "Good night, roomie."

I couldn't help it; I smiled back. "Good night. Thank you for dinner. It was…banging."

Even after I crept under the covers of his luxurious bed, I couldn't wipe the grin off my face.

Sunlight streamed through the windows, and I rolled away from it. But since I'd had Ellie, I'd lost my ability to sleep in. I opened my eyes a little, hoping that I'd slept long enough to be refreshed. I squinted at the clock: seven a.m. That was actually late for me!

The prince stretched out on the couch, grabbing my attention. He was still asleep. He'd thrown his covers off, and was sprawled out, all six-foot-three of him, somehow even more glorious and sexy in his sweatpants.

Speaking of his sweatpants...*oh boy*. I wasn't trying to check his stuff out, but he definitely had something going on underneath them. I sat up a little, careful not to make any noise. *Woo boy!* Prince Clive appeared to be quite large *down there*. Huge, perhaps.

I laid back down and pulled the pillow over my head. I was a bad, bad girl.

Something *pinged* from the nightstand, and the prince cursed. I peeked out at him.

"Bloody hell." He rubbed his face and lunged for his phone. "This better be important," he croaked.

His brow furrowed as he listened. "Fucking Izzie! Send it to me at once." He hung up and then glared at his phone.

"What's wrong?"

He sighed. "They leaked a picture of us from the party last night. The press is going bonkers."

I bit my lip as he glared at his phone. It buzzed, and Clive cursed again as he looked at the picture. "Oh boy," he groaned.

I was almost afraid to ask. "What? Is it bad?"

"No…" He scrubbed a hand across his face. "But I can't bloody read this without coffee. Do you want some?"

"Yes, please." Although there might not be enough coffee in the world to deal with my picture being featured in the tabloids.

He called the kitchen and ordered breakfast. Then the prince grabbed a nearby tablet and powered it up. He scrolled, then read for a moment. Then he sighed again and handed the tablet to me. "Look at this while I'm in the shower. The food will be here in a minute."

"I thought I wasn't supposed to read the news about us?"

He scrubbed a hand over his still sleepy-looking face. "I think you need to see this. If this is the way the press is starting off, we need to be prepared." His voice softened as he asked, "Do you need anything?"

I couldn't help but smile at him. "I'm fine, thanks." But as soon as Clive disappeared, my nerves flared.

I clicked on the tablet and stared at the picture on the screen. It was of the prince and me. His hand was protective around my waist. He beamed down at me as his mother and the Duchess stood nearby.

PRINCE PRESENTS AMERICAN FIANCÉ TO THE QUEEN, the headline screamed.

Fiancé? Say *what?* I scrolled to the following picture. It was the same shot from a different angle, this one showing the Queen beaming at us. *AN AMERICAN PRINCESS IN ASTOS?* It read.

The next picture showed Izzie hugging me. *PRINCESS IZZIE WELCOMES TARRYN TO THE FAMILY.* Woah. I pressed my fingers against my temples. Seeing my name in print like that was unreal and also more than a little unsettling...

The last picture was of the prince and me leaving the party, our hands entwined, our heads held high. Both of us were smiling. *ALL HAIL THE NEXT QUEEN?* The caption screamed.

Oh boy. Oh dear. The press was going bonkers, all right.

There was a knock on the door. "Breakfast, Your Highness!" A cheerful attendant opened the door, humming to himself, and deposited silver trays on the table, along with a large pot of coffee. "Ah, Ms. Clayton. Lovely to see you." The attendant grinned at me and bowed. "Have a good morning!" He didn't stop smiling as he left.

At least *someone* was cheerful. Aside from the pit in my stomach, I had no clue how I felt about the stories in the news. What on earth did His Highness think? Our cover story was that we had a *casual* relationship. But the press was making it seem like we were already engaged!

I poured myself a giant mug of coffee and added a hefty amount of cream. Then I went and sat by the windows. The headlines had unsettled me, but that didn't mean I needed to miss out on the view.

And what a view it was! The sun had crested the horizon, its glorious rays spreading out across the green lawn. The grass was so thick and lush, it looked like a blanket. There were more statues in the interior courtyard and a bubbling fountain. Its water sparkled in the early morning light, and I longed to go outside and throw a penny in it, all the better to make a wish.

I wish Ellie is good—and that she knows I love her!

I wish no one recognizes me in the photos!

I wish the prince would like me!

I surprised myself with that last one, but that was silly. Of *course*, I wanted him to like me—he was paying me enough money that I'd feel guilty if he didn't.

Plus, I liked *him*. Not to mention his beard and those biceps…

Prince Clive hustled out of the bathroom, his hair still wet. He'd changed into a fresh, dark T-shirt and yet another pair of sweatpants. These were slightly more fitted, all the better to check out his muscular backside when he faced the trays.

"Thank fuck for coffee." He poured himself a cup and then stalked over to me.

Why was his stalking so *hot*? I shook my head as if to clear it. *Drink your coffee, Tarryn*, I scolded myself.

He dropped into the seat next to me, then scowled out at the grounds. "You saw the pictures?"

I nodded.

"And read the headlines?"

I nodded again.

"Hand the tablet to me, please?"

I gave it to him, and he scrolled through the pictures again. When he finished, he stared into space for a moment. "No one was supposed to take pictures at the party last night. There were no phones allowed. So all the guests who came from outside the palace had to check theirs in before they went to the party."

"Someone isn't following the rules, I guess." I had another sip of coffee. "Are you…mad?" The stalking and scowling indicated yes, but there was also a glimmer in his eyes.

"Not exactly." He frowned out at the grounds. "It had to have been my sister who leaked these—I'm sure of it. Izzie is in charge of everything, and she doesn't make mistakes. So she knew exactly what she was doing."

"And what's that?"

He grimaced. "Drumming up even *more* excitement about her wedding. You'd think she's had enough of the spotlight, but apparently, my sister's ego knows no bounds."

I hesitated. "You don't think it bothers her that the stories were so focused on you, not her? It's *her* wedding, after all."

"Nah." He leaned forward. All the better for me to ogle his big shoulders. He smelled like shampoo, soap, and coffee, *mmmm*. "Izzie has the spotlight anytime she wants—she's the press's darling. But she really wants to whip the whole *world* into a frenzy over this event. It's her dream in life to have everyone obsessing over her wedding. And she's done it! Christ, I played right into her hands."

I blew out a deep breath. "What do you want to do?" I asked. "Do you want me to…leave?"

"What? *No*." He shook his head. "Absolutely not."

I nodded, relieved he hadn't accepted my offer. Of

course, I should *never* have suggested it, but I didn't want to make his life even more difficult.

"If my sister wants a spectacle, we're going to give her a spectacle. That is, if you're up for it."

I raised my mug in a toast. "I'm like a genie—your wish is my command."

He coughed a little. "Good. Perfect."

"So, what's the plan?"

"First of all, if the press wants us to be engaged, let's not spoil it for them."

I blinked at him, surprised. "Really?"

"Yes. If they want to play the relationship up, let them. You and I can keep acting as though we're the real thing. We can play it up. They will go absolutely mad, of course." Clive smiled.

"And…I had another idea while I was in the shower." He seemed to relax a little, warming to the topic. He sat back and put his feet up, having another sip of his coffee before continuing. "Remember how my cousin, the Duke of Clifton, was asking if you had any hot friends?"

"Of course. I liked him, by the way."

Clive smiled, and it was like the sun coming out. "Cliff's a great guy. Terrible taste in women, but that's another story. He really wants a proper date for the wedding. So I was thinking…why don't we import one of your friends from the agency?"

I raised my eyebrows. "Really?"

He shrugged a big shoulder. "Like my sister said, the more Americans, the better. I'll import more frickin' Americans than she'll know what to do with!"

"Um…" I bit my lip. "Don't you think it's a little risky to bring in another escort? The Chief made it sound like he almost didn't let me come to Astos," I said gently.

"Trust me when I say this—and I mean no offense to my dear cousin—but the tabloids don't give a crap about him. Her picture will make the news, for sure, especially if she's as half as hot as you. But no one will dig deeper. Cliff's had plenty of scandalous girlfriends. None of them have ever made the headlines, although several have given his parents migraines."

"It's an interesting idea…"

Clive grinned at me. "It's a *brilliant* idea. So." He handed me his phone. "Which one of your hot friends do you want to fly to Astos?"

CLIVE

PERHAPS BRINGING YET another prostitute to my sister's wedding was a bad idea. But then again, this was *Izzie* we were talking about. She deserved it.

I'd been initially pissed when I saw the pictures, but it shouldn't surprise me. My sister loved attention more than anything. The fact that the entire nation was freaking out about my date was a *massive* coup for her. I could picture Izzie picking out the pictures to send to her contacts at the press, knowing exactly which ones would make the internet blow up…

PRINCE PRESENTS AMERICAN FIANCÉ TO THE QUEEN. I shook my head. You had to give it to those bastards: they knew how to sell a story. And even *I* had to admit I looked besotted in the photo. I'd been staring at Tarryn, a genuine smile on my face…

I sighed as I waited outside of her door once again. She was getting ready for our day of touring the grounds. Back in my suite, we'd had coffee, fresh croissants, and bacon and then sat around, each of us checking our email. It was strange, but it had been quite pleasant.

Odd how things were working out.

I texted Cliff, letting him know I was working on a date for him for the wedding. He sent me back an emoji of a smiling face wearing a party hat. *See you tonight*, I wrote. He didn't know that I'd have a surprise waiting for him!

Tarryn had spoken to Elena briefly, and they'd arranged everything. Now I would be out *another* colossal sum of money, but it was well worth it. I hadn't decided whether or not to tell Cliff the truth. On the one hand, I felt like he should know that Tarryn's hot friend was an escort who I'd paid to accompany him to the wedding. On the other, if he knew about the friend, he would find about about Tarryn. And I wasn't ready to share that news with anyone.

Like the Security Chief had said, keeping the circle small was crucial. If *anyone* found out about Tarryn, *everyone* might find out.

It was funny, but I felt oddly protective of her. I still knew nothing about her background, except that she liked that burrito place. She was a mystery, one that I intended to unravel.

My phone pinged. *A word, please.* It was from my father. At least he hadn't sent Herbert to find me.

I have plans, I texted back. *Can it wait?*

No. Come to my study.

Groaning, I knocked on Tarryn's door. "I'm almost ready!" she called.

"I have a quick errand to run—I'll be back in five minutes."

"Perfect!"

I imagined her smiling, and also possibly naked, behind the door. *Fuck.* I already knew I was going to ask her to sleep in my room again tonight. We needed to keep up the good work. But that wasn't the only thing that was going to be up…

I shifted my sweats uncomfortably. *Down boy,* I thought. Then I remembered that I had to meet with my father, and let me tell you, nothing was less sexy than that.

I grimaced as I entered his study. "Father." I bowed. Because he insisted everyone bow to him, the prat.

"Close the door, please."

My stomach dropped with a sense of foreboding. Father rarely called me to his study—and when he did, it wasn't usually for happy purposes.

"Please, sit."

I sank down across from him and waited. I'd learned, from a young age, to let him speak first.

"I assume you saw the papers this morning?" My father still referred to news on the internet as "the papers."

"I did."

He sat back in his oversized leather chair, which looked a bit like a throne. "And?"

I blinked at him. "Someone obviously leaked the pictures."

The King glowered. "That's not what I'm asking you about, and you know it—don't play dumb. I need to know if the headlines are right. Are you serious about the girl?"

I shrugged. "I'm serious about having her here for the wedding."

"The press is going to need more than that."

"The press can sod off, as far as I'm concerned." I smiled at him without warmth.

"You are going to be King someday. And you know it's over my dead body—quite literally," he sniffed. "But you are going to have to grow up, Clive. You can't be a bad-boy prince forever."

"No, because then you turn into a bad-boy king. Nothing's tackier than *that*." My tone turned icy.

The silence stretched out between us. My father knew exactly what I was referring to, but we never spoke of it. He'd made a deal with the press long ago: he would continue to allow them access and feed them stories and tidbits from inside the palace, and they would never report on his extramarital…endeavors. It was a delicate balance, one he sweated to maintain.

Come to think of it, Izzie was probably following the same model. I couldn't picture her staying faithful to boring old George for too long, even when he livened things up by choking on Parmesan crisps…

"Did you hear me?" my father asked sharply.

"Sorry, I tuned out there for a second. What were you saying?"

"I *said*, it's high time you assumed a more public role. If you're serious about this girl, take her out in the capital. Let the press photograph you. If she is to be their Queen someday, they have a right to know her."

I shook my head. "I'm not going to do that."

"Because you're not sure of her? Or because you're being stubborn?"

"Both," I admitted. "The relationship is new. And I like her. I wouldn't put my worst enemy under that sort of pressure, let alone a friend."

"How much do you know about her?" My father's tone was casual, but I knew better than to trust that.

I shrugged. "I know she's a student, her father's deceased, her mother lives with her in Boston. I know that our security team fully vetted her and that she passed with flying colors."

He nodded once. "That's the only reason she's here."

I raised my gaze to meet his. "Stay out of my affairs, Father. Who I choose to spend my time is my business, not yours—and not the public's."

"They already have you marrying this girl."

"Which is bloody ridiculous! I've only started seeing her."

He leaned forward. "You did this to yourself. You never brought anyone out in public, and everyone's been wondering for *years* if you were ever going to settle down. So don't cry about it. And pay attention—if the public reacts well to her, they've made it easy for you: you've found your Queen."

I shook my head. "I'm not choosing my bride based on a public opinion poll."

He shrugged. "You have to understand that being King means you have two faces: one for the people, one for yourself. So you could do a lot worse than the pretty American. And in private, you can, of course, do whatever you like."

"Do you even *know* what you sound like?"

His stare didn't waver. "I sound like a man who is satisfied, who takes from life what he wants."

I rose to my feet. "You *disgust* me, Father. I will never be like you. I will *never* have two faces, nor would I ever treat my wife the way you treat yours. She's always deserved better than you, and I think deep down you know it."

"And I deserve what she's given *me?*" He raised his voice. "Drinking and pills, and never leaving the house? You think that's what *I* wanted?"

"At some point, you might want to consider that you have some responsibility for what's become of her." I backed toward the door. "I have to go."

I bowed and turned to leave.

"Just remember son: you might judge me, but walk a mile in my shoes," he said, his voice cold. "Marriage isn't about moonlight and roses. It's about duty. You'll understand soon enough, I expect. I can only hope that we get day passes in Hell—someday I'd like to see how my mighty, holier-than-thou son has fallen."

"Always a flair for the dramatic, eh?" I left before he could say more. *My bloody father.* He wanted my allegiance, my obedience, and now my…what…my *pity*? As far as I was concerned, that was a new low.

I stopped halfway down the hall, stepping inside an

empty room to collect myself. Tarryn shouldn't see me like this.

No one should.

But the truth was, I would never be free from my father or from my duty.

And that was all the more reason for me to keep my distance.

TARRYN

THE PRINCE HAD SAID to dress casually, but I still wasn't sure what "palace casual" meant. His Highness might be able to pull off sweatpants, but his American guest was likely another story altogether…

My phone pinged with a text from my mother. It was a picture of Ellie at the table, eating Cheerios and waving. I couldn't help but smile—every time I saw my daughter, my heart soared. I loved her more than I'd ever loved anything. *We're having a great time, but we miss you!* Mom texted. My eyes filled with tears. I loved my mom so much, and I was so lucky to have her.

Taking Ellie for her checkup at 10—keep you posted.

Okay, I texted back immediately. *Don't forget to ask about the dose, okay? Thank you.* I added three hearts, but I really should add a million. My mother was amazing, taking care of Ellie, managing her medications, and taking her to her appointments.

When I'd come to her four years ago and said I needed to leave our hometown in Minnesota—in the middle of the night, no less—she nodded. And then she asked if she could come with me.

We packed our things that night and never looked back.

God bless my mother. She'd left her part-time job, her friends, and her apartment that night. And she never asked me anything, because of course, she knew everything. She'd been the one who'd begged me to call the police, to get help, to run. And each time she saw me too afraid to leave him, she still loved me. She was still my rock, never wavering.

We never spoke about what happened. But I told her on the twenty-four-hour drive to Boston that I was pregnant, and that I was scared, and that I was never going back.

And you know what my mother said? "Good for you, honey."

And through everything that followed—Ellie's surgeries, me turning to AccommoDating when I realized we were never, *ever* going to get ahead—my mother supported me. She told me she was proud of me. She said I was a wonderful mom and a terrific daughter.

And then she'd make dinner.

I sniffled a little as I deleted the text. How lucky was *I*? I couldn't wait to tell my mom the good news when I got home: that we'd be able to pay off our debt and buy a cute place. That we could afford to buy Ellie new clothes, enroll her in preschool, and maybe my mom could even take a night off from making dinner because we'd have enough money to *go out to eat.* Imagine that!

I hadn't told her about the money yet because I didn't want to jinx it. After everything she'd done for me, I wanted to deliver the good news after it was a done deal. My mother had been through enough— I *never* wanted to disappoint her.

All I had to do was get through the next ten days. Then everything was *finally* going to go our way.

I tore through the closet, looking for the perfect thing to wear. If I was being honest with myself—which I wasn't—I would admit that my desire to find a cute outfit had less to do with adhering to palace-casual than it had to do with looking good for a certain royal.

I chose a pair of tight-fitting black pants and a relaxed yet still insanely expensive cashmere top, then did my makeup. I kept it simple, with mascara, blush, and lip gloss. The fact that I was wearing a sexy, lacy bra and matching underwear underneath the outfit?

That was nothing! It was fun to wear La Perla, that was all.

I *might've* found myself reminiscing about seeing His Highness in his sexy sweats this morning and the smell of shampoo in his hair…

I'd tell myself to get a grip, but that would only make things worse!

There was a knock on the door, and I opened it with a grin. "Hi!"

But it wasn't Prince Clive. It was his mother, the Queen.

"Oh! Your Highness!" I dropped into a quick curtsy. "I'm so sorry. I thought you were your son."

"No worries. May I?" She motioned inside the suite.

"Of course." I quickly got out of the way, mind racing a mile a minute. What on earth did the Queen want with *me*?

She swept into the room, and I noticed how thin she was, far too frail-looking for a woman her age. She wore a floor-length blue day-dress with a high collar. Her hair was pulled up into a bun, and she wore her crown. I wondered if she was tired from always being so refined, so dressed up.

She turned to face me. Confronted with the lines on her face and her faded-blue eyes, I immediately knew that the answer was yes.

"I hope I'm not overstepping—well, I'm *certain* I'm overstepping, so I guess my wish is that you'll forgive me for it." She wrung her hands together. "I should start by saying that I am delighted you've come to Astos. I haven't seen my son smile like that in what seems like forever."

"T-Thank you."

"But that's part of what I wanted to talk to you about. Will he be here soon, my son?"

When I nodded, she continued, "Then I must be brief. You saw the headlines this morning, I assume?"

"Yes, I did."

"Of course." She seemed satisfied by that. "You can hardly get away from the press. They're wretched. I swear they're vampires—they'll suck the life right out of you."

Curious, I waited for her to go on.

"You seem like a nice young lady, so I wanted to impart some…wisdom…that I've learned from my years at the palace," the Queen continued. "You see, I was an outsider, too."

Her hands twisted nervously again. "I don't mean that in a bad way—I only mean that I married into the royal family. I was from a middle-class upbringing in a small town. I'd always dreamed of being a princess…"

She smiled again, but now it was a sad smile.

"Dreams and reality have very little to do with one another, of course. When I married His Highness, I believed we were in love. It was like a fairytale. But fairytales are for children. My real life here has been very different from what I'd dreamt."

I nodded. "I imagine it's been difficult."

"That's one word for it—oh, I'm all over the place. I need to get to the point." She started pacing. "What I wanted to say is that you seem like a nice, normal girl. And nice and normal do not always flourish under these conditions. These *royal* conditions. I know this from first-hand experience."

We eyed each other for a moment. Her face was pale, but determined.

"My son seems quite taken with you," she continued. "Clive has never been able to hide his true feelings. But, as his mother, I am here to beg you to consider *all* the ramifications of having a relationship with him. I do not want his heart broken, do you understand?"

"I think so…?"

The Queen stopped pacing and took a deep breath. "Had I known what it would be like, this is not a life I would have chosen for myself. Or for my children. I only wish someone would have had the compassion to tell me the truth before I came down this path. Of course, I would do it all over again—it got me my Clive and my Izzie."

She looked straight at me as she said, "But I couldn't hide what was in my heart. After all these years, I wouldn't be able to live with myself. I wanted to tell you the truth before you let my son fall madly in love with you, but it may already be too late for that."

"He's not—don't worry. Our relationship is very new." For a moment, I longed to tell her the truth. "But…thank you for being so honest with me. It means a lot. And for what it's worth, I think you're very brave."

"You would be the *only* one to think that." She gave me a curt nod. "Now, if you will excuse me, I need to go before my son returns."

I curtsied, but she didn't seem to notice as she fled from the room.

I stared out the window, mulling over the Queen's words. Her honesty shocked me. Even though she was a royal, living with every luxury, I felt sorry for her. *This is not a life I would have chosen for myself. Or for my children.*

She'd been kind to come and talk to me, but I knew she had an ulterior motive: she loved Clive. *I haven't seen my son smile like that in forever.* Again, I wished I could tell her the truth about us. It would be one less thing for her to worry about.

Clive showed up a minute later. "Was that my mother I saw in the hall?"

"No." I smiled at the prince. "At least, I don't think so."

∽

The morning air was warm and lovely. We sat by the fountain in the inner courtyard. The sun-dappled the water, flowers blooming all around us, and the lush, green grounds stretched out as far as the eye could see.

With His Highness sitting next to me on our sunny perch, the Queen's words drifted away. Her concerns touched me, but they were misguided. The Queen had my sympathy; I reminded myself that I didn't need hers.

I smiled at the prince. "This is the first time I've been outside without a coat in six months."

Clive widened his eyes. "You're joking."

"No, really." I laughed. "In Boston, it gets cold in the middle of October, and I'm still usually wearing mittens until the end of April. No word of a lie."

He wrinkled his nose. "Sounds miserable."

"It probably is, but it's all I know. I grew up in Minnesota, and that was even worse." I raised my face to the sun. "I could get used to this."

"We'll have to enjoy as much time outside as possible

while you're here. Perhaps we can steal away to the coast after the wedding." He smiled at me, and my stomach somersaulted.

Steal away to the coast... Oh boy. Imagine staying in a sexy hotel with His Highness? And him in his swim trunks, riding the waves, water dripping off his massive muscles... *Unf.* I resisted the urge to fan myself.

"That sounds nice." My voice was a little shaky.

"Doesn't it?" His crooked grin winded me.

I smiled back at him, basking in the glow of his good mood. Being attracted to His Highness was inconvenient, but it was nothing I couldn't handle. I just had to keep my hands to myself!

"Would you like to visit the lake now?" the prince asked. "I had the staff bring out some lunch for us. It's quite pretty. Are you up for a walk?"

"I'd love to." I hopped up, grinning up at him.

He leaned closer, and my heart rate kicked up. "You know they're watching us, right?"

I looked around. "Out *here*? In your *yard*?" But yard wasn't exactly the right word for the massive, sprawling grounds.

Clive arched an eyebrow. "Whoever took those pictures last night is definitely back in action this morning. So what story shall we spin, Ms. Clayton?"

His tone was playful, inviting. And *ooh*, I wanted to play.

"A *gripping* one." I laughed, even though only I could understand the joke.

But as he casually threw his arm around me—and my stomach did yet *another* somersault—I worried the joke was most surely on me.

CLIVE

I had my arm around her shoulders, and it felt right, so right. Having her so close was…an event unto itself. I was *very* attracted to her. Heat kicked up between us, and I wondered if she felt it. I definitely did.

Might as well burn…

"I think we should be extra-demonstrative today." I tilted my chin as I gazed down at her. "Especially since I'm certain we're being watched."

I was definitely playing with fire. So why did I have no fucks to give about that?

Her eyes brightened. "You do, Your Highness? Aren't you at least a *little* worried about causing a feeding frenzy by the press?"

I shrugged. For some reason, I couldn't stop staring at her mouth. "My sister will be thrilled."

"And you?" Her tone was suddenly serious.

That snapped me out of my lust-filled trance. "What do you mean?"

Tarryn bit her lip as she seemed to gather her thoughts. "I *mean*, I think we really need to think this through. I want to do right by you—and you said you wanted to whip the press into a frenzy, but what happens after that?"

"I'm not sure." My dick definitely hadn't been thinking that far in advance.

"I'm leaving after the wedding. Elena told me the official word would be that things just didn't work out between us," Tarryn said. "But what about your subjects? What will they think? And what if it's worse for you after I'm gone?"

Her concern touched me, but I didn't answer right away—I didn't *have* an answer. That was the problem with not thinking things through.

"I'm here for *you*, to do what you want," she continued. "But I don't want to leave you in the lurch when I hop on a plane back to America in ten days."

We continued toward the lake. It was about a mile, so we would have plenty of time to analyze the situation. *Fuck.* I'd been hoping to hold her hand and maybe kiss her, all under the pretense of us being watched. And then perhaps I'd let my hand roam down her back, all while not thinking about the consequences... Instead, she was asking me Hard Questions.

Since we were in this together, I owed her answers.

I sighed. It was a beautiful, warm sunny day. It was officially early summer in Astos, my favorite time of year.

"I don't know what message I want to send," I admitted. "But I know how to drive the press crazy—my sister's not the only one who's talented in that department."

Tarryn nodded. She looked gorgeous in her pale pink sweater, her hair pulled up into a casual ponytail. "I remember what you said—if Izzie wants press, you're going to give it to her."

I nodded.

Tarryn glanced at me as we walked. "I'm just not sure what *you're* getting out of it, Your Highness."

Her use of my official title made me feel like a jerk. "Please, call me Clive. And to answer your question, what I'm getting out of it is…"

I get to touch you with immunity? I get to play my family for fools?

"I'm not sure," I said. "I guess I feel like I'm pulling one over on everyone, which is satisfying. But, I guess that also makes me an immature prick."

She laughed, a bright, appealing sound. I loved how easy it was to make her laugh.

"Well, there's that," she said. "But I think it's also fair that you feel that way. You've been in a difficult position for a long time. And now you're doing your 'duty' by having a proper date for the wedding, but the truth is, I'm hardly proper."

"I don't think that's true," I said quickly.

"Well." Tarryn shrugged. "*I* don't think we need to pretend to each other."

Silence fell between us, but it wasn't awkward.

She lifted her face to the sun. "I'd like to ask, if I may...*why* did you hire me in the first place? I imagine lots of women would want to be your date for the wedding."

"There was no one I wanted to take. I haven't been in a serious relationship for a long time, and I'm not involved with anyone." I shrugged. "Izzie is the one who pressured me to bring a date, so in one sense, I guess I feel like hiring someone was my opportunity to give her a big middle finger, at least behind her back. But, like I said, I'm an immature prick." Admitting my motivations out loud made me feel ridiculous.

"Please—no, you're not. She put you in a tough spot. But...how did you hear about the agency? Elena mentioned you had a friend or something."

Did I imagine it, or was she blushing a little?

"That's right—Chase Layne, the quarterback. He's a buddy of mine. He met his wife through the agency." For some reason, that made me cough.

"Right. I heard about that." Tarryn's tone was neutral.

"Anyway." I coughed again. "He recommended the service, and here you are. And as for what I want the press to believe… I guess it's nice they think I'm involved with someone, for once. The headlines are usually something along the lines of: *Will the scowling, reclusive prince ever meet anyone and settle down?*"

I sighed. "I half-hoped this arrangement would get them off my back, but you're right: as soon as you're gone, it will be back to business as usual. But first, they'll question what I did wrong. That will probably take a few months."

"But I get it," Tarryn said. "It's like you're giving them something, but it isn't something *real*. I bet that probably feels like winning."

I nodded. "That's exactly right." To have her understand me so perfectly was almost disarming. My complicated feelings about the press weren't exactly something I could talk to many people about.

I glanced at her. The sunlight glinted in her hair and

made her perfect, pale skin shine. "Can I ask *you* a question?"

"Of course." But that little line between her eyebrows appeared.

"Can you tell me more about yourself?"

She exhaled. "Sure—but I'm pretty basic. I live in Boston with my mother. We used to live in Minnesota. My father passed away when I was young. He had cancer."

"I'm sorry to hear that."

She smiled at me. "That's okay—I don't remember him much. But thank you."

When she didn't say more, I hesitated.

"You want to know why I work for the agency," she said.

"I *am* curious," I admitted.

"I needed the money." She turned and looked me in the eye. "My mother was sick, and we had a ton of medical bills. I don't have a college degree. I was waitressing, but…"

"But you could work a million shifts and never get ahead."

She nodded. "I've only been at AccommoDating for a few months. I'll be able to quit when I get back, thanks to you."

I winced. I'd no idea that this arrangement would be

life changing for the woman I'd hired, and that made me feel like a colossal prat. *But, of course*, it would be. The money was practically nothing to me, but to someone actually *with* nothing...

"You don't have to feel guilty," Tarryn said as if reading my thoughts. "I made a choice to work for the agency and to take this job. And I'm grateful for it."

The tone in her voice was practical, which made me ache for her. Tarryn—or *any* woman—shouldn't have to make a choice like that to avoid financial ruin. "I'm so sorry."

She stopped walking. "For what?"

"That you were in that position. That you felt you had to go to the agency in the first place." My heart literally broke for her.

She watched me carefully. "You don't believe in it, do you?"

"Believe in what?"

"In what I do for a living." She kept her voice low.

I shook my head. "No, I don't. Of course not."

She tilted her head and studied me as if she were calculating something.

I tugged at the collar of my shirt. "Why are you looking at me like that?"

"It's nothing." She smiled at me, but it wasn't the same open smile. "Ooh, is that the lake?" She started walking ahead of me, and feeling very much more than several steps behind, I hustled to catch up.

The water spread out before us, calm, blue, and sparkling like a sapphire in the sun. "It's so beautiful." Tarryn's face lit up again.

"It is." But I was looking at *her*.

"Listen." I went closer and took her hand. She turned to me, surprised. "I hope I didn't offend you just now—it's nothing against *you*."

"Oh, I know." She nodded. "You are very high-minded, Your Highness. You have ideals. That's admirable."

I squeezed her hand. "Not everyone can afford to have ideals."

"But I already knew that." She smiled one last time, then gently took her hand away. "Is that our picnic basket? I'm dying to see what they packed for us."

She was off again before I could speak, her blond ponytail swinging as she headed down the gentle hill to the lake.

Fuck. I'd gone and done it, now. I wasn't sure exactly what I *had* done, only that she was pulling away from me. I watched Tarryn's ponytail as it swished. The intelligent thing would be to let her go.

I watched her, my hands clenched into fists.

Then I followed her down the hill.

TARRYN

HE WAS BEHIND ME—I could *feel* him closing in—but I at least had a few moments to compose myself. *Easy, girl.*

The lake was gorgeous. There was a weeping willow on the other shore. Ducks swam in a row, quacking to each other, and the bright sky shone above. The green grounds spread out in every direction. Had I been in a different frame of mind, I would have been in awe.

Instead, I had a knot in my chest. His Highness had rejected me—and quite soundly, too. Clive hadn't insulted me, but his words still stung. *I'm so sorry.*

He *pitied* me. And there was nothing less sexy than pity!

The picnic basket was a welcome distraction. I headed directly toward the provisions the staff had left for us, neatly packed by the shore. I would definitely find comfort in some food right now if nothing else…

My mind raced as I stayed several steps ahead of the prince. He'd been the one to hire me, but now I knew why he'd told Elena the arrangement would be strictly business: he would pay for a fake date, but he wouldn't pay for sex. Because he didn't believe in it.

His ideas were stronger than his attraction to me, if any. Perhaps I'd been wrong thinking that he felt some sort of spark—he was likely above it. *Fair enough.* I would be his genie for the next ten days, make all his tabloid wishes come true, and then disappear back to America with my new riches. It wasn't as though I would whine about it—this arrangement would be life-changing for my family.

If I was being honest with myself, which of course I wasn't, I would admit that his pity made me feel ashamed.

But as His Highness himself had said, not everyone could afford to have ideals.

I vowed not to think about it anymore. *Game face, Tarryn.* I thought of Ellie and my mother. I thought of the money. He could pity me all he wanted, so long as he paid me.

"Sandwiches on baguettes and a bottle of rose—that's my guess." Clive's voice was suddenly in my ear.

Why did his proximity make me shiver? *It's officially never going to happen, girl!*

"You think? Let's see." I smiled at him, hoping to return us both to the playful mood we'd had by the fountain. I was going to play my part, and it would be a Golden-Globe-worthy performance, dammit.

I opened the cooler as he spread out the blanket the staff had left for us, a colorful quilt covered with purple paisleys. "Aha! You were correct. One lovely bottle of rose."

I handed it to him, and he unscrewed the top, pouring us each a glass while I brought out the sandwiches. He was correct again—the kitchen had prepared two fat sandwiches on fresh, crusty bread. I spied mozzarella inside and fresh basil. "These smell like heaven."

Clive's eyes twinkled as he handed me my wine, trading me for his baguette. "I think Chef enjoys impressing you."

We sat down on the blanket, and I had a bite. "I think I might love him—or her?" I asked.

"Her. Mmm. She's French, and she can be a little testy, but she's worth it." We ate in silence for a moment, and then he raised his glass to me. "I'd like to make a toast. To *you*. I have managed to put my foot in my mouth several times; you have met my *very* trying family, and yet, you have not run away screaming. I appreciate you more than I can say."

We clinked glasses, and I laughed. "It's my pleasure." The wine was as delicious as the food, and in the warm sun, it went straight to my head. The knot in my chest loosened a little.

Maybe I should quit with the wine while I was ahead.

Instead, I had another reckless sip. He might pity me, but he *needed* me. Plus, I wanted to see something…

"Should we continue with our plan?" I asked.

He arched an eyebrow, which he somehow made look sexy, the devil. "Which plan was that?"

"The one where we're openly affectionate."

Clive looked mildly surprised, but then he smiled. "I'm game if you are."

He might not want me like that, but a public display of affection had been *his* idea. So we should stick to the program, as awkward as it might be. *Golden Globes, here I come.*

"Grab your wine? And then come here." He patted the quilt next to him.

Oh boy. I had another large sip of rose first, and I noticed Clive did, too. I scooted closer, and we both leaned back, looking out at the lake. "It really is lovely here," I said. "Thank you for bringing me."

"It's very peaceful. Izzie and I used to come here a lot

as children with our mother. It almost felt like another world."

I nodded. "What was it like, growing up as a prince?"

"Well, I suppose I didn't know any different, so it was normal for me." Clive shrugged. "But even as a little boy, I hated wearing dress clothes. Mother used to insist because it's highly irregular for royals to dress casually. But you can't climb trees in a suit coat." He laughed. "I ripped enough of them that she finally gave up."

"Good for her."

"I don't think she was happy about it, but at least Izzie always wanted to dress up." He glanced at me. "What about you—what was growing up in Minnesota like?"

He remembered what I'd said? "Cold, mostly. But like you said, I didn't know any different, so I was used to it. And I had fun. There was a park near my house—I used to swing every day. I loved the feeling! Ooh, and I used to have a contest with myself about jumping off. I tried to get a little higher every day, then jump and try to land on my feet. I had *lots* of scabby knees to show for it."

"I bet you were adorable."

"I think I was usually dirty, and my hair was a mess. But, I loved playing outside—my mom was always picking leaves and twigs off me." I giggled. Ellie was like that, too. She *loved* playing outside. Even in the winter, we'd just bundle her up and bring her out…

"What are you thinking about?" he asked. "You had the happiest look on your face."

He needed to stop being so damn perceptive. And handsome. I shrugged. "Just the swings, I guess. Being a kid was great, wasn't it?"

"It *was* pretty great." He jutted his chin toward the lake. "I used to pretend that I was a pirate, and that was the ocean. I played by myself for hours. My mother always said I had an overactive imagination."

I could picture him as a boy, muttering to himself and battling imaginary enemies. "That's so cute."

"Ha—I'm glad you think so. Izzie used to tell me I was weird. But then again, she'd be busy with her dolls, arranging lavish wedding ceremonies." He glanced at me, a wry smile on his face. "Not much has changed."

He watched me for a moment before he asked, "Will you be all right, being with me like this?"

"What do you mean?"

He sighed. "If we get closer. I don't want to do anything that makes my new American friend uncomfortable."

"Your new American friend isn't the one we need to worry about." I tilted my head at him. "My royal friend from Astos is the one we need to keep an eye on."

"Ah, I'm fine. This was what I wanted, after all."

"Okay then." I smiled at him expectantly. Then, when he didn't move, I boldly climbed onto his lap and threw my arm around his neck. I trailed my fingers through his thick hair, relishing the feel of it. "Let's let the professionals handle this, shall we?"

He nodded, but the muscle in his jaw looked taut. And his pupils got larger.

Aha. I'd wanted to see something, and there it was. Heat kicked up between us. I looked up at him from under my lashes and parted my lips a little. Did he feel it, too?

I'd be outright lying if I said *I* didn't feel something. In fact, I felt a literal *wall* of muscle as I pressed up against his chest. He wrapped his arms around me, big biceps holding me firmly in place.

And beneath me, he started to get hard. I could feel him stirring. I wriggled on his lap, and he bit back a groan.

So, bad girl that I was, I went in for the kill.

I kissed him tentatively at first. He didn't move for a moment, so I stopped. Still, electricity shuddered through me. We stared at each other, time stretching out. His length hardened beneath me, solidifying, and I *knew* he wanted me. That heat was undeniable. Clive could say what he wanted, he could be too good for me, he could pity me, but he *still* wanted me.

I was pretty enough and experienced enough to know that his hard-on meant little, but it still meant something to *me*.

I wriggled my ass against him. Then, when he moaned, I kissed him again.

This time, he didn't hesitate. He took my face in his hands and deepened the kiss, his tongue seeking mine. When they connected, fire lit up my core. He released my face and sank his hands deep into my hair, pulling me closer against him, his mouth devouring mine.

A speedy, hot feeling took over. I couldn't stop kissing him. Our bodies rubbed together, creating a delicious friction. I moaned, and he laughed—a deep, satisfied sound—as his hands roamed down my back.

I felt…*wet*. And *fiery*. And entirely out of control, like I'd never been in my life. If he wanted to lay me down right there, in broad daylight, I'd have little will to stop him. Even though we were being watched!

That snapped me out of it. A picture of the prince having sex with his fake American girlfriend was *not* going in the tabloids!

I broke our kiss and scooted off his lap. "Well…ha." I put my hands on my face: it was hot. "That was affectionate, all right. All out in the open."

Clive's massive chest was rising and falling rapidly. His hair was a bit wild. "You can say that again. I'm sure whoever is watching us got an eyeful."

I adjusted my sweater and fixed my ponytail. "Yes, Your High—Clive. Well played."

There were two hectic spots of color in his cheeks. "Well played, indeed."

As I was studiously avoiding being honest with myself, I ignored the small—but *very* satisfying—sensation of smugness that bloomed in my chest.

Well played, indeed. *Golden Globes, here I come!*

CLIVE

JERKING off in my shower was *not* how I'd expected to get ready for the party that evening, but alas, there I was.

I closed my eyes, remembering the feel of Tarryn on my lap. Her sweet ass rubbed against me. My cock lengthened, growing thicker. Different images from our time by the lake ran through my mind, making me crazy.

my hands in her hair

electricity shooting through me as we kiss

Tarryn sitting on my lap, grinding herself against my erection

the smell of her skin

Jesus, I wanted her. I wanted her *bad*. So bad that I had to whack off in my shower, so I didn't have a raging hard-on for her all night, straining against my tux—

I shoved the thought away and imagined us by the lake again. *Tarryn's naked underneath me on the blanket. The sun dapples her creamy skin, her perfect tits bounce as I enter her, and then she screams my name—*

Fuck. I fisted my cock as I came, hard, but not hard enough. I was momentarily sated, but *real* satisfaction eluded me. This orgasm was merely a placeholder, a cheap counterfeit of the real thing. I wanted her. I wanted the way she smelled, the feel of her skin, her hair fanning out beneath her as I made her cry out in ecstasy.

Fuck! What was I going to do? From the outset, I'd been firm that I wouldn't have physical relations with her. And then today, I'd told her how I felt about what she did for a living. That I felt *sorry* for her for being forced into such a choice. Masked as concern, I'd pissed on what she did to take care of her family.

Great work, mate. I really had a way with the ladies! I needed to make it up to her.

But even after what I'd said—and my bumbling attempt to apologize to her—she'd played her part down by the lake. If anyone had been watching, we'd given them quite the show. But how much of it was pretend on her part?

When she'd kissed me, I'd been completely undone. I hadn't wanted someone that badly in…ever. My desire for her was like a stranglehold around me. My cock stirred again. *Down boy*. Christ, how was I supposed to function like this?

I stuck my face under the water and turned it to cool. More than needing to make things up to Tarryn, I needed to get my shit together. Otherwise, I was no good to anybody.

For better or for worse, we were headed to yet another party. With alcohol. And my family. And Tarryn, most likely in another killer dress. And she'd be sleeping over in my room, of course. Because everyone would expect her to sleep over. Again.

I wanted her, but I wouldn't take her like this. She was vulnerable. She'd accepted the job because she'd desperately needed the money. Part of me wondered if I should just pay her and send her on her way back to America. But I immediately shot that idea down—I needed her. She was my ruse. What would the press say if she disappeared before the wedding?

Not that I gave a flying fuck.

Still, it was convenient to pretend.

And I refused to think about it any more than that.

THAT LITTLE LINE was back in between Tarryn's eyes when I went to her room to pick her up. Her hair and makeup were done, but she was still wrapped in a thick robe. Her eyes were wide with worry.

"What's the matter?"

"Ugh, I'm sorry I'm not ready yet—I got sucked into the internet." She pulled me inside her suite.

"It's okay. I'm early. But what's wrong?"

She held up her phone. "Did you go online this afternoon?"

"No." I was instantly on alert. "Is it pictures from the lake?"

She nodded. "They're pretty…graphic."

I snatched the phone from her hand. The browser was open to an image of us from earlier today. "Oh. Wow."

I gaped at the photo, which was indeed graphic. Tarryn sat on my lap. We were locked in a heated embrace, kissing, my hands sunk deep into her hair. The headline read: *IS A ROYAL HEIR ON THE WAY?*

"Oh boy. Here we go." I flicked to the next story, which had the same image. *PRINCE CLIVE AND TARRYN CLAYTON CAN'T KEEP THEIR HANDS OFF EACH OTHER—AND IT'S SO CUTE.*

"Cute." I scowled at the headline. "Yes, you could say so."

I scrolled through the other sites; it was more of the same. But it wasn't the headlines that rankled me, though they were pretty annoying—it was the pictures and not because our privacy had been violated. We'd *staged* the photos, for fuck's sake—so why did they look so real?

I handed Tarryn her phone. "Well done."

She raised her eyebrows, but to her credit, she didn't say a word.

I shrugged. "We knew they were photographing us. This is to be expected."

"Well, if you're okay with it, then…" She smiled. "I'll just go and get dressed. We should hurry."

She hustled off, long blond hair trailing in her wake, and I longed to follow her into the dressing room and lock the door behind us.

Fuck. How many times in one day could a man think the same word?

I was perseverating, and I knew it. Which was not a good look during a dinner party thrown by my sister.

At the thought of Izzie, my mind started whirring. On the one hand, it surprised me that neither my sister nor my father had called me that afternoon to talk about the coverage. On the other, they were probably pleased with the way the story was playing out. In fact, they might be directly responsible for its tone…

What were they playing at? It was likely they actually wanted to marry me off. One less thing to worry about, I supposed.

Izzie wanted Tarryn to sit next to her at dinner. Tarryn could handle herself, but I worried my sister would cross-examine her in great detail. Had she not been a princess, Izzie would have made a highly skilled prosecutor. So I needed to insert myself next to them—even though I knew Izzie would put up a fight.

What did she want with Tarryn? Was she in fact rooting for us, or was she against us? I mean, there was no 'us' but…

Done with thinking myself in circles, I located the bourbon and poured myself a glass. Just as I was finishing it, Tarryn came out in her gown. It was strapless, pale yellow, and made her look like a…princess.

"You look beautiful." I couldn't stop myself from telling her the truth.

She smiled broadly, pleased, and it was like the sun coming out. "Thank you, Clive."

I poured myself another bourbon. Because I was in some fucking trouble, all right.

THANK goodness there was a cocktail hour before dinner. Not because I needed more bourbon—I definitely didn't, not that I let that stop me. Instead, I needed a few minutes to develop a strategy to deal with my sister, and yet, a plan eluded me.

The other guests gave Tarryn and me a wide berth. Perhaps they thought we needed space to grope each other?

"How are you, Cousin?" Cliff was suddenly beside me, a sour expression on his face. "Ms. Clayton." He bowed to her stiffly.

"What's wrong with you?" I asked.

He scowled. "I *thought* you were going to find a date for me. It appears I'm in need of Freya Wilson, after all."

"Poor thing." Tarryn patted his arm.

"Thank you, My Lady." Cliff had a sip of water. "You know, it *does* make it a little better when you give me a sympathy pat."

I puffed my chest, but Tarryn winked at me. "I've got something even better for you."

The Duke looked hopeful. "You do?"

I was probably going to punch Cliff soon. He sounded *way* more hopeful than was appropriate.

"Yes! Just one second—be right back." Tarryn hustled off, and we both stared after her.

After a moment, when I realized Cliff was *still* staring, I punched him in the arm.

"Ow! What'd you do that for?"

"Stop trying to steal my girl." I straightened my jacket. "She's off-limits."

Cliff arched an eyebrow. "You really *do* have it bad, Your Highness. I saw those pictures today." He let out a low whistle.

I cleared my throat. "You and everyone else."

"What does Izzie have to say about all this?" He scanned the room for my sister, who was surrounded by admirers, holding court.

"You heard her last night—the more Americans, the merrier." I spotted Tarryn with an attractive young woman, who was shorter and curvier, with long, dark hair. They were laughing and chatting happily as they headed for us. "Speaking of Americans…"

"Holy crow." Cliff gaped as he watched the crowd part for the beautiful pair of females coming toward us. "There *is* a God."

They reached us, and when Tarryn smiled at me, I had to agree with him.

"Your Highness, Your Grace, may I introduce my friend?" Tarryn asked. "This is Vivian Park. Vivian, this is my boyfriend, Prince Clive. And this is his cousin, the Duke of Clifton—the one I was telling you about."

Vivian was lovely and petite, with long, dark hair, copper-colored skin, and curious, sparkling eyes.

"Your Highness. Your Grace." She dropped into a flawless curtsy. When she rose, she gave Cliff a million-dollar smile. "I am so *thrilled* to meet you. Tarryn's been gushing about you ever since she got here."

"She has? What a wonderful friend you have." Cliff shook her hand, his eyes never leaving her pretty face. "It's an honor, My Lady. Would you care for some champagne?"

"I'd prefer seltzer if that's okay with you."

He held up his water. "I'll drink to that." When she smiled at him again, looking up at him from under her thick lashes, he appeared to be a bit dazed.

"Perhaps you could get her that seltzer, and maybe show her around, Cousin," I urged him gently.

Cliff nodded. "Would that be all right with you, My Lady?"

She tossed her hair and beamed at him. "I'd love it. This is my first time in Astos, and I've *never* been to a real palace. *Or* met a real Duke. It's an honor, Your Grace."

"The honor is mine." He beamed back, and, offering his arm, they disappeared together toward the bar.

"Nice work, My Lady." I bowed to Tarryn. "He's already completely smitten."

"You think so?" She watched them with interest. "Vivian was *so* excited when I called. She's obsessed with dukes, no word of a lie."

"Really? More so than with…princes?"

Tarryn nodded, eyes wide. "Dukes are apparently a *thing*. They're all the rage right now. She screamed so loud I had to hold the phone away from my ear."

She turned back to me, a massive grin on her face. "I'm *so* glad Viv's here. She's my best friend back in Boston. Viv's good people—the Duke will enjoy his time with her."

"We should have a double date with them tomorrow," I said, though I instantly regretted it. I didn't want to share Tarryn with anyone, not even for a moment.

Fuck, I was doomed.

"Your sister's looking at us," Tarryn whispered. "Do you have any last-minute tips for dealing with her at dinner?"

I sighed. "She's very clever—she will remember everything that you say, and she will analyze it to death later if it suits her. So be careful. It may seem as though she's rooting for our relationship, but you never know with Izzie. She often has a plan that's invisible to the untrained eye."

Tarryn gulped some champagne. "I'm nervous."

I took her hand and squeezed it. "Don't be. I'll be next to you, whether Izzie wants me there or not."

"Hello, darlings!" Izzie tripped over to us, enveloping us in a cloud of perfume, carefully orchestrated hugs, and air kisses. Tonight she wore a champagne-colored column gown which skimmed her slim figure; George really ought to encourage her to eat more.

"How are you, Princess?" I asked her formally.

"You're so silly, *Your Highness*—and I am lovely! The wedding is so soon, and all of our dear friends are here." She turned to Tarryn, her megawatt smile firmly in place. "And how are *you*? How does it feel to be the belle of the ball—or at least, of the tabloids?"

Tarryn shook her head. "I think there's only one belle here—and that's you, of course. So what's it like having a fairytale wedding? Would you please tell me all about it at dinner?"

Tarryn's eyes were wide in her face. I was pretty sure that even though she was a solid actress, she wasn't feigning interest in the nuptial details.

"Ooh, I'd love to." Izzie linked her arm through Tarryn's and led her away toward the dining room. "But you mustn't tell a soul, okay? I don't want the details being leaked out before the big day."

I trailed after them as my sister chattered to my date. Was it insane that I was jealous that my *sister*—who was not only a pain in the ass but also a hetero *female*—had stolen Tarryn away from me?

I grabbed yet another bourbon as I left the party, following the two women, anxious to stay nearby.

For fuck's sake, this was not working out the way I'd planned *at all*.

TARRYN

⚜

THE PRESS often described Princess Izzie as "dazzling"—and they were right. I stared as she chattered away at me, talking about the dresses for the flower girls and what type of appetizers they'd be serving at the reception. But all I could focus on were her corkscrew curls, sparkling eyes, and charming smile.

"...What do you think of that?" Her bright eyes searched my face.

"Um." I bit my lip. "Can I be honest with you? I was so busy staring at you I didn't hear what you said—you're *so* beautiful."

"Ha! You are a *love*! I'm so happy my brother finally met a nice girl, thank goodness!" She squeezed me closer and happily started chatting again.

This time, I paid attention. There was going to be a

symphony playing outside the chapel when the bride and groom arrived. Her nine bridesmaids were wearing pale pink; didn't I think that was a universally flattering color? I did. Her mother's dress was a mint green, which Izzie had picked out herself because she was tired of seeing the queen in blue, blue, blue. Had I seen her mother's eyes? They were faded blue and a bit depressing, and hence the mint green to shake things up.

Did I like escargot? I'd never tried one. They were being passed during the cocktail hour after the ceremony; I'd have to sample one then…

We entered the dining room, and I gaped at the space. It was massive, with an enormous table set with china, fresh flowers, crystal goblets, and dozens of blazing white candles. Speaking of crystal, the largest chandelier I'd ever seen glittered above the giant table.

I stopped, stunned. "Princess Izzie, this is…amazing."

She raised her shoulders, grinning in pleasure. "It *is* rather festive, isn't it? Here we are."

She ushered me toward two seats in the center of the table, and liveried servers appeared out of nowhere and pulled out the chairs for us. With a nod, the princess sank gracefully into her seat. I tried to imitate her poise, but how could I? Princess Izzie was in a league of her own.

She watched, pleased, as the guests filed in and took

their seats. "Ooh, who is that with the Duke of Clifton? She's quite pretty."

I mentally ran through Elena's instructions before I answered. I wouldn't waiver one iota from the plan. "She's a friend of mine—from America," I added quickly.

The princess's eyes widened. "Ooh, do tell."

"When you said that the Duke should have an American date, Prince Clive asked me if I had any single friends," I explained. "Ms. Park—Vivian—is my best friend back home. She *loves* the royal family. Your brother was kind enough to fly her over here to meet your cousin."

I held my breath, waiting for the princess's response.

She reached for my hand and squeezed it. "That is *brilliant*. Clive did that for me?"

"Well, yes. I think he also wanted to help the Duke out—he seemed pretty sad he didn't have a date."

Izzie's eyes were wide in her face. "I truly believe you're having a positive effect on my brother. This is quite unlike him, I assure you."

"In what way?"

"He's doing something for someone else—I love my brother, you see, but he's *very* self-centered." She blinked. "Maybe it's *you* he wants to make happy, as much as it's the Duke. Or me, for that matter."

I tilted my head. "Me...?"

"He wouldn't fly over one of *my* friends if I danced a jig, stood on my head, and then begged," she said simply. "But apparently, my brother is *very* interested in what makes you happy. And so tell me, what is it?"

"I'm sorry?"

"What is it that makes you *happy*?" Izzie accepted a glass of champagne for each of us. "I think I should like to know, too. You might be my good-luck charm after all these years."

"What makes me happy? Let's see…" I immediately thought of Ellie—the way she smelled after she'd taken a bath and was in her pajamas, wanting to read a book. But of course, I couldn't talk about *her*.

"I like food. And champagne." I tilted my glass toward her.

"But what makes you *tick*? You're an American—all Americans are motivated, aren't they?"

"Er…" I had the sense that the princess's brain was moving a million miles a minute, and I was at a loss to keep up. "I like being outside, and I love the ocean. I like my classes at school," I added as an afterthought.

She arched an eyebrow.

"I'm sure that makes me pretty basic, but I'm a simple person."

"Food. You like *food*. And the ocean." Her eyebrow crept a fraction higher.

I nodded.

She leaned closer, and I was once again confronted by her beauty, so natural and yet somehow elevated. "You know, my dear, my brother is also a simple sort of man. So you two might very well be a match."

"Oh…thank you." My cheeks heated.

"Are you serious about him? I mean, the tabloids already have you two engaged—"

"It's still very new." I swallowed hard. I didn't want to disappoint her, but I also didn't want her getting it into her head that her brother would be the next one heading down the aisle.

"But when you know, you know—ah, when George and I first started dating, I knew it right away. He was just so…*dependable*." She leaned closer. "We like to have our spouses be reliable, you see. George likes numbers, cigars, and horses. You like *food*. And the ocean. That's the sort of woman I'm looking to add to the team, you see?"

I nodded, even though she was confusing me. *She* was looking to add to the team?

"So I want you to consider how you see yourself fitting in around here," Izzie continued, her cool, minty breath wafting over me. Even her breath was immaculate. "Do you think you can be a team player?"

"I—"

ESCORTING THE ROYAL

"Is that my girl *Tarryn*? My friend from the plane? Can you believe it?" A cloud of musky perfume that made my eyes water suddenly enveloped me.

I looked up, shocked. *"Mindy?"*

"As I live and breathe"—Mindy Fitz bent down and pulled me in for a tight hug against her ample bosom—"I *thought* that was your picture on the internet! I said to myself, Can you believe it? Your new friend from first-class is dating the *prince*!"

She released me and laughed loudly, an alarming honking sound. Princess Isabelle looked quite astounded by the sound—and as though she might go into cardiac arrest.

Mindy Fitz—my new "friend" from the first-class flight from Boston—stood before us in all her glory. She was spectacularly put together for the evening. Her frosted-blond curls were voluminous, framing her face like a helmet. She'd applied smoky eye makeup to match her black velvet gown. An enormous diamond necklace and earrings so large they made her earlobes sag weighed down her compact, curvy frame.

"You must be Princess Isabelle." Mindy gave a surprisingly nimble curtsy. "It's an honor to finally meet you."

Isabelle gaped, and I came to Mindy's rescue. "Your

Highness, this is Mindy Fitz, from America. I met her on my flight to Astos."

"It's a...pleasure," Isabelle said weakly. She looked pretty scandalized. "How is it you came to the palace tonight?"

"Your father sent a car for me." Mindy smiled broadly, her hot-pink lipstick contrasting with her blinding-white teeth. "He and *my* father are longtime business associates—my family owns World News, the media conglomerate. I'm sure you've heard of them?"

Isabelle immediately straightened her spine. "Yes of *course*, Mindy, shame on me for not recognizing you. The King can be remiss sometimes about sharing details with me—you know how men are! But, please, have a glass of champagne with us."

Mindy did one better—she parked herself right next to Isabelle. She started chatting, asking all sorts of questions about the royal wedding. I sat nearby and watched, fascinated. Each woman's body language told a different story. Mindy's was excited and aggressive; Izzie's was defensive, masked as warm and friendly. It was a complicated dance, indeed.

A few minutes later, the dinner bell rang. Mindy rose, grinning, in a triumphant cloud of velvet and perfume. "Princess Izzie—I *hope* it's okay that I call you

Izzie—it's been a pleasure. Can you believe we have so much in common? I can't wait for the wedding, gah!"

Mindy winked at me on her way out. "See you around, kid. And let me know if that handsome chauffeur is anywhere? He had such a nice smile!" She hustled off, hips swaying.

Princess Izzie looked flustered, as though Mindy Fitz had taken her on a wild ride. She watched as Mindy sashayed toward the end of the table, where the King and Queen were already seated.

"Is everything all right?" I asked.

"Of course." Izzie's smile was instantly, firmly reattached to her face. "Mrs. Fitz just surprised me, is all. I didn't know my father had invited her to the festivities."

"She seems nice enough." I shrugged. "All I really know about her is that she likes champagne."

"Then I shall have to keep her flute full." Izzie drained her own glass, and a server immediately swooped in and replaced it with a fresh one.

George joined us. He lovingly patted his fiancé's back as he took the seat next to hers. "Hello, darling. Everything all right?"

Izzie chugged her entire fresh glass of champagne before answering. "Of course, darling. Of course." Still, she raised her empty flute, signaling for it to be filled.

I wondered what exactly had the princess so rattled.

CLIVE

I BULLIED the random Countess sitting next to Tarryn out of her seat. With a sniff, she swept off, nose stuck into the air. Much to my surprise, my sister didn't argue with my insistence on being close to my date.

Izzie seemed busy discussing something with George, so I leaned closer to Tarryn. "How are you holding up?"

"I'm not sure." That tiny crease formed between her eyes again, and I longed to do something, anything, to ease her strain.

I immediately tensed. "What happened? Are you okay?"

"Oh, I'm fine!" she assured me quickly. "It's just been…interesting, is all. Let's talk about it later, okay?"

"Of course." Unable to stop myself, I put my hand on her back and rubbed it. For some reason, touching her made me relax. "I'm here now—I'll rescue you if necessary."

"You're the best." She smiled. "I'm really glad you're here. I missed you, Your—Clive."

A little jab hit me in the heart. "You did?"

"Of course, silly. You're my knight in shining armor." She whispered, "Listen... If dinner is super fancy, can we order something basic later? I'm starving."

"My lady." I grinned at her. "Your wish is my command."

She grinned back. "Excellent."

Someone coughed loudly next to us. I looked past Tarryn to my sister, who watched us with her eyebrows raised.

"I don't expect that you two need to have any more public displays of affection—at least, not during dinner. Tarryn is *my* plus-one for the evening," Izzie said pointedly. "Ooh, here they come with the first course. Does everyone like caviar?"

The servers brought out the platters, and Tarryn stared blankly at the gleaming, onyx roe on her plate. She hesitated, watching as I squeezed some lemon juice on mine, then ate it with a cracker.

She hesitantly followed suit. She was smiling and nodding at something Izzie said, but as soon as she had a bite, she reached underneath the table and squeezed my hand hard. Tarryn looked mildly panicked as she continued to chew. *Uh oh.* Someone didn't like caviar.

"Don't you love it, darling? It's *beluga*, the finest kind in all the world." Izzie was gushing about the food, but she'd barely taken a bite.

"It's delicious." Tarryn nodded with enthusiasm, but she gripped my hand with desperation.

Liar.

I needed to come to her aid. "Not to interrupt your enjoyment of the extraordinary caviar, Iz, but I wanted to point something out. Our cousin and his new American friend seem to be getting on well." I tilted my head in Cliff and Vivian's direction.

Izzie blinked at the new couple. "That appears to be an understatement."

My sister was correct. Cliff was feeding Vivian caviar from a spoon, and she was sucking on it suggestively as they eye-fucked each other.

"Good lord." Izzie fanned herself. "Perhaps you should try feeding *me*, George."

George's cheeks were full of caviar. "What's that, love?"

"Nothing." Izzie shook her head. "Try not to choke tonight, okay?"

Tarryn was pushing the food around on her plate. She looked as though she wanted to crawl under the table to hide from the caviar. I needed to keep my sister distracted.

"Who is that woman talking to father?" I asked Iz. "She was over here earlier."

"Oh, that's one of his business associates. Mindy Fitzwilliam, or something." She waved her hand dismissively. "She's American, too. Funny story, Tarryn met her on the plane."

She turned to Tarryn, a curious look in her eye. "Who did she ask about, again? Was it Clive's chauffeur?"

Tarryn nodded. "Yes—Stellan. She was quite taken with him when she saw him at the airport."

"Interesting." But Izzie sounded bored.

But it *was* interesting that my father was spending time with this foreign newcomer at such an important dinner. Usually, he would surround himself with the other royals, happy to lord his position over them.

But tonight, the king was the captive audience of the American. He nodded in agreement with something the frosted-blond said, and she honked with laughter, shoulders shaking. My mother watched them from her nearby seat, fastidiously sipping from her martini, a stony expression on her face.

At least we weren't sitting at *that* end of the table.

The other good news? The servers cleared the caviar away; Tarryn blew out a sigh of relief. But her respite only lasted for a moment. They served the main course: an artfully arranged tower of lobster, scallops, and clams.

She squeezed my hand one last time, but smiled gamely. Then, fine actress that she was, she bravely dug in.

~

"Will you sleep over again?" I asked once we'd finished with the blasted dinner. "I think it would look funny if you didn't." It was an excuse, pure and simple. What was that old American song? *Burn, baby, burn!*

"Of course—I just need to brush my teeth, first. Maybe I'll do it twice." Tarryn shivered. "I've never seen that much seafood in my life."

"You didn't *have* to eat it."

Tarryn's eyes got wide. "Of course I did! Your sister raved about the caviar and how the clams were dug from special mudflats in the Pacific Northwest! How was I supposed to say no to *that*?"

"You get an 'A' for effort." I chuckled.

"Ugh! Hopefully, I can get a grilled cheese from Chef if she's feeling generous." Tarryn smiled at the thought. "I'll only be a minute—I just need to grab a couple of things. You can come in."

"No, it's fine. I'll wait out here." I bent down and kissed her cheek—in case anyone was watching, of course. "See you soon."

She was still smiling as she went inside and gently closed the door behind her.

It's a fake date, I reminded myself. So why was I pacing as I waited for her, anxiously awaiting her return?

I decided to stop thinking so much. It was only causing me trouble.

Voices drifted from down the hall; damn, I did *not* feel like talking to anyone after such a long evening. I stepped into a small, darkened room, which the staff used to store seasonal items and art out of rotation.

The voices came closer. I instantly recognized my father's. "You know, I've been considering your request. I don't think it's a good idea, I'm afraid. It might seem highly unusual to have outsiders seated so prominently at the reception."

I could tell, in an instant, that he was uncomfortable. That piqued my interest—my father was usually the one to make people squirm, not the other way around.

"I understand that, but *please?*" It was a woman, American, with a somewhat nasally voice. "This is the opportunity of a lifetime!"

"I can assure you that this whole arrangement is highly unconventional." My father sighed. "Would you consider sitting at a table with the Duke and Duchess of Idrid? They're quite popular."

The woman groaned theatrically. "Aw, Your Highness, this isn't what we agreed to. I want front and center. I want kings and queens. I want in on all the action!"

"Of course—as you wish." Their voices disappeared down the hall.

I stood in the darkness for a moment, thoughts racing. Who in the *hell* had my father been talking to? It had to be that American businesswoman from dinner. But why was he giving in to her demands?

I stepped out of the room just as Tarryn opened her door. She still wore her yellow gown and clutched a small overnight bag.

Suddenly, I forgot all about my father. He could wait.

Tarryn was another matter altogether.

∽

I sat on my bed, legs stretched out, watching as she ate. It was great to be out of my tux, and it was even better to be locked in my room with my gorgeous, albeit pretend, girlfriend.

"Oh my goodness, that was delicious." Tarryn put her hand on her stomach. She'd changed into her pajamas, pale-pink cotton, disappointedly modest, and she'd washed her makeup off. She once again looked young, innocent, and incredibly beautiful.

She'd just inhaled the grilled cheese Chef had prepared for her and was now eyeing a platter filled with cupcakes. "Have one," I ordered. "They're heavenly."

"I might not fit into my dress for the wedding if I keep this up. But I hate to waste them…" She selected a chocolate cupcake with white frosting.

"We need to tell Izzie that you don't like seafood," I chided.

Tarryn's shoulders slumped. "She was already raving about the escargot they're serving at the reception."

"You need to be firm—just tell her the truth."

"I want your sister to like me."

"Speaking of that. You said you were going to tell me something," I reminded her.

She nodded. "Your sister said something that I thought was strange."

I immediately tensed. "What was it?"

"Nothing bad—she just asked me if I thought I could be a team player. And I had the feeling she meant for *her* team." Tarryn frowned. "What do you think she meant by that?"

I sighed. "I think she meant exactly what it sounds like. She's the de facto leader of our family. She wants to know whether she can control you."

"Maybe you're being harsh. Maybe she just wants to make sure that I wouldn't cause trouble." She looked as though she were about to say something else, then stopped herself. "Anyway, it doesn't matter. Mindy Fitz interrupted us and Izzie didn't say anything else about it. But I just wanted you to know—I feel like it's the sort of thing you should be aware of."

"Thank you." But the insinuation was plain: Tarryn didn't think it was something *she* needed to be concerned with because she was only in Astos for ten days. She wanted to warn me so that it could prepare me to bring the next woman home.

It made sense. Still, it didn't sit well with me.

"So…these cupcakes." She had a bite of one, then

moaned. "Mmm, but I want Chef to like me even more than your sister. How does she make everything so good? She's giving my mother a run for the money!"

I immediately perked up. Any mention of Tarryn's life back at home interested me. "Your mother's a good cook?"

She nodded. "She's amazing. She makes me dinner every night. I'm so lucky." She held up the cupcake. "Although you're pretty lucky, too."

"I am."

Her brow furrowed for a moment, as if she was considering something. "I can sleep on the couch tonight—I don't want you to be uncomfortable."

"I'm fine on the couch," I said quickly. "Don't be silly."

"Your bed is *huge*—there's plenty of room for both of us." She raised an eyebrow. "We're adults. I think we can handle it."

I'd been thinking the same thing, but I hadn't wanted to suggest it. "I don't want to make you uncomfortable."

She raised her other eyebrow; now, she had a matching set. "I don't want to make *you* uncomfortable."

"Listen, about what I said earlier…about what you do for a living…" I sighed. "The way I said it sucked, but I promise you—my heart's in the right place. I care about you, Tarryn."

That little line formed between her eyes. "I appreciate that. But I can assure you, I'm doing just fine." Her tone was all business. She finished the cupcake, wiped her hands, and stood up.

"I'm going to brush my teeth and go to bed now. You're welcome to sleep in the bed, too—I promise I'll stay on my side." With that, she hustled off in her pink pajamas.

I stared after her and sighed again. Where TF was my "A" game? I just kept digging myself deeper and deeper into no-man's-land... I glanced over at the bed. It *was* huge—there would be plenty of room. But how was it physically possible that I was going to sleep next to the most beautiful woman I'd ever seen and not even *try* to touch her?

I mean...it was a dumb idea. I should definitely sleep on the couch.

Tarryn came out a minute later, still eyeing me with what I ventured to guess was mild disdain. I wish I could *command* the right words, in the proper order, to come out of my mouth. But apparently, my authority didn't extend that far.

"I'm going to brush my teeth."

She nodded once, then climbed onto the bed.

Fuck. What did I say that had irked her? *I care about you?* Was it wrong that I said it out loud? Was it bad that I meant it?

Fuck, I thought again as I brushed my teeth. Now I would have to ask her what was the matter, which seemed an awful lot like a question I might not want to know the answer to.

Stop thinking, I reminded myself. *It only gets you into trouble!*

I sighed when I returned to the room. Tarryn was in bed, turned on her side, facing away from me.

I clenched my fists, nervous. "Did I say something wrong?"

"No," she said immediately.

"Then why are you... Tarryn, are you *mad* at me?" I felt like a teenaged girl asking a stupid freaking question like that!

She rolled over and frowned. "No."

"Then why're you frowning like that?"

She tried to stop frowning and failed.

I sat down on the bed. "You might as well tell me. Remember, we're in this together. I'm sorry if I said something wrong."

She sighed and sat up. "It's just when you talk about what I do for a living—I don't know, I guess I just feel judged. And *I* understand if you don't understand or approve, but... You could keep it to yourself."

I opened my mouth and then closed it.

"That's good!" She smiled at me, a glint of humor

returning to her eyes. "Keeping your mouth shut is a great first step!"

I couldn't help it; I laughed.

"Are you sleeping in the bed, roomie?" She snuggled back underneath the covers, careful to stay well on her side.

I don't think it's a good idea, I thought.

"Sure," I said.

TARRYN

THE PRINCE amiably climbed under the covers, and I mentally kicked myself.

Me and my big mouth! *The bed is huge,* she said. *We're adults,* she said. That was the problem! I was old enough to know exactly how hot His Highness was and, even worse, that I liked him. Even though he was judge-y. Even though it appeared he felt sorry for me—which I hated.

Still, and very much against my expectations, I liked him.

He stayed on his side of the bed, near the edge; I stayed on mine.

He rolled over and faced me. "I *am* sorry if I seem like I'm judging." His dark eyes were pleading. "I really don't mean to be such an ass."

"You're not," I said immediately. "I'm sorry if it seems like I'm sensitive about it—I guess I am, and maybe I didn't know it. I just don't want you to feel sorry for me."

He grinned, lightening the mood again. "I feel sorry that you have to put up with me."

I grinned back. "Fair enough. Although you do have Chef in your corner."

He laughed. "Thank goodness for that."

I relaxed, buoyed by his laughter. And the fact that we were amicably sharing his gigantic bed. "So… The Duke and Vivian seemed to hit it off pretty well, don't you think?"

"I'll say. Cliff texted me a hugging emoji at dinner. He looked smitten with your friend."

"Vivian texted me, too! A smiley face surrounded by hearts." I beamed at him. I hadn't gotten to talk to Viv much, but knowing she was near made everything better. "She mentioned they might want to do something with us tomorrow. Would that be okay?"

"Yes, I suggested as much." Clive gave me a lopsided grin, and my stomach did a somersault. "Izzie has another blasted party planned, but we have the day to ourselves. I'll think of something splendid."

"Splendid? Wow, you're really rolling out the red carpet."

"Of course. It's not every day my hot American girlfriend and her best friend get to visit Astos." He winked at me. "Speaking of Izzie, who was that American woman you two were talking to? You mentioned her name. Mindy."

"Right—Mindy Fitz." I settled in against the ridiculously comfortable pillow. "She seemed to make your sister a little off-kilter."

Clive frowned. "What do you know about her?"

"I met her on the plane. She seemed nice enough." I shrugged. "When she introduced herself to your sister, Izzie seemed surprised—not in a good way—that she was there. But when she found out who Mindy was, she changed her tune."

"Who *is* she?"

"Oh. Her family owns…let me see…World News." I wrinkled my nose. "The media conglomerate? That's what she said."

"Huh." His brow wrinkled as he mulled over the information.

"Is that bad?" I asked. "Like I said, she seemed nice enough."

"No, it's just interesting." He frowned. "My father loves the press. Mindy might be his new best friend."

"Hmm." From my blessedly brief experience with the King, Mindy didn't seem like a best-friend match for him. "I'm sure I'll be seeing her around. I'll let you know if she says anything."

Clive sighed and settled in under the covers. "Don't trouble yourself with it. Now, let's forget about Mindy the American and my father. Instead, tell me more about *you*. You said your mom's a great cook? What does she make that's so special, huh?"

"My favorite is her lasagna. She makes garlic bread to go with it, and it's, like, the best thing *ever*. Although those cupcakes were pretty good," I admitted. "What about you? What's your favorite meal? Did your mother ever cook, or has it always been the staff?"

"*My* mother? Never. I think the cooks would pass out if she ever went into the kitchen." He chuckled. "No, my mother was never involved with anything like that. In fact, I wonder if she's made tea since she's married my father—I doubt it."

He appeared to be deep in thought for a moment. "But my favorite meal, let's see… Okay, this is going to make *me* seem basic. But I love a good steak. And a twice-baked potato with chives."

"Oh my goodness, I love twice-baked potatoes."

"Right?" the prince asked. "With cheddar cheese and chives sprinkled on top? I could eat a hundred of them."

"Me too." I laughed. "I guess we have a new request for Chef!" The only thing that got me more excited than food was, well…food. There was the hot prince in my bed, too, but he was firmly planted on his side.

"Love it." Prince Clive's eyes twinkled. "I suppose I should let you get some rest. Good night, roomie."

I smiled. Part of me longed to reach out to him, but that would only spoil the moment. Like this, he really was Prince Charming.

Like this, there was no chance of him rejecting me.

"Good night." Even though this was a genuinely odd situation, I smiled as I drifted off to sleep, knowing that he would be there when I awoke.

My eyes drifted open early the following day. No matter what, I knew I would never sleep in again after having Ellie.

Ellie. My heart twisted because I missed my daughter so much. Maybe I could sneak away today and FaceTime her when no one was around…

His Highness was across from me, still sleeping. His massive chest rose and fell rhythmically. His face was softened with sleep—he reminded me of a little boy, innocent and peaceful. I longed to snuggle against him, to feel his big arms around me, strong and protective.

But it was never going to happen, and I had to accept

that.

Still, I watched him as he slept. I wasn't sure, but it might be more fun than watching tv. Why *was* that?

I decided not to dig deeper. It was definitely safer that way.

He groggily opened one eye. "Are you staring at me?"

"No," I lied.

He rubbed his eyes and then sat up a little. "Stalker."

I couldn't help it—I winced.

"Hey." Clive was suddenly alert. "What's wrong?"

"Oh—nothing!" I quickly hopped out of bed. "I'm going to take a quick shower, okay? We have a busy day."

I locked myself in the bathroom and leaned against the door. *Stupid, stupid, stupid.* Why had I reacted like that? Robbie hadn't been a stalker—at least, not at first. I hoped Clive didn't notice my reaction, but he seemed pretty perceptive. Hopefully, he'd just forget about it.

I turned on the water, lost in my thoughts.

I'd noticed, over the years, that I had reactions to the casual use of violent language. *Stalker. I'm going to beat the crap out of him. I'm going to kill you.* I understood people didn't mean these things literally, but still, it could be jarring, just like violence in movies. I couldn't bear to watch...

I looked at myself in the mirror. *Get it together, Tarryn.* On the outside, all was well. I looked good. Well rested, well-fed, and... But there was something else, something I didn't care to acknowledge. *Hopeful?*

Ugh. I feared it was precisely that. *Not a great time to get your hopes up, girl.*

I climbed into the shower, letting the hot water run over me. I was playing a dangerous game, and I knew it. I'd begun to...*like*...the prince. In fact, I liked him quite a bit more than I should.

He was kind; he was tall, strapping, protective, and caring. It would be *so* nice to have a guy like that in my life for real. I couldn't even imagine it—I'd never had a relationship like that before, and I probably never would. It was easier, better, to be alone. I *knew* I could rely on myself. Other people were a different matter altogether.

My whole life now was Ellie, and I would rabidly protect *her* and her happiness above all else. I didn't need anyone, or anything, else.

Still, there was just something about Clive—how physical he was, how powerful—that made me want to throw myself into his arms. *My knight in shining armor.* Had I winced just now on purpose, so he would ask me what was wrong? Deep down, did I *want* to tell him the truth—about Robbie, about everything that had happened—so that he would kiss my boo-boos and make everything better?

You're an idiot, Tarryn. A theatrical one. My cheeks heated with shame. I didn't need Clive's protection or big arms around me; I needed his money.

I would do well to remember that.

I finished quickly in the shower, blew my hair dry, put on my mascara and some lip gloss—even though we'd be eating soon, I was sure—and went out to face the prince. He was still in bed, a mug of coffee on the nightstand. He stared out the window at the grounds.

"Hey." I forced brightness into my voice. There would be no more wincing, no more mistakes. He was paying for a fantasy date—not a basket case. I poured myself a cup of coffee, eyeing the enormous croissants Chef had prepared. They looked delicious. Today was going to be a great day; I refused to let it be anything else.

"Come here." Clive patted the bed.

I went and sank down onto the edge, feeling wary.

He watched me, a thoughtful expression on his face. "I don't know much about you."

I nodded. "That's because there's not much to know."

"I doubt that." He tilted his head, his dark eyes inspecting me. "I just want you to know something—I respect your privacy and your boundaries. But you can tell me anything, okay?"

"Okay."

He jutted his chin at me. "And if you ever need anything, and I mean *ever*—you call me. I'm your knight in shining armor, remember? It would be my honor to defend you, My Lady."

I smiled, but my stupid, traitorous eyes filled with tears. I blinked them back. "Thank you, Your—Clive."

He laughed. "Your Clive says You're Welcome. Come now, let's eat our breakfast. I've already had five texts from Cliff—he and Vivian are anxious to start our day. How do you feel about boating?"

I blinked at him—which thankfully helped the tears recede. "Boating?"

"Yes. Although we'll be on the water, it does *not* involve seafood, lucky for you. Just sun. And the bay. And…bikinis. Lucky for *me*, ha!" At that, he grinned. "Do you think you Americans are up for an adventure like that?"

I couldn't help it; I grinned back. "Of course we are, Your Clive. It sounds great."

It actually sounded terrific. My heart leaped at the idea of spending the day on a boat with the prince and our friends.

But all that heart leaping was…a problem. A real one.

And although I knew it, I couldn't wipe the smile from my face.

CLIVE

My favorite part of being a royal was traveling to different villages in Astos. I got to know the locals, and I often stayed for months to work on various infrastructure projects. It was a way I could serve my country that made me feel proud.

Part of my training for this aspect of my position was community outreach and health education. Over the years, coaches and leaders had trained me about effective communication and cultural responsiveness. On the healthcare side, I'd taken courses on such things as adolescent health, family planning, and…domestic violence.

I was no expert, of course. But I knew a little. So when I said the word "stalker" and Tarryn physically reacted, it struck me immediately.

Perhaps I was being paranoid. But she'd flinched, and I was sure I hadn't imagined it. Had someone hurt her in the past? Who was it? Where was the fucker now? Could I locate him so that I could beat him to a bloody pulp?

Maybe I *was* just being paranoid, but I made a mental note about what happened—real or imagined—and filed it away. I would find out more later. Somehow. Where there was a will, there was a way.

That had indeed been the case last night. Sleeping next to Tarryn without touching her had been near impossible. Still, I'd done it. She'd fallen asleep quickly, and I'd watched her for almost an hour. Even as she slept, that little line creased her forehead. It seemed as though deep down, she was worried about something. Or was it someone?

My phone pinged again. It was another text from Cliff.

I owe you, Cousin. Best night of my life! Winking emoji.

I sent back a puking emoji. *Spare me the details, but meet us out front in an hour. Bathing suits. Sunscreen. Etc. We're taking the boat out.*

He immediately sent back a gif of a frog fist-pumping.

Christ, Cliff could be annoying when he was in a good mood. I wasn't sure if I could handle spending the day with him and his date, but Tarryn had seemed excited to be reunited with Vivian. Therefore, I would suck it up.

Plus, I had an ulterior motive. *Bikinis.* Everyone knew Americans loved their bikinis!

I called Chef while Tarryn went to grab her things. "What food can you pack a prince, a duke, and their two American girlfriends for a day out on the water? Mind you, we want to be *impressive.* I need you to show off a bit!"

Chef replied energetically in French. Something to the effect of she was not a machine, but I *was* a demanding boor. "Just make it delicious," I begged, "and I know you're not basic—but keep it simple, okay?"

I hung up before she could yell at me more. Then I went to collect my fake American girlfriend and her bikini.

And I could not keep the smile off my face.

∽

It was my first trip out on the water since last summer. I loved my large motorboat—which was technically a yacht. The crew had cleaned it until the hull was a spotless, gleaming white against the aquamarine bay.

Tarryn and Vivian had been talking non-stop since we'd met the other couple, but they stopped in their tracks as we reached the launch. Vivian let out a low whistle. "That's quite the boat."

"Do you know how to drive that thing?" Tarryn asked. "It's a beast!"

"Of course, I know how to drive it." I grinned. "I used to steal it when I was younger when Cliff and I would skip school."

Cliff laughed. "Those were some fun days."

"C'mon." I held out my hand for Tarryn. "Let me bring you aboard."

She wore a white coverup with what appeared to be a tiny black bikini underneath. *Yay!* She was fair, so she'd quite sensibly worn a hat. Jeweled sandals finished the look—I couldn't help staring at her long, toned legs.

This might be the best day ever.

I gave her a tour while Cliff and Vivian came aboard, laughing, talking, and holding hands. I couldn't wait to get my cousin alone to find out what he thought of his pretty American date. He seemed utterly besotted.

Tarryn and I reached the bow and stared out at the bay. It winked like a jewel in the mid-morning sun.

"It's so beautiful. And *warm*, oh my goodness, it feels so good to be warm." She looked out across the water to the city beyond. "Astos is beautiful. I love how colorful it is. What's that building over there?" She pointed to a modern, pink structure facing the water.

"It's a museum—lovely, really. If the press would leave us alone, I'd love to take you some time."

"Speaking of the press..." Tarryn wrinkled her nose. "How did we get so lucky that no one followed us here today?"

"It wasn't luck—I had my security team go out and barricade the route. My whole team will follow us in a separate boat, and we'll have security lining the shore, too." I sighed.

"The yacht club's private, so no one can come on the property. But I expect we'll see a helicopter or two—they'll be anxious to take a picture of you in your suit—I imagine that will sell some serious ad space." I waggled my eyebrows at her.

"Ha." But her cheeks turned pink. "Do you ever get used to it—the constant attention? The pictures?"

I scrubbed a hand across my face as I looked out at the water. Its deep-aqua color was a shade I'd only ever seen in Astos. "No," I admitted. "It doesn't ever stop being a nuisance. Which is one reason I prefer to visit the remote villages—they leave me alone out there."

"What are the other reasons you enjoy it?" She sounded genuinely curious, which for some reason, cheered me.

"I like the people." I shrugged.

"You?" Tarryn teased. "You like *people*?"

"When they're not my family, and they're not giving me a hard time—yes, I actually enjoy spending time with people." I shrugged. "I also like the work. A lot of it's physical—digging ditches for water filtration systems and breaking ground for medical centers, that sort of thing. I like working. It's better than sitting around in a parlor, eating tea-cakes and wearing a suit."

She grinned at me. "I'm sure it is."

I glanced behind us, where Vivian and Cliff were busy making out. "I hate to tear old Cliffie away from your friend, but I need his help at the stern for a moment. D'you think you can pry her away?"

Tarryn outright laughed. "Maybe. But…aren't they kind of showing us up?"

We watched the couple for a moment. The Duke had his hands on Vivian's backside, and he was squeezing her as they passionately kissed. Her dark hair was flying everywhere. Cliff grunted, then moaned.

"Yes. Yes, they are." I coughed. "Well… Should we… you know…?"

She threw her arms around my neck. "Of course, Your Highness. They're not stealing my prince's thunder!"

I laughed again, and then she kissed me, and then it wasn't funny anymore. I felt a pull toward her, deep in my belly, as our lips connected. I ran my hand down her sides—touching her made me feel sparks, as though she might light me on fire.

When our tongues connected, a shock went all the way down to my core.

I stiffened against her. *Christ.* But she didn't pull away—instead, she deepened the kiss, her mouth hungrily exploring mine. *Bloody hell.* Emboldened, I trailed my hands down her back, pulling her closer still. My cock thickened, poking her in the belly. *Good luck hiding that!*

She knew the truth: I wanted her.

But instead of being embarrassed, Tarryn seemed encouraged. She rubbed herself against me as we kissed, tongues lashing. I longed to throw her over my shoulder and take her somewhere, anywhere that was private, and bury my cock inside her until she screamed my name.

Fuuuuck. This was impossible.

Tarryn pulled back—pupils huge, breathing hard—but she gave me a wicked grin.

"I don't know if there are any paparazzi around, but..." She looked as though she'd won something. "Nice work."

I stared, dazzled by her gorgeous face. "Er...thank you?"

Her grin widened as she leaned forward and whispered, "I think we're back on track, Your Highness."

I felt a bit dazed. "I'm sorry?"

She tilted her chin toward Cliff and Vivian. "We're *winning*. They can't compete with us!"

I shook off my lust-filled confusion, finally catching on to what she was saying. "Of course not. I'm a *prince*. And you're *blond*. With legs for days. Love to my cousin and your attractive friend and all, but they don't stand a chance."

"Ha, I love it!" She winked at me. "We'll have to keep up the good work."

"A-Absolutely." Fuck, if she winked at me while she had her bikini on, I might come in my swim trunks. How *exactly* had I kept my hands off her last night?

I tore myself away. But something inside me felt on the edge of snapping as I went and pried Cliff off of Vivian, bringing him to the helm with me. How much more abstinence could I take? And for what purpose—who was benefitting?

I'd had a reason. I knew I'd had a reason for vowing not to sleep with her...

I shook it off, willing myself to calm down. Cliff and I talked briefly with the security team, agreeing on a route and a preferable place to moor on the bay. Then I started the boat and headed out into the beautiful day, trying to will my raging hormones to retreat.

"So," I said after a minute. "How are you getting along with Vivian?"

My cousin's eyes were bright. "She's amazing," he gushed. "I've never met someone like her before."

"Someone so...American?"

He shook his head.

"So short?"

He scowled.

"Someone who appears to like you?" I inspected him, pale and ginger-haired, beneath his large protective hat. He wore a sun shirt and pink plaid board shorts. "Even dressed like that?"

"Ha, ha, ha." His scowl deepened into a thoughtful frown. "I mean, we hit it off *right* away. I've never been so attracted to someone—or so comfortable."

"Not even Freya Wilson?" I teased.

He wrinkled his nose. "Freya Wilson can't hold a candle to my Vivian."

I steered slowly into the bay, and the security team followed close behind in their boat. I was lucky I'd convinced them to let us come out today; Tarryn's presence had whipped the press corps into an absolute feeding frenzy.

"So is it just…physical…with you and Vivian?" I asked.

"Not at all." Cliff's eyes were wide. "She's so sweet and kind. But firm, you know?"

I raised my eyebrows. "Not in this context. What do you mean?"

He leaned closer. "She's very…dominant."

"In conversation?"

His eyes were wide. "In bed."

I coughed. "I thought you said it wasn't just physical?"

"It's not—it's so much more than that." He stared at Vivian, who was laughing at something Tarryn said. "But I'm still in awe of what she did to me last night."

I coughed again; this felt more like choking. "What did she do to you, mate?"

He shook his head. "I don't think you want to know."

I nodded in agreement. "Probably right, Cliffie, probably right."

"How's it going with Tarryn?" he asked. "You two seem like you're being quite romantic."

I smiled as I steered into open water, the sun shining down on us in glorious intensity. "She's a great girl."

"Is it serious?" The teasing tone was gone from his voice.

I sighed. "I don't know. I'd like it to be, but she has a

whole life back in America. I'll probably be a bachelor prince for quite some time." This was true; it also made me feel sour.

"I didn't even know you were seeing somebody, but you two seem quite close." Cliff arched an eyebrow. "How were you staying in touch with her while she was in the States?"

"Texting, phone calls—you know." I shrugged. "We FaceTimed."

He raised his eyebrows. "That sounds boring. And celibate."

"Ha. Well, yeah." He didn't know the half of it. "But we did what we had to do to make it work."

"Hmm." He was watching the women again, an intent expression on his face. "Have you asked *her* what she wants to do after the wedding?"

"No," I admitted. "I guess I've just been riding the wave. Why be so focused on the future? I just want to live in the moment." *Because I only have a few more days with her. That's all I'll ever have.*

"I don't know, Cousin." He was still watching the women. "I think if you find someone special, you shouldn't let them go."

I nodded, but an alarm sounded in my head. I knew Cliff was taken with Vivian, but in less than twenty-four hours, he sounded utterly devoted to her. And then there was the small matter of what she did for work and the fact that I'd hired her to be his date…

"Let's just have fun today, okay?" I asked. "Live in the moment."

"Live in the moment—yes." The Duke was smiling, but he wasn't looking at me. He still stared at Vivian.

Oh boy. He's got it bad.

My gaze flicked from my cousin to Tarryn, who threw her head back and laughed at something Vivian said. My dick twitched—but what was worse? My freaking heart, so long dormant, twisted.

The Duke wasn't the only one in trouble.

TARRYN

"Watch me do a backflip." Vivian stood at the edge of the boat, her tip-toes the only thing anchoring her toned body in place. She wore a tiny blue bikini embellished with crystals, and her coffee-colored skin was flawless in the bright sun. If I wasn't so busy fretting about her impending flip, I'd be telling her how gorgeous she looked.

"Don't get hurt!" I clutched my heart.

"Ha!" Her eyes sparkled. "You're cute to worry. Watch this, T." She bent her knees, then threw her feet back over her head, executing a flawless backflip. Viv disappeared into the aqua water with a small splash. When she came up for air, she was grinning. "Told you! Now *you* try."

"*No.*" My voice was firm—the same tone I used with Ellie when she tried to touch something dangerous.

Viv arched an eyebrow. "Can you at least do a pencil dive? The water's awesome!"

I peered over the edge. "Are there any fish?"

"Nope. All clear."

I frowned at my friend. "How do you know?"

"I just know," she snapped. "Now, will you come in the freaking water and live a little? It's thirty degrees in Boston. Get *in* here."

They didn't call Viv the Dominator for nothing—she sure was bossy. "Fine. But don't make fun of me when I hold my nose."

I cautiously climbed to the edge of the boat, examining the aqua water. I loved to swim but feared that something shiny and slimy might brush up against me and then drag me down into the darkness and eat me for breakfast. *That* was what I wanted to avoid.

I took a deep breath. One, two—*three!* I jumped in, holding my nose, and was surprised and delighted to feel the warm yet refreshing water envelope me. I smiled at Viv when I broke the surface. "The water's amazing!"

"Told you." She grinned as she paddled water. "It's like the Caribbean."

"I've never been."

Viv arched an eyebrow. "I could've guessed that—you're a chicken, and you hold your nose like my mother!"

We laughed and swam around the boat. The water was so clear, it was easy to keep an eye out for shiny and slimy things. Nothing came near me, and I let myself relax enough to float, the sun on my face.

"So while we're out here, we should talk." Vivian paddled over and floated next to me, sticking her toes above the water, her blue toenail polish sparkling in the sun. "What's the deal with you and Prince Clive? He's *seriously* hot. And a little broody, which is *also* seriously hot."

"Mmm, I know." I caught sight of His Highness on the deck—he'd taken his shirt off, and I could finally see that sculpted chest. "He's *totally* hot."

"Wow." Viv blinked at me. "I can't believe you just said that."

"What do you mean?" But I didn't look at her—I refused to tear my eyes away from the prince's toned pectoral muscles. How much time could one man spend at the gym? And how on earth did he already have a perfect, light tan?

"I *mean*—first of all, you're practically salivating because he just took his shirt off."

"Am not."

"Are so," Viv said firmly. "Second of all, I've never heard you talk about a man like that before."

I squinted at her. "That's ridiculous."

Viv squinted back. "Is not. I've never once heard you say someone—a *real-life* person, not the MVP of all MVPs, Tom Brady—was hot. The prince is the first."

"Well," I said defensively, "Binky isn't exactly someone I'd write home about."

"We're not talking about Binky—who sends his regards, by the way—we're talking about *you*." Vivian's all-knowing gaze flicked to me, then to the prince, then back to me. "Because *third* of all, you two seem like you're actually a *couple*. Like, if I didn't know any better, I'd say he's totally in love with you. Is he?"

"No." I snorted. "That's ridiculous. It's not like that between us at all—we're just for show."

"Um, I saw you grinding against him earlier. That didn't look fake."

I stuck my nose in the air—as much to avoid getting water in it as to feign superiority on the subject. "It's just for the paparazzi. Trust me. I spent the last two nights in his room, and nothing happened."

"What?" Vivian looked stunned. "You haven't slept with him?"

"No. Did you sleep with Cliff already?"

She looked at me as though I had three heads.

"Of *course* I slept with the Duke! I made all his dreams come true last night. The Duke of Clifton was putty in my hands."

"You like using his title, huh?"

"Of course! He's a *Duke*. That just makes everything better." Vivian's eyes were wide. "As in, the *Duke* said I turned his legs into Jell-O. The *Duke* said I'm the most beautiful woman he's ever met. Doesn't that just make it even more awesome?"

"It does." I tried not to be jealous that she'd turned *her* royal's legs into Jell-O while I'd been busy staying on my side of the bed. "Good for you, Viv. He really seems like he likes you."

"Of course he does. I introduced him to the male G-spot—he thinks he's in *love* with me!"

I spluttered a little. Vivian was so matter-of-fact about sex; I wished I could be more like her.

"You are such a prude it's *adorable*." Vivian winked at me. "But why're you two in the no-sex zone? I saw His Highness last night—he couldn't stop looking down your dress. And he's been following you around with a huge boner all day. So I'm guessing this isn't *his* choice."

I frowned. "Actually, it is."

"What?" Vivian's eyes got even bigger in her face. "Is he *gay*? What about the boner?"

"No, it's not that." I sighed. "He doesn't want to sleep

with me because he thinks it's…*wrong*. He doesn't believe in prostitution."

Vivian always had a comeback, but even *she* seemed stymied by this news. She scowled at the water, at the boat, then at the sky. Then, finally, she said, "*He's* the one who hired you!"

"As a fake date," I reminded her. "Not for sex."

Her pretty face twisted almost comically. "I'm, like, *boggled* right now. He's into you. I can tell."

"It doesn't matter. He has ideals." I watched the prince as he laid back in a lounger and closed his eyes, relaxing in the sun. He was so gorgeous and sculpted, he was like a Greek god. "He won't touch me like that—in public, he will," I said quickly, "but it's just for the press."

Viv shook her head. "I need to process this. It doesn't make sense."

We floated in silence for a minute.

Vivian finally turned to me, frowning. "So are you saying that he won't have sex with you for ethical reasons?"

"Moral, ethical…" I nodded. "Something like that."

"Do *you* want to have sex with him? Or is it better like this?"

She eyed the boat, where the prince and the Duke sat together. They were talking about something, and the Duke laughed. "Because *I* thought you guys were really into each other. *Both* of you. He has the boner, but you have the *look*. Like you wanted the boner."

"He's handsome, obviously," I said, trying not to ogle him and failing. "And I'd be lying if I said I hated kissing him."

"He *is* handsome." Vivian waggled her eyebrows. "And those big arms! It wouldn't suck having those holding you down!"

I frowned at her. "He doesn't want to hold me down. Because he feels *sorry* for me."

"That's dumb." Viv closed her eyes and floated. "You have everything in the world going for you, you know that?"

"I don't think that's exactly true, Viv. The prince and I—we're from two different worlds."

She snorted. "There's only *one* world. And in *that* world, you're the total package. You're smart, you're gorgeous, and you have a heart of gold. So why the hell would he feel sorry for you? I feel sorry for *him*."

Viv shook her head. "All that money, living in a palace and all—and he can't even recognize a true work of art."

I winced. "I appreciate you sticking up for me. But don't judge him like that, okay? He's a good guy. He just thinks what I do for a living involves me being trafficked."

Viv's eyebrow raised a fraction. "Tarryn Clayton, you are *defending* him. You know what that makes me think?"

"No..."

"You *like* him. You have a crush on Mr. Princey Biceps."

I scowled at her. "No, I don't. I mean, I *like* his big biceps. And the beard. But who wouldn't?"

"Ha." Vivian spread her arms as she floated, a satisfied look on her face. "*I* wouldn't. I prefer my ginger-haired Duke, thank you very much. I might keep him."

"Cliff, the Duke of Clifton?" I teased. "Are you going to live happily ever after with a *ginger*?"

"I might." She opened one eye and stared at me. "What about you, huh? Are you going to let Prince Charming call all the shots, or are you going to be honest with him?"

"Honest about what?"

She opened her other eye, all the better to give me a *you-are-dumb-as-a-box-of-rocks* stare. "That you *like* him. God forbid you let your guard down."

I crossed myself. "God forbid is right."

～

"Chef outdid herself again—how am I supposed to fit into my cocktail dress tonight?" I moaned, pushing the plate away. She'd prepared *homemade* potato chips, Coleslaw, and something she'd labeled a "California club wrap," which had turkey, bacon, avocado, fig jam, and…yum.

Clive eyed me in my bikini. "I think you'll manage just fine."

"Says you." I fake-pouted. "Hey, where did Viv and Cliff sneak off to? They didn't even finish lunch. Did they go back in the water?"

"Um, I don't think so." A sheepish expression crossed his handsome face. "I think they're below deck."

"Really? Why…?" But then I heard a thump, and a moan, followed by a strangled scream. "Oh boy."

A half-grimace, half-smile engulfed Clive's handsome face. "They've certainly hit it off."

A smack, followed by another holler, issued from below. "That's one way of putting it."

We both started laughing so hard, my stomach hurt worse.

But the whirr of a helicopter overhead interrupted us—at least it masked the sounds coming from below deck. "I knew they'd show up." Clive nodded toward the chopper. "That's the press."

"Darn, I can't believe they found us. Now we have to

give them a show." But I didn't even pretend to sound sorry. Being photographed meant another chance to touch the prince, to feel his arms around me, to relish the feel of his tongue in my mouth. And *unf*—an added bonus? His shirt was off.

Come to mama!

"Shall we, Your Highness?" I fluttered my eyelashes at him theatrically.

Clive grinned. "We shall."

Goody! I wasn't really sure what 'fun' meant to me anymore, but I was pretty sure I was about to have some.

There was a spark in his eyes as he held out his big arms for me. "C'mere."

The helicopter circled us overhead as I slid directly onto his lap, his bare skin against mine. This was new—and dangerous—territory. The prince wasn't wearing a shirt; I was dressed only in my bikini. I trailed my fingers down his muscled chest, feeling like it was my birthday and Christmas all at once.

"Well, *hello*." He put his arms around me, then tenderly brushed the hair back from my face. Clive beamed down at me. "You've got a bit of sun, Tarryn. It suits you."

"Thank you." I felt him start to stiffen beneath me; I

held very, very still, savoring the sensation. *I did that to him.* No matter what he'd said, he wanted me.

The truth grew between us, as did the heat.

"Thanks for taking us out today—it's beautiful." My voice was husky. "It's not something I'll ever forget."

"Me either." He smiled, but there was something else behind his eyes, something I couldn't quite decipher. He ran his hands over my bare shoulders and down my arms. Electricity tingled between us; it was increasingly hot, and it had nothing to do with the sun.

Moving closer, the prince inhaled the scent of my skin. "You smell so good. Sunscreen, the water, sunlight."

I smiled up at him. When our gaze connected, I felt as though someone squeezed my heart. *Oh boy.*

The helicopter hovered directly overhead.

Clive lifted my chin and leaned closer. My heart thundered as I gazed up at him. *Steady, girl.* This was allowed. This was for show. He didn't have to know the truth: that I *meant* the way I was looking at him, that being in his arms felt right—that it was everything I'd been yearning for.

I refused to let the opportunity slip away. He was finally mine to touch. I reached out and stroked his beard, which was both scratchy and soft. I loved the feel of it.

Clive leaned into my hand, then bent closer, brushing his lips against mine. I fought back a moan—I wanted this, but I wanted so much more.

Our lips connected again, and he deepened the kiss. His cock throbbed beneath me, but I didn't react to it. Not yet.

"You're so beautiful." He broke the kiss and trailed his lips down my jaw, my neck, my shoulder. *Holy hell.* Even his lips were muscular! Hot and cold at the same time, I shivered beneath his touch. When he kissed my collarbone, I couldn't help it—I ground myself against his erection.

Clive groaned, a deep, low sound, and pressed himself against me. I could feel him—*all* of him—hot, hard, and throbbing. He wrapped his massive arms around me, holding me close, his touch filled with an undeniable yearning.

We kissed again, and it left me breathless. It was like he was happening *to* me. I was helpless to pull away, to stop my hands from roaming down his spectacular muscles.

I wanted. I wanted *him*.

He pulled back, breathing hard. "Fuck, Tarryn."

He looked up at me, dark eyes tortured. "I don't think I can do this anymore."

CLIVE

"I don't think I can do this anymore."

The look of shock—of *hurt*—on her face practically undid me.

"We have to go." I unceremoniously removed her from her lap. I stood and adjusted my board shorts, which were ridiculously strained from my huge, heat-seeking erection. *Must. Get. Back. To the palace.*

If I didn't, I was going to slide her bikini bottom over and take her right on the boat for all the paparazzi (and subsequently the rest of the world) to see.

Without a word, I threw on my T-shirt and hustled to start the engine. I immediately headed back for shore. I didn't care if Cliff and Vivian got jostled below deck—it sounded as though things were being smacked around down there, anyway.

Tarryn glanced back at me, still with that hurt expression on her face. But I couldn't talk to her. If I said *any*thing, I might blurt out all *sorts* of things, none of which would be a great idea.

When you're in my arms, it just feels right.

I take back everything I said about not sleeping with you. Even though I care. Even though I know it's wrong.

Once isn't going to be enough.

I wanted her. I wanted her more than I cared about doing what was honorable, what was good, what was *right*. Some sort of fire had started burning in me, and I knew that no matter what my good intentions were, getting inside of her was inevitable. I *had* to. *We* had to.

My cell phone buzzed with a call from security. "Your Highness—is everything all right?"

"Yes, we just need to get back to the palace."

"Is there some sort of emergency? You're driving fast." My guard sounded tense.

"No." *Yes.* "I just have some business I need to take care of."

And it was no one's damn business but mine.

* * *

"I'll leave a car for you," I hollered below deck. A minute later, Cliff texted me a thumbs-up sign. He was obviously doing just fine.

I gripped Tarryn's hand and practically dragged her into the SUV. She was quiet, her eyes wide. She waited until Stellan put up the privacy screen and began navigating toward home before she asked, "What's the matter?"

I was still holding her hand. I stared at our hands together, and then I looked at her. "I'm not sure."

That little line appeared between her eyes. "Okay…?"

"I'm worried I'm going to say the wrong thing here."

She shook her head. Her cheeks were pink from being out on the boat, and she smelled like the ocean. "You don't have to say anything." She tried to take her hand back, but I held on for dear life.

I longed to hold her, to kiss her, but I didn't dare. I needed to get her back inside the palace. Then maybe I could explain…

Maybe I could show her.

We pulled down the drive, and I lowered the screen. "Take us to the side entrance, please, Stellan. I don't want to get intercepted."

"Of course, Your Highness."

The line deepened between Tarryn's eyes. She probably thought I'd gone mad, and she wasn't wrong.

We *finally* reached the bloody side entrance. I still gripped her hand, practically dragging her into the west wing and hustling to my room. I locked the door behind us and started pacing while Tarryn wrapped her thin coverup against her skin, shivering.

"Bloody hell—I'm such an ass." I ransacked my closet and handed her a thick, fluffy robe. She pulled it on, and I caught another glimpse of her pale skin, her unforgettable figure in that bikini.

"Fuck." I paced the room again.

Tarryn stood with her arms crossed against her chest, watching me.

I kept pacing.

"Use your words, Clive." She tilted her head.

"Right, bloody hell…" I scrubbed a hand across my face. "I need to talk to you about something."

She nodded. "You said you couldn't do this anymore—go back to that. What do you mean?"

I stopped pacing and stood there. "I can't keep pretending."

She nodded again, more slowly this time, as though she were reckoning with something. "All right. I understand. We don't have to keep kissing like that in front of the press if it makes you uncomfortable—"

"Christ, I am royally fucking this up."

"Haha." But it didn't sound as though she thought it was funny.

I took a deep breath. *Steady, mate.* She'd told me to use my words, but they were inadequate. They were failing me. I crossed to the room, closing the distance between us.

Tarryn didn't move. She watched me, eyes wide.

I tentatively put my hands on her shoulders, then her arms, then her shoulders again. But I didn't know what to do after that. So finally, with a heavy sigh, I let them hang down at my sides. "Tarryn."

"I'm right here."

I reached for her hand and gently held it. "Forgive me. I'm afraid I'm a bit of a mess."

"It's okay." She pursed her lips and stared at me. "But... Are you firing me?"

"*No.*" Although part of me wanted to. If I fired her, then I wouldn't feel so guilty about what I wanted…

I moved closer, but the easy heat between us had dissipated. Now I felt a strain, a lump in my throat. "I don't want to hurt you."

"Hurt me how?" Her voice was husky.

"I don't want you to do anything you don't want to do."

Her eyes widened. "Honestly, I'm more worried about *you* at this point."

I couldn't help it; I laughed. "You might have a point."

She didn't move. She let me hold her hand, but she didn't say a word. She wasn't letting me off the hook here or making it easy. And I couldn't blame her for that.

I moved closer. I wanted her so badly, I almost felt sick—and she was the antidote I desperately needed. If we did this…if *I* did this…

Don't think about it, said the voice in my head.

I pulled her against me. I was already so hard, dammit. My cock jutted between us, heavy and undeniable. There was no hiding my intentions now. Tarryn's eyes were still wide, watching me, taking my measure.

"Are you going to make me say it?" I asked, my voice hoarse.

She shook her head: *no*.

But I had to say it. To tell her. "I want you. I *need* you."

"Then take me," she whispered.

I leaned down and kissed her once, her full lips a shock against mine. *Fuck.* Our tongues connected, and my cock strained against her, throbbing. It wanted in. *I* wanted in.

I roughly took her robe off, throwing it to the side, and ran my hands down her glorious body. Her nipples pebbled beneath her cool suit, and I worshipfully put my hands on her breasts. For fuck's sake, she was perfect. Her suit still had a damp trace of the ocean. I kissed her more deeply, molding her luscious body against mine.

Yes. This was everything I wanted. I sank my hands into her hair, and she ran her hands down my body, exploring, and then somehow my shirt was off.

I pushed her back against the bed.

I wanted to be gentle, to be tender, but our kisses were urgent. I undid her bikini top and was confronted by her pale, perfect breasts, with just the outline of a tan around them. I suckled her nipples greedily, and Tarryn moaned beneath me, arching her back. She was kissing me, too—my shoulders, my biceps, her fingers trailing down my back.

She undid the tie of my swim trunks, and I shimmied them off. My cock sprang out, enormous and heavy, between us.

There was no going back now.

I took a deep, shuddery breath. "We don't have to do this if you don't want to."

"Clive…" She wrapped her hand around my hard length and started to milk me.

Oh fuck. My eyes almost rolled back in my head.

I couldn't wait. I roughly pulled her bikini to the side, and she guided me against her slit—soaking wet and hot.

Our gazes connected, and she nodded. "See? I want to." Her voice was raw, vulnerable.

I devoured her with a kiss, and she stroked my erection against her. We both moaned—it felt incredible. I was close, so close—

She positioned me at her entrance. And fuck if she wasn't already so wet, I almost came right there. But I inched inside her, making sure that she could accommodate every bit of my thickness. She was tight, but she greedily sucked me in, bucking her hips so I notched inside her fully.

Once I was all the way in, we both moaned in relief.

I thrust once, her body tight around me. Her bathing suit caused friction, rubbing against the base of my shaft. She was so wet that we slid against each other easily, her muscles clenching me, making my whole body shudder.

The combination of sensations and having her underneath me—*finally*, our bodies entwined—almost undid me.

Tarryn's body was so tight, so hot. I thrust again—hard. *Fuck.* I buried myself in her, and she threw back her head and moaned. Deep, primal satisfaction settled in my gut. And a desire to make her come so hard, she screamed my name. *Mine. She was mine.*

I thrust again, harder. My balls were heavy. I wanted to go slow, to make it last. But she writhed beneath me, moaning, begging, her hair thrashing all over the pillow. *Fuck.* I thrust again and again, unable to stop myself. Tarryn groaned, a deep, low sound, and I felt her own orgasm start to build. She reached down, her fingertips grazing my balls. *Unf.* She squeezed them once, lightly, and began to do it in time with my thrusts.

Oh fuck. I was going to come so hard, I might die.

"Yes—Clive—*yes!*"

I started fucking her hard. Both of us cried out. She kept her hand around my ball sack, owning me, cradling them and squeezing them as they naturally contracted.

I was going to fill her with so much of my cum, she wouldn't ever be able to forget me—

"Clive!" she screamed my name as she came, her hot, tight body spasming.

It undid me.

I buried myself into her and orgasmed hard, shooting my seed deep inside. *"Fuck."* That was the only word for it. I collapsed on top of her, not pulling out, and kissed the top of her head.

She was mine, now. She just didn't know it.

TARRYN

⚜

I was surprised—and alarmed—by what happened to me after His Highness made me come so hard, I almost passed out: my eyes filled with tears.

The prince collapsed on top of me, our sweaty bodies still connected. "Am I crushing you?"

"No." That was when the stupid tears sprang to my eyes. He sounded so boyish, so trusting. I felt close to him, and not just because his massive, sweaty chest was pressed up against me.

I felt close to him because this felt like it was…real.

I ran my fingertips through his thick, springy hair. I didn't want him to roll off me. I didn't want him to pull out. Even as his erection receded, I *liked* the feel of him inside me. I liked being connected to him.

I was so fucking doomed.

We lay there for a few minutes—recovering, relaxing, basking. At least, *I* was basking. I'd never had an orgasm like that in my life! The shock waves still emanated through me.

I ran my fingertips from his hair, down his back, over his shoulders. My touch was greedy. I'd been longing to let my hands roam over him, to explore.

I didn't mean to kiss him on the cheek. But I couldn't help myself—he was just so *delicious*. And *cute*. I kissed him again, and then again, and then he turned to me, eyes burning.

His cock stiffened inside me.

Oh boy.

We didn't say a word. But he kissed me tenderly, and I got a lump in my throat.

Our bodies started moving together. We were slower this time, but with every thrust, he was more urgent. He was so *big*. He loomed over me, claiming me deep inside. I could already feel another orgasm building. I felt that I was falling and that Clive was catching me each time, and then we were flying back up together.

He thrust slowly, deeply, burying his enormous cock in me. He looked me in the eye as he fucked me. I didn't even know what to think, I was so lost in him. I heard a grunt. I guess that was me? I didn't even care. I surrender myself to the sensation of the prince owning my body. With every thrust, he claimed it. I gave myself to him. Freed from my normal inhibitions, I ran my nails down his back, boldly and greedily grabbing his thickly muscled ass as he pumped into me. *Yes!*

Fuck me. Take me. Come in me. There was something raw about how I felt, the urgency of it, a craving I'd never experienced before. It started low in my belly, then radiated everywhere, making me insane.

He drove deeper, cradling me with his big biceps as he pumped. I started to come. "Oh my God, *YES!*"

He chuckled, a deep, satisfied sound, as he held me down and fucked me. His thrusts were steady, deep, determined. There was almost a savage quality to it. "That's a good girl. Come for me," he commanded.

Your wish is my command, Your Highness. I shattered beneath him.

"Fuck, Tarryn." The urgency of his thrusts increased as he fucked me through my orgasm. "My turn."

He exploded inside me, his cum fueling my own off-the-charts, out-of-body whatever the hell it was that was happening to me. I didn't even know my own name anymore.

But I sure as hell knew his. I was screaming it.

"You're glowing." Vivian's eyes narrowed in on me. She looked fantastic in a strapless violet mini dress, her copper-colored skin flashing with a light tan. "Why do I feel like that's not just from being on the boat?"

"Because you're being silly." I had a sip of champagne. It tasted magnificent.

She leaned closer, a knowing look in her eyes. "You *slept* with him. You gave it to Mr. Princey Biceps *good*."

I giggled.

"Ho boy." Viv looked me up and down. "I think he gave it to *you* good."

I didn't answer. Instead, I had another sip of champagne. I felt eyes on me and glanced across the room—Clive was talking to a group of men, but he was staring in our direction. In *my* direction.

Viv snapped her fingers. "Earth to Tarryn," she was saying. "Stop eye-fucking His Highness for one freaking second and dish to your best friend. *Now.*"

I sighed. She wasn't nicknamed the Dominator for nothing. "Okay—I slept with him."

"Duh." She leaned closer still, inspecting me, and I could see her expertly applied eye-makeup up close.

"How many times, what positions, and did you… you *know*?"

Feeling trapped, I sighed again. I had never enjoyed being an escort. In fact—and this was something that only Vivian knew—I'd never once had an orgasm while on assignment. I'd faked lots of them, but the real deal was definitely harder to come by. Pun intended, haha!

"Four times, missionary, and yes, I…*you know*. A lot."

"Tarryn Clayton." Her eyebrows rose higher than I'd ever seen them. "Are you telling me that you had multiple orgasms in the missionary position this afternoon?"

I felt like she was quizzing me on something and that I was about to fail. "Y-Yes. Why are you looking at me like that?"

She stared suspiciously at me, then at the prince, then back again. "Ooh boy. The way he's looking at you—hon, it looks like he's going to eat you alive."

My stomach twisted—I half-hoped Viv was right. I very much hated being away from him. I very much wanted him to come over here, pick me up, throw me over his shoulder, and take me back to the orgasm cave. Then we'd be alone again, and I could tear his clothes off, run my hands down his big muscles, and pretend that we were going to live happily ever after.

Vivian fanned herself. "Did you two talk about anything?"

I swallowed hard. "He said he didn't want to make me do anything I didn't want to do."

Vivian laughed, a throaty sound. "He's a fucking idiot. Has he *looked* in a mirror recently?"

"Hah. I don't know." My prince still stared, a dark look in his eyes. My insides went all hot and squishy. I started to throb *down there*. Geez Louise, how much sex could I have in one day?

He crossed the room toward us; I had a feeling I was about to find out.

"I'm out of here—I'm going to go find my Duke and ride him like the ginger stud he is." Viv fanned herself on her way out. "I think whatever you two've got is catching!"

"Maybe." But I couldn't focus on the conversation. All I could focus on was Clive, who swiftly closed the distance between us. He loomed over me in his tuxedo, and I gaped up at him. The party completely fell away. The gowns, the tuxedos, the piano music—all the glamor, all the tiaras, that I was in a foreign country away from my family, the truth about my circumstances —everything dissipated.

Except for *him*.

Holy hell…what had I gotten myself into?

He put his palms on my hips, and I thought I might catch on fire.

"Let's get out of here." His tone was urgent.

"Can we?" I tried to care about what Princess Izzie would think, or the Queen, and failed.

"Yes we fucking can." He put his hand low on my back, dangerously low, and guided me out of the party. The other guests stared, then politely looked away. I had a feeling everyone knew exactly why we were leaving so early. The heat radiating off of us was palpable.

Clive pulled me aside in the hall and buried his hands in my hair. Then he kissed me. I felt like I was drowning in him—I wanted to pull him through me, for him to take me down, and for us to never get back up. Our tongues lashed, and I moaned.

He pressed me up against the wall, kisses growing more urgent. He was already hard. His erection pressed against me, and my body shook with need.

"Do you see what you do to me?" He nudged me with his cock. "I couldn't stop staring at you all night."

"We were only at the party for thirty minutes."

"See?" He smiled. "You make me *crazy*. I had to get you alone. I can't stand it, Tarryn. You're so fucking gorgeous."

"Thank you. But we're not alone." I looked around the blessedly empty hall. "We should—"

"We should go, right." There was a wild look in his dark eyes. "Before I try to take you right here. Like I almost just fucking did."

He put his hand on my backside again and hustled me to his room. Good thing it wasn't far. As soon as we were inside, he unzipped my dress. It fell to the floor in a pile of pink sparkles. He kissed me hungrily, hands roaming all over, and suddenly my bra was off, my panties, everything stripped and thrown to the side. I yanked his jacket off him. I don't know how we got the buttons undone on his shirt, but he was finally, gloriously naked, our bodies sliding once again against each other.

He pushed me back onto the bed. His heavily muscled body rose above me, Greek-God-like, and his cock sprung out straight and proud. And pointing at me.

Unf.

Vivian had made fun of me for the missionary position—so I turned around and got on all fours. I crawled up the bed, and Clive let out a strangled moan behind me. "You're trying to kill me, aren't you." He didn't even bother to make it sound like a question.

"Not at all." I shivered with anticipation. "But I know you'll be so deep like this. I want to feel it—I want you."

The words coming out of my mouth shocked me, as did my behavior—still on all fours, I opened my legs a little so he could see me. I had never, as in *never ever*, been so honest with someone in bed. And maybe that was because I'd never wanted someone like this. But I wanted Clive, oh boy, I wanted him *bad*.

He was immediately behind me. His big hands ran over my back, my ass, my sides, grazing and pinching my nipples. *Fuck.*

"I'm not going to last long like this." Clive notched the head of his cock at my entrance and pulsed there.

"Please." I felt like I might go insane. "Just do it."

He slid all the way into me, all at once. I cried out. He stopped thrusting at once. "Babe, are you okay?"

"Yes." I shook my head. I was sore from earlier, but somehow it made it feel even better—he'd marked me. I was *his*. The pain made it more real. He would never know it, but I would cherish this day for the rest of my life. I'd never felt this way about anyone, and I'd be kidding myself if it said it was just the mind-blowing sex.

Don't think about it. Blissfully, the sensation of his long, fluid strokes made everything else fall away. I'd been right—he was in *so* deep like this. Every thrust made me cry out. He was fucking me hard, just the way I liked it, the way I'd never known I liked it. He put his big hands on my hips and pressed down, so his hot, throbbing erection stroking me on multiple levels. My pussy spasmed around him. *Oh fuck.* He hit the spot deep inside me, again and again. I could feel an orgasm building, almost frightening me with how powerful it was, how swiftly it overtook me. I relished the feel of him, the sensation of him, of fucking, of being fucked. His balls were heavy as they slapped against me. His thrusts got deeper, harder, all the way in.

He trailed his fingers over my sex and gently circled my clitoris. But there was nothing gentle about what he was doing behind me. My body felt out of control, ravaged in the best possible way. He fingered the tender bud and then pinched it lightly, in time with his deep strokes.

I didn't even realize I was screaming his name, but *someone* was…

"Clive!" I hollered as my body shattered around his cock, vibrating and shuddering with an overwhelming pleasure I'd never experience before.

"That's right—you're *mine.*" He slammed into me and came in a torrent. My bodily greedily sucked up everything he gave, making me come again, our bodies vibrating together in a spasm.

Once the shock waves passed, we lay down on the bed. Clive drew me into his enormous arms, cradling me, and kissed the top of my head. "Thank you." His voice was thick.

"For…?"

In answer, he just kissed my head again. My handsome prince pulled me closer, hanging on tight as he immediately, adorably, fell fast asleep.

And as I watched him, safe in his arms, I didn't know whether to laugh or cry.

CLIVE

The headlines the next day were surprisingly accurate.
PRINCE CLIVE'S OBSESSION DEEPENS
IS TARRYN CLAYTON PREGNANT?

Was she? I hadn't bothered to ask her about birth control before repeatedly plunging my dick inside her. The truth was, I'd do it again—and I probably would, just as soon as she woke up.

I peered down, feeling her warm body close to me. Tarryn slept as I scrolled through the newsfeed. I had her tucked protectively beside me, not even wanting to be inches away from her.

I was so fucked. And not just because of all the sex we'd been having…

Sighing, I continued to scroll. The following headline grabbed my attention. *EXCLUSIVE: WHAT PRINCESS*

IZZIE REALLY THINKS OF TARRYN CLAYTON. It was a tabloid called the Daily Chat, which happened to be owned by World News, Mindy Fitz's company.

My stomach churned as I clicked the link. Had my sister given an interview?

There were two pictures—an older one of Princess Izzie with an icy smile, wearing her tiara, and one of me and Tarryn from the day before on the boat. She straddled me, her long blond hair blowing back in the breeze, and we were both laughing.

Oh boy. What did my sister have to say about these latest sexy photos?

I scanned the article, quickly finding her quote. "Well, I have to say, I think the fact that they're so publicly affectionate is *adorable*. We're usually more reserved than that in Astos, aren't we? But the Americans have a different take on such things. They're more free. If I'm being honest, I'm *thrilled* for my brother. It seems that he's found love at last. No one is happier about that than me."

When the reporter asked if the new couple's popularity with the press was drawing too much attention away from the royal wedding, Izzie quickly shot the idea down. "Nonsense! I'm happy to share the spotlight with my beloved brother, who will someday be King. My happiness is complete because he's found someone wonderful—and she *is* wonderful. My only hope is that they make it official soon!"

I turned my phone off and tossed it on the bed. I was in deep trouble here, and I hadn't even taken a moment to process it. Everyone was entranced by my relationship—my *fake* relationship—even my sister.

I'd wanted the press to make a big deal out of my date. I'd wanted to break the sob-story cycle of the handsome prince, destined forever to be alone and aloof. What was that saying…be careful what you wish for? Now I felt like a fool. What had been important to me as recently as last week no longer mattered.

Now *Tarryn* mattered. And that was something I'd never anticipated.

She was a prostitute. There was no way around that. I'd had zero intention of having any sort of interaction with her other than a strictly for-show, professional one. I'd hired her to help me out, to keep my family at bay, and to alleviate the annoying news cycles that centered on me.

And now I'd gone and slept with her.

But it was so much worse than that.

I eyed the gorgeous woman next to me, who was still peacefully sleeping. She'd earned her rest—I'd never had sex like that in my life. And it wasn't because it was kinky, or remarkably different, or anything other than mostly pure-vanilla goodness. But the depth of my orgasms had shocked me to my core.

And I had a bad feeling I knew what that meant.

Tarryn burrowed beneath the blankets. I still knew little about her, but I knew how she made me feel: lighter, better, happy. I hadn't had fun in…ever? I couldn't remember a time—save those afternoons years ago by the lake, playing pirates, or perhaps when I was older, cutting school with Cliff and taking the boat out —that I'd felt carefree. But even though we were surrounded by my cloying family and the paparazzi hadn't given us a moment's rest, I felt great. Tarryn was my ally. She was my *friend*. When she was by my side, I felt like I could handle the rest of it.

For fuck's sake, I was making a mess of things.

I carefully picked up a tendril of her hair just to have something to hold on to. What was I going to do now, huh? I had feelings for her. *Real* feelings.

Being a prince was a duty I'd never asked for. I'd been born into this, the same way Tarryn had been born into her circumstances. But I couldn't deny what I was— what *either* of us was.

Her phone was on the nightstand. Out of the corner of my eye, I saw the screen light up. Someone had sent her a picture. Curious, I bent closer as the screen flashed again.

It was a picture of Tarryn. She looked about five years younger. She wore a button-down shirt and a strained smile.

I sat back against the bed, ashamed of myself. I shouldn't be looking at her phone like that. It was rude—even worse, it was sneaky. She started to stir, and I nudged her. "Good morning."

She adorably opened one eye and smiled at me. "Good morning."

"I did something bad."

She immediately sat up, alarmed. "What happened?"

"It's okay." I gently patted her arm. "But you got a text, and your phone lit up—I looked at the screen."

She froze for a moment. "You did?"

"Someone sent you a picture, that's all." My tone was soothing, but I was alarmed by how anxious she looked.

She reached for her phone, glancing at the image when the screen lit up. Then a deep frown lined her face as she protectively held it against her chest.

"I'm sorry—I didn't think about it," I said quickly. "I just looked."

She shook her head, but her eyes were a bit wild. "It's fine. It's nothing. I'm going to go take a shower, okay?"

Before I could say another word, she disappeared into the bathroom, still clutching her phone. I had a sick feeling in my stomach, and not only because I'd done something wrong.

Tarryn was hiding something from me. What was it?

A montage of possibilities swirled in my mind. She was married. She was in a relationship. She was in love with someone else. She was engaged to someone else. There was a theme, see? And it revolved around me being jealous as fucking hell.

She didn't owe me anything—not even the truth. I'd hired her as a fake date.

That fact did not make me any more rational.

My temples pounded as I slid from the bed and threw some clothes on, scribbling a quick note to her. *Be back soon*, it read.

But not before I had some answers.

∾

"WHAT DO YOU MEAN, it's been destroyed?" I looked at Chief Phillip in disbelief.

He calmly stared back from behind his desk. "Like I said, it's protocol."

"Since when is it protocol to incinerate the records of someone"—I leaned closer and kept my voice low, even though the door was closed—"who is employed by the palace?"

"She's not technically employed by the palace," the security chief reminded me. "You paid for these services in cash out of your own pocket."

I sat back and glared at him. "I want to know what was in those files."

The Chief raised his eyebrows. "Why don't you ask Ms. Clayton?"

"I will—of course, I will." I struggled to keep my voice under control. Like most things these days, I hadn't thought it through when I'd hustled to the Chief's office and demanded to look at Tarryn's file. But I'd had an overwhelming desire to find out more about her real life without hounding her to her face.

Was that...sneaky? Was it wrong?

It was both. But I suspected that more than anything, I was acting out of cowardice. What if I asked her more about herself, and she pushed me away? Or worse—what if she told me there was someone else, someone she loved?

Hounding my security chief was the cheater's way to the information. I'd come up with nothing when I'd searched her name on the internet.

"Your Highness," the Chief was saying, "it's not a good look."

"What isn't?"

"The way you're approaching this. Listen, if you

want to know more about her, ask *her*. I'm not a matchmaking service."

"I don't need the attitude, Chief."

I gave him an ugly look as I left. *Not a matchmaking service. Not a good look.* If I didn't like Philip so much, I'd punch him in the jaw.

I straightened my shoulders as I headed down the hall. Who had sent her that picture? It seemed innocent enough. But why had she reacted that way? Was it because I'd been snooping? Did she want to hide something from me? Or was it something else?

Yes, I wanted to know more about Tarryn. Yes, I was afraid to ask her to her face. Perhaps I was scared to find out about her past. More likely, I was worried she'd want to know why I was asking…and then I'd have to admit it not only to her, but to myself.

Familiar voices drifted from down the hall from one of the libraries. My sister and my father sounded as though they were arguing about something. Izzie was trying to keep her voice down and failing. "I did exactly what you asked. Now it's your turn!"

"I don't see why you think it's appropriate to throw a temper tantrum at your age," my father snapped. He sounded annoyed, which was unusual when he was speaking to his favorite child. "Relax, Isabelle. You don't want those lines on your forehead to become permanent!"

I surprised myself by knocking at the door and entering, unbidden. "Are we having some sort of a family meeting? Why am I not surprised that no one told me—or mother, for that matter?"

My father and sister blinked at me. I never joined them of my own volition. They stood at the opposite end of the room, near the floor-to-ceiling windows, the early morning sun outlining them.

My father smiled at me without warmth. "To what do we owe the honor?"

I joined them, flopping into an uncomfortable wing-backed chair. My mood was *just* sour enough from my encounter with Philip that I felt like annoying them. It would only make me feel darker, just what I deserved at the moment.

"Why are you here, exactly?" My sister looked vaguely annoyed and also like she was trying to keep her forehead relaxed.

"I heard you arguing. If you're trying to keep secrets, you might want to close the door."

Izzie huffed and puffed past me and slammed the door. "Now then—don't you have better things to do than snoop? Your pretty American will grow cold without your hands on her arse for five seconds."

"Ha." I chuckled. "Good one."

"How *is* your pretty American?" My father looked a little too interested for my liking.

"She's great." I waved my hand dismissively. "But I'm a little worried about you two. Having a bit of a quarrel, are we? That's not like you."

When they didn't say anything, I sighed. "What exactly are you up to?"

My father's face was a smooth mask, but my sister frowned. She looked to me, then to Father, then away.

"What is it, Izzie?"

"Er…" She wrung her hands together.

"Not one word, young lady. Don't you dare." My father's voice was ice.

Izzie groaned and started pacing. "We've got to tell him sometime."

"Isabelle—"

"What is it, Izzie? I'd rather hear it from you than read about it in the Daily Chat. You'd best tell me now."

My father's nostrils flared. "You'll be involved when you need to be, son. Not right now."

Izzie gave him a pleading look. "I don't think leaving him out is in our best interests."

A heavy tension filled the room as I waited. My temples started to pound again.

My sister took a deep breath. "We're worried about Mother, Clive. She's not well."

"Did something happen?"

"No, not exactly." Izzie resumed pacing, twisting her hands together. "It's just that things have progressed. She's gotten worse. I'm afraid she's never going to get better."

"You mean her agoraphobia?" It petrified my mother to leave the house. "That's because the press eviscerates her every time she sneezes."

"It's not just that," Izzie said quickly. "It's her drinking. It's gotten much worse over the years."

"That's true, but she's not so different from a lot of other people who are deeply unhappy." I looked at my father; he was inspecting his hands. "She could probably use someone to talk to."

"That's exactly it." Izzie nodded. "We've been thinking—"

"Woah, *we*? As in, you and Father?"

"Yes. We've been thinking that she needs more help than that." Izzie stopped pacing. "She's not happy here, Clive. She might be better off someplace else, where there's a lot less stress."

I looked at my sister. Her expression was pleading. I turned to my father—*his* was impassive. "Does Mother know about this?"

"No, and we mustn't upset her before the wedding. We'll handle it as a family once the festivities are over."

"If that's the case, then why…" The throbbing in my temples increased. "Why are you arguing about it now?"

"Like I said, son, don't concern yourself with it. I must take my leave." With a nod, my father disappeared.

"I have to… I must… So busy…" Izzie tripped after him, probably afraid to be alone with me.

I didn't blame her. My mood, already dark, had blackened. I *hated* it when people kept things from me.

But that seemed to be exactly what everyone around me was doing.

TARRYN

Oh my god. Oh my god, oh my god, oh my god.

I locked the door behind me and lifted my phone with shaking hands. The picture was from years ago, another lifetime, in Minnesota. I looked awful in it—pale, my hair a mess, my youthful face taut with stress.

Robbie had taken that picture. The last time I'd seen it was tucked into the side of his mirror in his bedroom. It was a warning, a reminder. He'd taken it the day I'd try to break up with him for the first time.

Feeling like I was going to throw up, I clicked on the message. But it was blank except for the picture. There was no text. The sender information was a number I didn't recognize—I wasn't even sure it was a phone number.

I heard the door to the bedroom close, and I

quickly peered into the room. Clive had gone out. Locking myself back inside the bathroom, I called my mother.

She answered on the first ring. "Is everything okay?" she asked immediately.

"Everything's fine." I tried to mask the strain in my voice. "Did Ellie's appointment go all right?"

"Yes. Dr. McManus said that she sounds *terrific*. They lowered her dosage on the medication. She still might need the surgery, but she's hopeful that we're on the right track."

I breathed an enormous sigh of relief. At least there was *some* good news. "That's great."

"Yes, it is—and she's doing just fine, honey. We're keeping our routine, and I read her your notes every night. She loves them."

I'd written Ellie a note for every day that I'd be gone, and my mother had promised to read them to her every night. "Thank you for taking such good care of her, Mom." Tears burned my eyes, threatening to fight their way out.

"Aw honey, it's my pleasure." She went quiet for a moment. "Listen, I saw something on the news…"

"What?" My heart twisted painfully in my chest.

"It was about the royal wedding. Honey, are you…are you *at* the royal wedding?"

Of course. Relieved, I said, "Yes, I am. Sorry I couldn't tell you before, it's very hush-hush."

"I should think so! That Prince Clive is certainly handsome. Is he nice?" A note of hopefulness crept into her voice.

"He's really nice, Mom. You'd like him. It's all very glamorous."

"You looked so pretty in the picture."

"Were there lots of them?" I clutched the phone. "Pictures?"

"There were quite a few. But I don't think anyone else would recognize you if that's what you're worried about. They didn't say your name, just that the Prince was dating a beautiful American student. You look different than you did before, sweetie. If your own mother almost didn't recognize you, it's fine."

"Thanks, Mom." I exhaled in relief. "That's good. Hopefully, no one will guess that it's me. But, listen… Has anything unusual happened? Any phone calls, any strangers hanging around, any…anything?"

"Not at all." She hesitated for a moment. "Are you worried because of all the press?"

"A little," I admitted. "I just don't want anything to happen to you or Ellie. I'd never forgive myself." I wondered if the Prince would give me some sort of advance so that maybe I could hire security for them until I got back...

"Don't you worry about us. We're *fine*. Do you want to talk to Ellie?" Mom asked.

"I'd love to." Tears sprang to my eyes when I heard her little voice.

"Mama. *Hi*, Mama."

"Ellie! Mommy loves you. Mommy loves you so much. Are you being good for Grammy?"

She babbled a bit. Something about the park and her stuffed bunny, Boo Boo.

"Tell Boo Boo I love her, too." Now the tears went ahead and rolled right down my face. "I have to go, okay? Mommy will be home soon. I love you, sweetie."

As soon as she hung up, I had a full-on breakdown. It lasted one minute. I couldn't afford to be puffy, to have Clive asking me questions, to let myself completely lose my shit.

It might have been very, very stupid of me to come here.

I started the shower and climbed in, numb to the hot water. To my credit, I reminded myself, I hadn't known what the assignment was until I was on my way to the airport. I could never have guessed that I'd be a guest at the palace, attending the royal wedding, the fake date of the world's hottest bachelor prince. Had I known, I *might* have said no.

I closed my eyes as the water ran over me. Ellie might still need another surgery. Who was I kidding? I'd risk my life to save hers—I wouldn't think twice. So in some respects, that's exactly what I was doing.

But I couldn't put my daughter, or my mother, at risk.

Who had sent me that old picture? There was only one answer, but I couldn't bear to face it. *Robbie.*

No one else would have access to it.

But how had he found my number? It'd been years since I'd cut off all contact. Feeling bewildered, I washed my hair in a daze. Could he have gotten my number? If yes, how?

I raised my arms to wash the shampoo out, surprised at how relaxed and loose I felt. And then I remembered what I'd done last night—all night—and all afternoon before the party.

And then I really wanted to cry.

I regretted having sex with Clive. Not because I hadn't wanted to—I had, badly. And if I was being honest with myself, I wanted him again, now, even though we'd had *all* the sex. But that was the problem. I wanted him in a way that scared me, that left me breathless and needy and all the things I could never afford to be. He was my client. He was a prince who lived in a foreign country. It was an impossible situation on so many levels, it was borderline ridiculous.

What was worse? I had feelings for him. Real ones. Ones that were currently twisting my heart as I rinsed the shampoo from my hair, cursing myself for getting attached. I didn't ever let my guard down, and here I was, pining for a prince.

And Robbie had texted me. And I had to get home to my daughter, who Clive didn't even know about.

I felt sick. I didn't want to lie, to hide things. But what choice did I have?

I didn't want Clive to know about Robbie—first of all, because I was ashamed. Deep down, I knew what had happened wasn't my fault, but still. That dark chapter of my life was painful to think about. Why hadn't I left Robbie sooner? Why had I chosen him in the first place? He'd been so nice to me when we started dating. Were there warning signs I'd missed? Why had he done those things to me when he said he loved me?

I rested my forehead against the cool tile of the shower wall, waves of pain crashing over me. This was why I didn't ever think about the past. I had no answers for Robbie's behavior, for why he was a monster. Probably someone had hurt him, too.

That didn't make it okay.

I didn't want Clive to know about Robbie. And I *couldn't* let him know about Ellie. I'd almost told him several times over the past few days that I had a daughter—a wonderful, amazing, beautiful daughter who was the light of my life. But I hadn't. Just like I'd never told Vivian! I shook my head, turning off the water and roughly toweling my hair dry. Sometimes I couldn't believe myself. Vivian was my best friend; I trusted her completely. Still, I'd never told her about Ellie. I was so paranoid that somehow Robbie would find out I'd had a child, and then he'd try to make some sort of legal claim to her.

There was no father listed on Ellie's birth certificate. When they asked me at the hospital where I gave birth, I said I didn't know who the father was.

I'd wondered many, many times if that made me a terrible person. That I'd lied and that I'd kept her from him. But then I made myself remember when he swore, his hand over his heart, that if I ever left him, he would track me down and kill me.

By that time, I didn't doubt it. He'd come close to killing me already.

My daughter was never going to be around someone like that. Biology be damned—and maybe me, too. Perhaps I'd burn in the fires of hell because I'd lied and hidden Ellie from her father. But you know what? Fuck it! I'd do it again.

No one deserved to be beaten. To be terrorized. *No one.*

I shivered, glancing once again at my cellphone. There had to be some way I could deal with this. Some way to protect myself, protect my family, to finish this assignment, take the money and run. I hated to hear myself think like that—it made me feel ugly, a mercenary who had spread her legs for cash.

With that, my thoughts came full circle back to Clive.

I'd made a mistake by sleeping with him. I'd let my guard down, let myself feel something. And it was something real.

Except that I'd lied to him because I hadn't shared the most important part of myself: that I was a mom.

And I'd lied to him again—when we'd had sex, he most likely believed I was simply playing a part.

But that was just another lie, maybe the worst one of them all.

TARRYN

I HUSTLED down the hall to the security office, careful to avoid running into anyone in the hall. I'd left Clive a note—*BRB*, it read. Hopefully, he'd understand it. I'd been in such a rush, I didn't have time to write more.

"Can I speak to the Chief, please?" I nervously scanned the office, hoping that none of the royal family was nearby.

"Of course." The man at the front desk buzzed him, then immediately waved me through. "Head straight back to his office, Ms. Clayton. He's waiting for you."

"Thank you."

Chief Philip met me at the door. "I've been expecting you."

My heart leaped into my throat. "You have been?"

He nodded, motioning for me to take a seat as he closed the door. "I might be breaching confidentiality by telling you this, but His Highness was here this morning. Did something happen?"

"Not exactly." My mouth went dry. "What did the prince say? Was he upset? Does he want to fire me?" For some reason, this kept coming up for me. Every time I did something wrong, I feared that His Highness would immediately let me go. The worst part? I found I wasn't thinking about losing out on the money. I was worried about having to say goodbye to him…

Stupid, stupid, stupid.

"Ms. Clayton?" The Chief was staring at me. "Did you hear what I said?"

"No, sorry—I was thinking about something else." I shook my head. "What was it?"

"I said that the prince was asking about *you*. And now here you are. So what happened?" He watched me carefully. "And don't tell me nothing."

I sighed. "I got a text message this morning—an old picture of me. It's from a number I don't recognize." I opened up the message and handed him the phone.

His brow furrowed as he inspected it. He wrote down the number. "That's not a cell phone number, it's a shortcode. Businesses use them for automated follow-ups. I can trace it, but it might be registered to a corporation."

He handed the phone back to me. "Do you think this is from your ex?"

I nodded, my chin wobbling.

"And this is the first time he's made contact in years, correct?"

I swallowed over what felt like a boulder in my throat. "Yes."

The Chief nodded. "He must've seen you online—there's no other explanation. I'm going to get approval to have private security sent for your family back in the States. There's no reason to worry, but there's also no reason to wait."

I gaped at him. "You would do that? For me?"

"Of course. Not only because we have unlimited resources but also—it's the right thing to do, Ms. Clayton. Being photographed is part of this job, it's something you can't get away from. You shouldn't be punished. Neither should your family. I'll take care of it. But I'm going to need your permission to reach out to your mother. I'd like her to understand what's happening. I might look into moving them to a safe house."

I sat there, gobsmacked. "You would do that?"

"I'm doing it." He wrote a note on his pad. "You

should call her first and tell her to pack light. The wedding's this weekend—the press will be all over this event, all over *you*. Pictures of you online could stir things up."

I nodded. "How did he... How could he... My number's private. How did he find it?"

"The internet makes all things possible." The Chief sighed and wrote another note. "Speaking of which, I'm ordering you a new phone."

"Chief?"

"Yes?"

"Thank you." When I sniffled, he handed me a tissue.

"You're welcome. But can I give you some advice, Ms. Clayton?"

I nodded.

"Remember what I told you before—about keeping our circle small?"

"Yes."

"Maybe I was wrong about that." He sighed, big shoulder sagging. "You might want to talk to His Highness."

I took a deep, shaky breath. "I thought we didn't want him to know about my background because it would protect the prince. I want to protect him."

The Chief sighed through gritted teeth. "We *all* want

to protect him. But maybe we should think about what he wants, you know what I mean?"

~

Clive texted that he was taking me to lunch. I'd thought that meant we were leaving the palace grounds, but when I met him in the lobby, I learned otherwise.

"I think we need a break from the paparazzi for one day, don't you?"

"Sure." It was as natural as breathing that I accepted his hand as he led me outside, down a path toward some gardens we hadn't explored yet.

"I'm giving Chef a break—I ordered Thai food. Basic Thai food." He pulled down his sunglasses and winked at me. "Is that all right? I should've checked with you first, but I lost track of you for a bit."

"Thai food sounds great." I smiled. With the sun shining down on his handsome face, his big hand engulfing mine, how could I not?

We made it halfway down the path when he stopped. He put his hands on my hips, palming them, which for some strange reason made me salivate.

"Listen." His voice was husky. "I was thinking this morning… I hope everything that we did yesterday was okay with you."

I arched an eyebrow. "It was more than okay."

He took a deep breath, as though he was going to say more, then stopped himself.

"Is something wrong?"

"No. It's just that…" The muscle in his jaw bulged. "Why did you act like that this morning when I saw your text? I didn't mean to snoop, Tarryn. I just didn't stop myself from looking when your phone lit up."

"I know." I nodded as I looked up at him. It was not in my nature to be secretive; I longed to simply tell him the truth. "That text surprised me. It caught me off guard."

He watched me closely, waiting for me to go on.

I sighed. "It was from an old boyfriend, I think. Someone I haven't heard from in a very long time."

"So it was out of the blue?" Clive asked.

"Yes—unexpected and unwelcome, if I'm being honest." Which I only partly was. "I guess he saw my pictures online." I shrugged. "So he felt the need to text."

The prince nodded as we resumed walking slowly down the path. "So this is an *ex*-boyfriend?"

"Yes." I looked at him quickly. "I'm not seeing anyone, Your High—Clive. I haven't been involved with anyone for a long time."

"Oh."

The relieved tone in his voice made me melt.

For better—or more likely, for worse—I squeezed his hand and moved closer against his side. Because even though my attachment was going to make saying goodbye so much worse, I just couldn't help myself.

CLIVE

I haven't been involved with anyone for a long time. Oh, for fuck's sake, thank *god*. I felt like someone had lifted an enormous weight from me. If Tarryn had told me there was someone else, I would have lost it.

Not that the situation wasn't still impossible; it was. But at least it was bearable. For now.

She stayed close by my side as we walked down the path to the interior garden. I'd had the staff set up a private oasis for us, something special, something intimate. Because…because.

We entered the private garden, and Tarryn sucked in a deep breath. "Clive, what did you do? This is amazing!"

They'd gone all out. They'd set up an enormous table with a deep-violet tablecloth; it was set with fine china and a gigantic silver candelabra in the center.

I chuckled. "I'd love to take credit for this, but it was my staff. I think they want to impress you."

"Tell them they've done it—mission accomplished." She smiled at me, a smile that went all the way to her eyes. "They're really incredible, the people who work for you."

"Your Highness—excuse me, pardon me—Your Highness!" Herbert, my father's stubby steward, burst into the garden.

"What do you want, Herbert?" I eyed him with disdain. Most of the palace staff was incredible, but then there was my father's steward.

"His Highness the King has requested that you and Ms. Clayton make a brief public appearance this afternoon with the family. The King is taking some questions about the wedding, and he wants the royal family present."

"I'll speak with him after lunch."

"I'm afraid he sent me now because he was looking for an immediate answer—"

"Tell him I'll speak with him when I return to the palace." My voice was final. "Thank you, Herbert. You're dismissed."

He opened his mouth and then closed it. He looked pretty sullen as he tottered off.

"You were saying?" I asked Tarryn. "About our amazing staff?"

She laughed, but it sounded a bit forced. "Is Herbert really that awful?"

"Absolutely." I pulled out her chair and sank down beside her. "He used to tattle on Cliff and me all the time. Anytime we tracked mud into the palace, anytime we took cookies from the kitchen without asking, any time we stole brandy from the decanters—"

"Maybe he *should've* tattled on you for that." She arched an eyebrow.

"I was in high school." I sighed and poured her some water from a chilled bottle. "I suppose I shouldn't be so short with him, but he's my father's spy. And I'm not at all happy with my father right now."

"Did something happen?" Tarryn asked.

"Yes." I blew out a deep breath as I started serving the food. Green papaya salad, Pad Thai, and a coconut soup with curried chicken. "I know this is a bit exotic, but you'll like it."

She inhaled deeply. "Mmm, it smells delicious."

It might seem odd—because Tarryn was super hot and sexy—but one of the things I loved best about her was how she enjoyed food. I could picture us eating dinner every night, trying new restaurants…

She had a bite of the papaya and moaned. "Why is this so good? I didn't even think I liked papaya!"

"Ha. Yes, it's delicious." But I pushed the food around on my plate. I wanted to eat it when I could enjoy it. "So about my father… I ran into him and my sister this morning. They were having an argument."

Tarryn stopped chewing. "About what?"

It surprised me that I wanted to tell her. I wanted to hear what she had to say; I wanted an ally, but more importantly, I wanted to share something with her. "They want to put my mother in some sort of…home, I think. They didn't get into too many details—just that her drinking has gotten worse, and they think she needs professional help."

Her brow furrowed. "And what do you think?"

I shrugged. "I think she could use someone to talk to. And I'm sure she wouldn't miss living in the palace."

"But doesn't that seem, I don't know…extreme?" Tarryn tilted her head. "What does your mother have to say about it?"

"She doesn't know."

Her eyes got big in her face. "They're planning this without even consulting her? Why wouldn't your mother have a say?"

"Probably because she'll say no, and that's not what my father wants to hear."

"What about your sister?"

I shook my head. "She seemed like she was being forced to go along with it. But I don't know—Izzie and my mom aren't close. Iz gets annoyed with her because she feels like Mother is melodramatic, to use her word. I wouldn't be surprised if she thought this might be a breath of fresh air."

"But your mother isn't hurting anyone," Tarryn said gently.

"It makes me sad to say it, but my father thinks she's bad for his image. The fact that she rarely goes out, she won't give interviews… To him, she's a failure. He views her as an impediment."

"To *what*? She's his wife."

I speared a bite of papaya with my fork. "I've wondered for years what motivates my father. It's the fame for sure—he loves it. And he loves lording his power over others even more. Being in control, calling the shots, being the one everyone looks up to, that's what he lives for. And if you're not eviscerating yourself before his throne with public gusto, you're against him."

"Does he consider you against him?"

"Yes," I admitted. "But he also can't do anything about it—I'm the heir. I've been better than I've wanted to be over the years. There's been plenty of times I've threatened to walk away."

"And what happened?" Tarryn's eyes were wide.

"My father knows how to get what he wants. Any time we've had a real rift, he's suddenly offered to give massive funding for one of my initiatives, something that will help thousands of people." I stared out, unseeing, at the gardens. "I've never been able to say no to that. And he gloats every time he gets what he wants, then tells me that I'm lucky to have such a benevolent father. But I'm not strong enough to walk away."

"That's not true," she said quickly. "You're selfless. That makes you a great leader. You would sacrifice your own happiness for the greater good of your citizens. Don't let him make you believe it's being weak."

She reached up and rubbed my back. "You're going to be an amazing king, someday."

"I wish that was true."

"It's true." She traced a pattern on my back. "I know it."

I turned to her, suddenly overwhelmed. I never talked to anyone about my family, our problems, my feelings. "Thank you for listening to me."

"That's what friends are for."

When she smiled at me, my insides twisted painfully.

"Is that what we are?" I asked, my voice almost cracking. "Friends?"

Tarryn suddenly looked serious. "I think so. I think of you as a friend."

"But not just a friend."

Her throat worked as she swallowed. Her eyes were suddenly bright. "No…not just a friend."

It was suddenly very, very hot between us. I stared at her mouth.

"A friend wouldn't do this." I devoured her sweet lips with mine. My hunger had nothing at all to do anymore with the delicious food spread before us.

She moaned as our tongues connected, arching her back, her pebbled nipples pressing against my chest. My hands were everywhere at once. Her hair, her back, her sides. I was desperate to have her again, to bind her to me, to claim her as *mine*. Didn't she understand what she meant to me? I took her shirt off in one swift motion.

Her eyes went wide with shock. "Clive. What if someone comes out here?"

"They'll bloody hear us, and they'll turn tail and run." I unclasped her bra, freeing her spectacular breasts, and greedily palmed them. Her nipples hardened further and I rubbed them, pinching the tender peaks. I first took one dusky bud in my mouth, greedily suckling it as she attempted to get my shirt off.

I helped her, yanking the T-shirt over my head, and the gleam of satisfaction in her gaze as she raked over my chest made every minute I'd spent in a boring gym worth it. She ran her hands down my pectoral muscles worshipfully, and it made me hard, so hard, as did seeing her naked tits bounce in the sunlight. *Unf.* I positioned her back against the table, slid down her skirt and her panties, and then spread her legs. Her sex glistened in the sunlight.

"You're already wet."

She raised her eyebrows, then playfully traced her fingertips along my erection. "And you're already hard."

"How could I not be? You're so fucking gorgeous, Tarryn. It's killing me." I felt as though it might. I kissed her again, my cock searing fiercely between us. My lips trailed down her neck, over her breasts, across the soft curve of her belly to the dewy folds of her sex. I ran my tongue along her slit, and she cried out, already so wet for me.

I was going to make her wait. Not for long, but still. I wanted to hear her need.

I wanted to hear her need *me.*

My tongue lashed against her clit, and she bucked beneath me. She sank her fingers into my hair as I lapped at her. With each stroke of my tongue, she cried out. Her body was trembling, all of her muscles quivering. "Clive, baby," she moaned, arching her back as I sucked her clit hard, then nibbled it, then sucked again.

"Don't make me come like this, I want you inside me—"

I increased the pressure with my tongue. She moaned and trembled violently. I gently placed two fingers inside her, fucking her in time to my lapping.

"Clive, wait—Clive!" She came, hard, shattering around my fingers as she cried out. Her body was still bucking against me as I unzipped my pants and pulled out my very hard cock, fisting it before I notched it at her entrance. Tarryn was *mine*. I was going to show her.

Her tight little body was still spasming with the orgasm I'd just given her as I bucked my hips and entered her. Then I began fucking her. *Yes. Fuck, yes.* She moaned and writhed beneath me as I flexed and entered her fully.

"Oh fuck. Baby. Oh my god." She clutched at my chest, but I grabbed both her hands, pinning them above her head. I grazed each of her nipples with my teeth, thrusting deeply the whole time. I loved having her like this, pinned beneath me, my cock driving inside her. I wanted to show her with every thrust that I owned her, *fuck* the dude who sent her that picture, *fuck* the fact that I'd hired her, *fuck fuck FUCK*.

I felt her body begin to quiver again. "That's my girl. Come for me again, baby." I increased my thrusts, my ass pumping as she screamed my name, her pussy spasming around my cock, squeezing it in a vice-like grip. I started to lose it, to unravel as she pulsed around me, wet and hot.

My balls tightened, and I came, hard, my orgasm chasing hers.

"Fuck!" I loosened my grip on her hands and gently took her in my arms, our foreheads pressed together. There was no other word for it.

And even though I'd been the one doing the fucking, it was clear to me that I was also the one who was fucked.

I clutched Tarryn in my arms. I kissed her hair, her cheeks, her eyelids. How was it that this stranger had become so important to me?

And what exactly the *fuck* was I going to do about it?

TARRYN

I WAS STILL SHIVERING from my climax.

"Shh babe, I got you." Clive wrapped his massive arms around me. His embrace made me feel as though I was in a safe, protective cocoon. He tenderly kissed my cheek, then rubbed his scruff gently against me. "I think I got a little carried away."

When he laughed—a deep, throaty sound, his breath cool against my neck—I shivered all over again.

"I hope you're not apologizing. I enjoyed every second of that—which I think you already know." I'd developed an embarrassing habit of screaming Clive's name whenever I came, which seemed to be every five minutes.

He laughed again, his big muscles shaking against me. Then he held me for another full minute. I luxuriated in the feeling of being safe and protected, of being cared for. But, there was another feeling, too, underneath these. It was intense, powerful, and it petrified me.

I refused to admit what it was, even to myself.

∼

WE MADE LOVE AGAIN. Slowly, intensely. Clive's eyes never left my face as he thrust into me, my orgasm building in intensity with each stroke.

When he came, he moaned my name. Pure female satisfaction bloomed inside me as his thrusts grew ragged, and he lost control, shooting his seed inside me. *I* did this to him. It was my name on his lips. He wanted *me*.

I wanted him even more.

Even though we'd had all the sex, my need for him didn't subside. I didn't understand why I still keened for him, deep in my belly and in between my legs. All I wanted was to be in his arms—to hold him, to be held by him, to run my fingers through his thick, springy hair.

The prince seemed to want the same thing. Once we'd finally gotten dressed again, he couldn't seem to keep his hands off me. We ate lunch slowly, side by side, his hand on my thigh. He kept brushing the hair back from my face, all the better to pepper my cheeks with kisses. I leaned against him, happily inhaling his masculine, spicy scent.

It was a simple, al fresco lunch. Still, I felt like I'd died and gone to heaven.

After we finished, we spent a languid afternoon alone wandering the grounds, hiding from the press, hiding from the royal family, hiding from the truth: time was passing quickly. We were lounging in another one of the many royal gardens when Clive asked, "Do you like horses?"

"Um, I think so?" I wrinkled my nose. "I've never ridden one. But I think they're beautiful."

"We should walk to the stables." He smiled at me. "We have some spectacular horses."

Ellie loved horses. I longed to tell the prince about how she liked me to read books about ponies in particular, but I couldn't force my mouth to form the words. What would he think if he knew? I guessed the thing I feared the most is that he would judge me harshly for working at the agency. What kind of mother earned a living as a prostitute?

One that wants to feed her family and pay for expensive, lifesaving surgeries, I reminded myself. But I still didn't say anything.

The walk to the stable was lovely. The weather was glorious, blue skies, warm sunshine, and a light breeze.

They impeccably kept the palace grounds. The lush grass felt more like a carpet than a lawn beneath my feet. The shrubs and trees were manicured to perfection, and birds chirped happily from their perches. And why wouldn't they be happy? It was paradise.

We held hands as we crossed the grounds. Every time Clive looked at me, he smiled. Every time he smiled at me, my stomach did a somersault. If I hadn't known the truth, I would've sworn that we were falling for each other.

Or that we already had...

We reached the stables and were greeted by a young man and his son, who was about six. "Your Highness. Ms. Clayton." The man bowed to us. "It's an honor. Will you be riding?"

"Not today. We just came to say hello." The prince bent down and addressed the child. "Hello, Matthew. How are you?"

The boy was adorable. He had tousled dark hair, ruddy cheeks, and chubby legs. He grinned at the prince. "Good. D'you want to see the horses? We could give them some sugar cubes—"

"Matthew, I am certain His Highness would like to be left alone—"

"Do you happen to have some sugar cubes, Matthew?" Clive winked at the father. "Because Ms.

Clayton and I were hoping to make friends with the horses this afternoon."

"I do have some." The boy beamed at Clive. "Follow me."

Clive patted the father on the shoulder as we followed him inside the stable. "I love to see Matty, you know that."

The man smiled. "And I appreciate how kind you are. But if you want a moment alone, just tell me. Please."

"We don't, but I would," Clive answered.

We went inside the cool stable, and it took a moment for my eyes to adjust to the darkness. Matthew was at the far end of the stalls, stuffing sugar cubes into his pockets until they bulged. The horses peered out of their stalls, watching us with interest. "I think you've got quite enough." Clive laughed.

The boy ran back to us, his shorts weighed down by his bounty. "Here." He immediately put a handful of sugar cubes into my hand, then into Clive's. "Let's see Rosie first." He went to the third stall, where a reddish-colored horse waited patiently. "Here Rosie." He held out several cubes, and the horse gently took them from his palm, snorting her approval afterward.

Matty turned back to me, smiling. "Your turn."

"Should I give some to Rosie too or a different horse?"

"Mmm, Star. Star's next." He came over and guided me to a black horse with, most appropriately, a white star on its forehead. Matthew put his hand underneath mine and offered it to the horse. Star waited, sneezed, and then gingerly took the sugar cubes, one by one.

"His lips feel funny against my skin," I told Matthew.

"They're not funny—they're horse lips!" He waved the prince over. "Your turn! You feed Bailey."

"Bailey, huh? How did you know Bailey's my favorite?"

Matthew's eyes glittered. "Because you told me, silly."

Matthew went and stood by the prince. They talked in low tones as the horse, an older-looking chestnut, approached them. Matthew laughed as Clive said something silly to the horse. Then they both petted its nose.

The way the prince looked at Matthew made my insides twist with longing. *Prince Clive would make a great father.* The thought, unbidden and unwelcome, suddenly landed in my head.

Clive glanced over his shoulder at me, still smiling.

I forced a smile back. But on the inside, I was breaking.

* * *

Let's hang tonight at the party, Vivian texted me. *I haven't talked to you all day!*

I read the message as Clive, and I made our way back

to the palace. After saying goodbye to Matthew and his father, we'd realized how late it had gotten.

Clive gripped my hand as he practically dragged me across the lawn. "I forgot—my father wants us to attend a press conference that he's holding."

"Oh!" I turned to him, concerned. *"Us?"*

"Yes. It's just a simple question-and-answer business about the wedding, but he wants everyone in attendance. So we'll have to dress."

My nerves started to thrum. "What do you wear for a press conference?"

Clive's brow furrowed. "Something…navy blue?"

I nodded. "Okay, I can do that." Elena had packed a ton of dresses for me. Something had to be appropriate.

His brow furrowed further, a thundercloud waiting to crack. "Then we'll have to change again for Izzie's stupid party. It's black tie, of course."

Isabelle was having her final cocktail party catered. The event would take place on the southern lawn under an enormous tent.

"There are worse problems," I chided. *Like falling in love with your fake date. And realizing he's excellent with children.*

"True, true." He squeezed my hand. "Enough about that—thank you for feeding the horses with Matthew. He loves to show them off."

277

"He's a sweetie."

"He is. He's been with us since he was a baby." Clive glanced at me. "D'you like kids?"

I swallowed over a lump in my throat. "I love them."

"Me too." He nodded, then looked straight ahead.

Coward that I was, I didn't say another word.

∼

Yes to hanging at the party, I texted Vivian when I was finally alone. *But I have to attend a press conference first!*

Viv texted back *WTF*, with a wide-eyed emoji, but I couldn't respond. I had to be camera-ready, and I didn't have long. So I took a quick shower, washing my multiple orgasms away, along with the prince's scent mixed with mine. I didn't want our sunny, lazy afternoon to be over, and yet, I knew it was for the best.

Seeing His Highness with the little boy had made my heart hurt. Clive was a sweetie; I'd already known that. But his patience and humor with the child made me ache. Ellie would never have a father. She would never have someone like Clive—strong, gentle, protective, and loving—to watch over her.

I tried to focus as I applied fresh makeup, but my mind wandered back to the picture I'd found on my phone that morning. Had the Chief found out anything? Had he spoken to my mother?

Suddenly I was flooded with guilt. I'd been out all day. I'd had rip-roaring, glorious, mind-blowing sex *outside* on a *table*. Twice! I'd had a glass of wine with lunch. I'd been holding the prince's hand, gazing up at him, while it was likely my mother and daughter were being moved into a safe house because of me.

Not you, said the voice in my head. *Him.*

Still, I felt terrible. I'd had more highs and lows in one day than I usually had in a year. I suddenly missed Ellie so much, I had to grip the countertop. Again, the guilt overwhelmed me. I thought about my daughter all the time—what she was eating, was she being good for my mom, was she going down easily for her nap—but there had been several times over the course of the past week that I'd been so wrapped up in Clive, I'd forgotten her for a moment. Not like I forgot I had a *daughter*— once you were a mother, you could never forget your child. But I'd been intensely focused on myself for the first time since she was born.

It made me feel like shit.

Everything was making me feel like shit.

I sighed as I smoothed my hair, then went out to find the proper navy dress I was certain Elena had packed for me. If nothing else, I would look the part for this press conference. That was my assignment; I was going to leave the palace knowing I had completed my work, a job well done.

That's why I'd come here in the first place. I'd do well to remember that.

Clive was waiting for me, pacing the hall outside my suite. He stopped in his tracks when he saw me. "How is it," he asked, "that you get more beautiful every time I see you?"

I melted, even though his kindness somehow hurt. "You're sweet."

He took my hand and kissed it. "I have ulterior motives."

"Oh...?"

He grinned and pulled me closer. "What if you and I snuck away for a few days after the wedding? Go to the beach, like we talked about."

My heart twisted. "That sounds really nice."

"Maybe you can stay for longer than we planned." Clive shrugged. "What do you think about that?"

"I think it sounds lovely." I smiled at him, but inside, I was falling apart. "We'll talk about it, okay?"

"Of course." He kissed my hand again, his lips lingering for a moment. "Now, onto less pleasant things: we have to go and meet the double firing squad—my family *and* the press."

I took a deep breath, then plastered a brave smile on my face. "Let's do it." But what I really wanted to do was run away, screaming.

He was offering me everything I'd ever wanted.

Which happened to be everything I could never have.

CLIVE

I'D SWORN to myself that I was going to play it cool, that I wasn't going to trip all over myself and beg Tarryn to stay, but I'd already gone and done it.

How could I not? I'd literally just spent the best day of my life with her. The sex was insane—I was still thrumming with the vibration from it. It was as though our bodies had been made for each other, two puzzle pieces that had been intentionally designed to interlock.

When I was inside her, it just felt right.

But aside from our incredible physical connection, I couldn't deny that my affection for her was growing strong. I loved hearing her laugh. I loved eating lunch with her, having a glass of wine. Sitting next to her was an event. And then, when I'd seen her with little Matthew, I'd felt something weird inside my chest—

like a seed that had been planted poked through, sprouting.

I'd never felt like this about someone before.

For the time being, I refused to think about the implications. *Come to the beach with me for a few days.* It would be heaven to be alone with her, uninterrupted. Maybe I was just thinking with my dick? That would almost be a relief.

Because even though I wasn't letting myself think about it, I knew that my feelings for Tarryn were a genuine problem. Unless we could somehow keep her past a secret, there would never be a future for us. Not because of my family, but because of *her*. The press would eventually find out about the agency. How could I ask her to expose herself? If I truly cared for her, how could I ever ask her to be so vulnerable in front of the entire world?

I *did* truly care for her. Still, I'd asked her to stay.

Don't think about it, don't think about it, don't think about it!

Cliff sent me a text. *Save me a dance tonight—we need to talk,* he wrote.

Didn't Cliff know? 'We need to talk' was every man's least favorite four words. *Ok*, I texted back. But I had a sense of foreboding. What was on the Duke's mind?

Before I could mull my cousin's cryptic text further,

we reached the front lawn. My father, sister, and faithful fiancé George waited. The press was seated on chairs spread out on the grass, everyone whispering and taking photos.

Izzie hustled over to us immediately, kissing us on the cheeks and clutching our hands in greeting. "Finally," she whispered. "I was worried you were going to be no-shows!"

"Where's Mother?" I asked.

"She couldn't make it." Izzie looked a bit flushed.

"Is everything all right?"

My sister straightened her shoulders. "I don't think so. But it will be, eventually." She went and stood by George, who put his arm protectively around her.

My father nodded to us from the podium, motioning for Tarryn and me to join them. We stood behind him on his left-hand side, my sister and George on his right. He raised his hand, and immediately the reporters went silent—which was precisely the sort of thing he lived for.

"Ladies and gentleman of the media, thank you so much for joining us today." The King beamed out at them. "My dearest daughter, Isabelle, will be wed in only two days. Can you believe it? The world has watched her grow from a little girl to a beautiful, strong young woman. I know you'll all join me in wishing her congratulations."

Everyone clapped. A few of the long-time, more boisterous reporters whistled, which made Izzie laugh. Tarryn seemed calm at my side, and I had to give her credit. Not just anyone could roll with an internationally televised press conference thrown at them. She looked flawless in a simple navy gown, her hair loose around her shoulders.

"Now, you have requested this conference to ask more questions about the wedding. We're here to answer them. Please keep your queries to the subject at hand—not my son and his beautiful new girlfriend!" The King laughed, motioning to us. My face grew hot as he said, "You can maybe ask them one question at the end, ha ha!"

A female reporter stood. "Princess Isabelle, is it true that the full Astos symphony orchestra will play at your reception? They haven't confirmed it!"

Izzie stepped forward to take the podium from my father. "Yes, it's true—and I'm so excited to tell you, the conductor is Franz Waltheim. Yes, the famous composer will play at my wedding!"

That got the press quite riled up. There were several follow-up questions about Franz Waltheim, who was a legendary European conductor. The next round of questions consisted of press attendance at the event, celebrities on the guest list, and several questions about how Izzie would wear her hair for the ceremony. She refused to tell. "I have to keep you guessing about *something*," she laughed.

It was refreshingly boring until another reporter asked, "Princess Izzie, where is the Queen? We assumed she would take part in the family press conference. Is Her Highness well?"

Isabelle cleared her throat. "I'm glad you asked that, Fred." She smiled at the reporter, but I noticed her hands were clenched into fists on the podium. "I'm afraid that my mother the Queen is not feeling well, not at all."

All the reporters started asking questions at once. I glanced at my father, but his face was its typical smooth mask.

"One at a time, one at a time," my sister commanded calmly. "Yes—Fred again. Go ahead."

"What's wrong with Her Highness? Is she ill? Is it serious? Will she be able to attend the royal wedding?"

"That was more than one question, Fred." She smiled at him, but I saw the strain on her face. "My mother is ill, yes, but we expect her to make a full recovery. It is my hope that she's better for the wedding, but we'll have to see. She's with her doctors now."

Now it was my turn to clench my hands into fists. My sister and my father were up to something, and I knew from experience that it couldn't be good. They were moving my mother out of the picture and swiftly. She was no match for their schemes.

I stood there, raging. My sister was lying to the press, but it was my father who had put her up to it. This was *his* plan, I felt certain. I wanted to grab him and shake him. But with the press corps filming and watching our every reaction, I was powerless to confront him. Which was most likely exactly why they'd planned it like this…

More questions followed about the Queen and her health, but Izzie had no further information on the subject. "We're just about out of time," she announced. "One more question—you, in the back. Go ahead."

An attractive young reporter with glasses stood, looking almost beside herself with excitement. "Your Highness, hello. I'm Mina Mays, from the Daily Chat. Thanks so much for the opportunity." She beamed at my sister. "I've actually got a question for the prince."

The other reporters started objecting immediately.

Mina Mays put a hand on her hip and gave her peers a challenging stare. "His Royal Highness said we could ask *one*, right? Boo hoo that it wasn't yours!"

"Go ahead, Ms. Mays." Izzie nodded at her. "The rest

of you, please behave. The King said one question was allowed about my brother, and here it is."

"Prince Clive, it is an *honor*. On behalf of News Corp, I was wondering..." Ms. Mays had a glint in her eyes. "When are you going to put a ring on it, Your Highness?"

Everyone laughed. Then they went silent as if they were holding their collective breath, waiting for my answer.

Izzie turned to me, eyes pleading. I knew what she wanted—for me to behave. No public meltdown, no chewing out of Mina Mays, reporter for the Daily Chat. Typically, this was the part of the interview where I declined to answer further questions.

But this was not a typical situation. A lot was hanging in the balance—more than I was even aware of, I felt certain.

The reporters were silent, waiting. I wanted to curse them. I wanted to tell them my father was a beast, one who'd tired of my mother's frailty, one who only cared about himself. I wanted to walk offstage and never come back, taking Tarryn with me. I wanted to tell everyone to sod off, once and for all, and let me have some peace.

Izzie watched me, her face strained.

I took a deep breath as the moment stretched out. My mind raced. If I behaved—even better, if I *distracted*

—maybe I'd have a bargaining chip when all of this was over. Perhaps I'd be able to rescue my mother from whatever scheme they'd constructed.

If I played ball, Izzie would owe me. So would my father. The ball would finally be in *my* court.

I released Tarryn's hand and stepped forward to the podium. My head was pounding. I hadn't planned a proper response to the question, but I had an answer in my heart.

I opened my mouth and then closed it; Izzie winced. I took another deep breath and said, "The answer to your question is that I will put a ring on it, as you said, whenever Ms. Clayton tells me to. Have a lovely evening, everyone."

The crowd erupted with questions, but I'd done my duty. I grabbed Tarryn around the waist and unceremoniously dragged her off-stage, desperate to be away from the circus.

But I might be the biggest clown of them all.

TARRYN

"The thing is, Viv, I think I'm in trouble. Big trouble." I sniffed. "Because he just told the whole world that he was ready to put a ring on it!"

Vivian raised her eyebrows. "Sometimes when you know, you just know."

I shook my head. "That's insane—we haven't even been together for a week. And I'm a...*you know*."

I sniffled again. "We can't ever have a future."

Vivian looked confused. "Does he feel the same way? Because if he's saying things like what he just said, at a *press conference* no less, maybe he's got a different take on it."

"Yeah, I know. I mean, I don't know." I had a huge sip of champagne. "There's some other problems, too."

"Listen, I need to tell you something first. Don't be

mad, okay?" Vivian swirled a lock of her long dark hair between her fingers. "I told the Duke the truth about me. And about you."

"Um…" I glanced across the party to the prince and the Duke, who were deep in conversation. "I'm guessing that Cliff is telling Clive about that right now. Oh boy. We should've told him upfront—I feel terrible."

Vivian's eyes got wide beneath her mink eyelashes. "I'm the one who feels bad. I should've talked to you first, but it just sort of came out."

"It's okay," I said quickly.

Vivian sighed. "I couldn't lie to him anymore. He's sober, you know? Lying doesn't fit into what he's trying to do with his life, and I didn't want to make him an unwilling accomplice. I didn't think that was fair."

I stared at my friend. The Dominator rarely, if ever, took such a personal interest in her clients.

Viv clutched her drink, which looked suspiciously like water. "What are you looking at?"

I narrowed my eyes at her. "You." Vivian looked even more gorgeous than usual. Her mid-length, tight-fitting corseted gown was a deep bluish-green, striking against her flawless, caramel skin. Her dark hair was pulled back in a ponytail, the long tendrils curling over her shoulders.

"Are you, like…*serious* about him?"

She shrugged. "Yes. No. I don't know."

"That's a whole lot of answers for one question. Which is it? And did you quit drinking?" It occurred to me that I'd only seen Viv drink water since she'd arrived in Astos, even out on the boat. She was known for doing Polar Bear shots in between dancing on tables. "Seriously, what is *up* with you?"

She pursed her lips. "I'd been thinking I should stop drinking for a while—it makes me puffy. Plus... I like supporting Cliffie. He's trying to do the right thing for his life, you know? I admire that. He's a good guy. It makes me feel good to be supportive of his positive choices."

I raised my eyebrows. "That's awesome, Viv. But again, it's a lot of words. I want the short version. Are you into this Duke? Yes or no."

Vivian fidgeted.

"Answer my question, and I'll spill *my* guts." I raised my glass to her. "I promise."

"I'll drink to that. Woo, okay, here we go." She faced herself, then finished her water in one gulp. "I've never met anybody like Cliff. He's literally the nicest guy. And he treats me like a queen—a *Duchess*. He treats me like a Duchess!" She started laughing.

"Have you guys talked about what's going to happen after the wedding?"

Vivian started twirling her hair again. "Don't tell Elena, okay? But I don't think I'm going back to Boston. He wants me to move into his castle with him. He wants to—he wants all sorts of things. So don't think your prince is the only one who's going a little overboard after only a few days!"

She laughed and glanced across the dance floor, where Cliff and Clive were still deep in conversation. "These royals…I don't think they can get enough of us American women, you know what I mean? They got a taste of something they like! More power to them that they're going for it."

Viv turned back to me, her eyes bright. "I feel like I've been waiting for a long time for my real life to start, for something great to happen. I'm sort of done waiting, you know? I think *this* is pretty great. I'm going to be brave and go for it, too."

"You're always brave, Viv. I've always looked up to you for that. You can face anything." It was true. Vivian was fearless, and she took no shit.

I smiled at her, even as tears pricked my eyes. "I'm happy for you. But I can't believe you fell for a ginger-haired Duke. Of all the scenarios, this is *not* the one I pictured!"

She shrugged. "Life has so few real surprises. But they're the good stuff, you know?"

"Sometimes..." I nodded, my mood suddenly dipping. "I had a surprise this morning. But it wasn't good stuff."

"Tell Viv," she said, ushering me back into a remote corner of the tent. "Tell me all about it."

"The thing is..." My heart felt heavy from all the things I'd been hiding. The skeletons in my closet were rattling their cages, eager to be free. If I couldn't trust Vivian, who *could* I trust? I was past the point of being able to figure this out on my own.

"I've been keeping some secrets," I said miserably.

"Honey." Vivian leaned closer, careful to keep her voice down even though no one was near. "We're *escorts*. All of us have secrets, that's part of the deal. Did you know I used to be a used-car salesperson? And that I waitressed at Fuddruckers for five years?"

"You did?"

"Yup, and let me tell you, I'd take working for Elena any day. So go ahead and tell me what's up—I'm your person. Use me at will."

I groaned and looked out at the tent, the beautiful guests arriving in their fancy gowns and tuxedos. A breeze refreshed the warm air; it billowed the edges of the tent. Soft music played from the string quartet, and fairy lights twinkled on the carefully arranged potted plants. How on earth had I ended up at this party?

I turned back to Vivian. "A guy I used to date texted me this morning. And it scared the crap out of me because I haven't heard from him in years."

"Is he a stalker?" Viv asked immediately. She always got right to the point.

I nodded. "He's not someone I want anywhere near me or…my family. He's dangerous."

"He hit you?" When I nodded again, Vivian cursed. "If that fucker comes within a hundred feet, I will pound his ass. And not in a fun way!"

I melted a little—I could tell she meant it. "Thank you. That means a lot. But hopefully, that won't ever happen. Palace security is aware of the text, and they're on the lookout. Also, they said they were going to move my family to a safe house, just to be sure."

"Wow, they're giving your *family* security? That's amazing." Viv's eyes widened. "The prince is a pretty good guy, huh?"

"That's the thing." My gaze tracked across the room to the prince, who was still deep in conversation with the Duke. "He doesn't know."

Her brows knitted into a V. "Huh? How does he not know?"

I sighed. "He knows that an ex-boyfriend texted me, but he doesn't know that Robbie…hurt me. Or that I'm afraid of him. Or that security is aware he's a threat." I almost had to force the words out. "I didn't get into all the specifics."

"Okay…" She watched me carefully. "Why not?"

"I didn't tell him because it's not something I talk about." My voice was hoarse; my throat felt funny, like the words were making it close up. "Not *ever*. You're the third person I've ever told in my life—my mother and the Chief of Palace Security are the only other two."

"Wow. Thank you for trusting me." Vivian rubbed my arm. "But it's nothing to be ashamed of, honey. You didn't do anything wrong."

"I—I know." I took a deep breath. "But there's another reason I don't tell anyone about my past. It's just that… I…"

The words seemed literally stuck in my throat. I didn't want Vivian to be angry at me for keeping the truth from her for so long.

I took a deep breath.

"You're my best friend, Vivian. Really, you're the best friend I've ever had. I'm sorry that I've kept this from you. The thing is, I have a daughter. Ellie. She's three." Relieved to have finally told her the truth and petrified that Viv would be upset with me, tears sprang to my eyes.

"Oh honey—I knew it." She pulled me in for a tight hug. "I knew it!"

"You… You did?"

"You do *all* the mom things," Viv explained as she released me. "When we're driving, you always put your arm in front of me if we have to suddenly stop. When we eat, you always arrange the drinks at the center of the table, so they don't spill. You won't cross the road unless there's a 'walk' signal—you check the light three times. And you always have wipes."

I couldn't help it; I laughed. "I do always have wipes."

Vivian nudged me. "I figured there had to be a really good reason for you to work at the agency. I know you said your mom had a ton of medical bills, but a girl like you wouldn't end up doing a job like *this* unless you were trying to keep food on the table for someone tiny and adorable. That's what moms *do*. I just figured you didn't want Elena to know or the Johns. I always knew you'd tell me when you were ready."

My tears threatened to spill over.

"Don't do it," Viv warned, "that's an awful lot of high-end mascara to be streaking across your face. The party hasn't even started!"

I sniffled, trying to get ahold of myself. "I wanted to tell you so many times. You'll love Ellie—she's the sweetest. But I can't ever let her dad find out about her."

A knowing look dawned over Viv's face. "Now I'm starting to get it. He hasn't texted until today, huh? He must've seen your picture online. I can see why you're freaking out about the press conference."

I nodded. "It's crazy. But the fact that we have security…I mean, thank God." I crossed myself.

Vivian surprised me by following suit. When I gave her a look, she said, "I can cross myself if I want to! I just need my best friend to be all right, alright? I'm going to finally be an Auntie. So I'm allowed to ask God for help even if we don't talk that much!"

"Fair enough." I laughed. "Thank you, Viv."

She tilted her head in the direction of the prince and the Duke. "So what are you going to do about…you-know-who?"

"I don't know. He can't have meant what he said at the press conference. But…" I bit my lip. "He asked me to stay after the wedding, to go away with him for a few days."

"And?"

"And I can't." Again, tears pricked my eyes. "He can't mean it, you know? There's literally no way we could ever be together. If the truth about what I am comes out, it will ruin his family. If the truth about Ellie comes out and Robbie somehow finds out about her, it'll ruin *everything*. I ran away from him years ago. I can't risk it. I need to cut things off with the prince and get out of here, so the press leaves me alone."

I looked around the party with the glamorous royals, the string quartet, and the champagne fountain. "I don't belong here," I mused. "I never should have come. But I couldn't say no to the money. Ellie has a heart condition—my mother isn't the one with the health issues. She's had to have multiple surgeries."

Vivian squeezed my hand. "Oh honey."

"I'm not just hooking to put food on the table, although I certainly have to do that," I continued. "I was going to have to file for bankruptcy. I can't be raising my daughter like that. I *have* to give her a better life."

Vivian nodded. "Of course you do. You're doing the right thing."

I shrugged. "But I'm *not*. Because someone's going to get hurt." My gaze tracked back across the room to the prince.

"Is it okay if I say he's not the only one?" Viv asked softly.

"No." My eyes filled with stupid tears again, and I blinked them back. "No, it is not."

"So what are you going to do?"

"I have to talk to him about his public word choices, obviously." I felt so deflated. "And I have to be straight with myself. I don't have a future with His Highness. I let myself get attached, and it was a mistake. See what happens when I let my guard down? Frickin' nightmare."

Vivian eyed me but didn't say anything for a minute. "What?"

"Nothing." Vivian shrugged. "I was just thinking, maybe you should let Mr. Princey Biceps have a say in all this."

"Why—so I can tell him that even though we've gotten close over the past week, the whole thing's been a lie? That he has no idea who I really am? That I kept the truth about my daughter from him because I can't trust him—because I can't trust *anybody*?"

Viv cleared her throat. "Might not be a bad place to start."

"Ugh, I need to stop talking about this. I'm going to lose it." I hugged her. "Thank you for being my friend."

She squeezed me. "Thanks for finally letting your guard down. You're a lot of work, you know that? Good thing you're worth it!"

"Stop." I pulled back and fanned my face. "My expensive mascara's about to run."

Viv shook her head. "I keep telling you to get lash extensions. You might want to start listening to the Dominator—I'm in charge for a reason. I'm never wrong."

"Ha. Okay, I'm going to head to my date. I'll send

over your Duke so you two can get busy living happily ever after."

"We don't have to be the only ones," Viv called after me, but for once, the Dominator *was* wrong.

There was no future for Clive and me.

There was just an uncomfortable, yearning present, which was going to leave me precisely the way I came to Astos: alone.

CLIVE

AFTER THE PRESS CONFERENCE, Tarryn had said little as we hustled back to our suites. There wasn't much time before the party, and Izzie had threatened us to be prompt. I kissed her cheek as I deposited her at her door.

She looked at me with wide eyes, but she didn't say anything. *Bloody hell.* Cursing myself, I headed to my mother's suite to check in with her. Then I ran for my room, threw on my tux, and proceeded to the tent. Tarryn was meeting Vivian; I was meeting Cliff. Apparently, they each needed to talk to us separately.

The party was being held on the south lawn. The enormous tent billowed in the light breeze; I would've thought it was pretty if I wasn't so tense. Echoes from the press conference rang in my ears. What were Izzie and my father up to? Why had I said that about Tarryn? For fuck's sake, *what* was I doing? I felt as though I was digging myself a grave with a spoon, one tiny, painful scoop at a time—an exercise in futility.

My cousin waited for me by the bar. He looked handsome in his tuxedo; his pale skin had a pronounced, unusual glow. Old Cliffie had been having all the sex, maybe as much as me.

"Wow Cousin, you sure know how to cause a ruckus." Cliff had a sip of seltzer as I ordered a double bourbon. "That was quite the surprise twist at the press conference—and what the bloody hell is going on with your mother?"

"I'm not sure." I sighed as I gratefully accepted my drink from the bartender. "And I have my reasons for what I said."

"Yeah, about that. We need to have a chat." Cliff practically dragged me to the edge of the tent, away from the arriving guests. "Listen, Viv and I have been talking. A lot."

The Duke's cheeks started to flush.

"And?"

"And… She told me what she does for a living. I know the truth."

I coughed, almost spitting out my bourbon.

He leveled me with a direct gaze. "Why didn't you tell me, mate? You're the one who hired her!"

"I…" I sighed. "Again, I had my reasons. And they were selfish ones."

Cliff leaned closer. "She told me everything—I know about Tarryn."

I stared at my cousin. He stared back.

"Your Highness?" A familiar voice called from nearby.

It surprised me to see Stellan striding across the party towards us. He wore a tuxedo, along with a sheepish expression on his face.

"Stellan, is everything all right?"

He bowed to me and the Duke. "Yes, Your Highness. It's just that… Er, I'm here as a guest of a guest tonight. It all happened at the last minute. I just wanted you to know before you spotted me on the dance floor and called security."

"Don't be silly—I'm happy to see you. Do you mind if I ask who your date is?"

"It's Ms. Mindy Fitz, Your Highness. The American. Your sister arranged the date, of all things." Stellan tugged on his jacket as the faintest tinge of red colored his cheeks.

"Are you…okay with all this?" I asked.

"Of course—she's a lovely woman. She's been very straightforward, telling me how *fine* she thinks I am," he confided in a low voice. "It's rather something. These Americans are quite direct, aren't they?"

"You can say that again, old chap," the Duke said.

"Some of them are," I muttered at the same time.

"I am sorry to have interrupted you." Stellan bowed. "I'll see you out there."

I raised my glass to him. "See you out there."

"Enjoy your American," Cliff called.

I sighed as Stellan rejoined the party. Mindy Fitz waited for him at the bar. She bestowed him with a tall vodka tonic once he reached her, then she thrust her chest out and gazed up at him adoringly. *Enjoy your American, indeed.* The fact that my sister had gone to the trouble of setting up Mindy Fitz with my driver gnawed at me. It was yet another example of how she and my father were bending over backward to cater to the media heiress's wants and needs.

Stellan beamed down at Mindy. At least *he* appeared to be having a good time.

My driver and his American heiress got my hackles up… *Something* was going on. Something more than a set-up, more than a seat for Mindy Fitz at the reception, more than giving Mina Mays from the Daily Chat the last question at the press conference. But what?

"Clive—earth to Clive," the Duke was saying. "Stay with me for a moment. I'm sure you think that Stellan's interruption saved you from this conversation, but I'm afraid not."

Bloody Cliff. Why had I bought a date for him? "I'm listening."

"Why didn't you tell me about Vivian? Or Tarryn, for that matter?" My cousin looked hurt.

I winced. "I didn't feel like it was my secret to tell."

"Except for the part where it's *your* secret, mate." The Duke sighed. "You know you can tell me anything. And also, lies are a big no-no for me. It's part of my sobriety, remember?"

"Fuck, I know that, Cliffie. I'm sorry. I was trying to protect Tarryn."

He clapped me on the shoulder. "I understand. And I get it—I'd do the same for Viv, course I would."

"So are you...?" I couldn't find my words. "How are things with you two?"

"Excellent." He nodded. "She's the real deal, my Vivian. And it doesn't matter to me about her past because that's exactly what it is—her past. I'm her future."

"You're *that* serious about her?"

He arched a reddish eyebrow. "You're *that* serious about Tarryn?"

I had a sip of my bourbon, not answering. "I want to be. But there's a lot of problems with the prospect, as I'm sure you can imagine."

"So why did you tell the press that you were ready to get engaged to her? I have to admit, even I was a bit shocked. It was a bold move."

"I think… I think I might be in love with her."

Cliff let out a low whistle. "Woah, that's the first time I've ever heard you say *that*. I never thought I'd see the day. Tough circumstances, though. Your father's going to be bloody difficult about it."

I stared as Tarryn came in with Vivian. Their arms were entwined, and they appeared to be deep in conversation. "Which is why what I said at the press conference was a terrible mistake—but like I said, I did it for a reason."

Cliff waited patiently as I continued to stare. She'd changed into a pale pink dress, which was light and airy, and she'd pulled her hair up into a topknot. Sparkly earring dangled against her pale neck, and I longed to reach out for her, to pull her against my side and keep her there.

I sighed. "I've made a bloody mess of things, haven't I?"

"Probably." Cliff gave me an amiable smile. "But why don't you tell me what you've done, first? Besides lie to your cousin, who doubles as your best friend. I forgive you, by the way. Vivian's totally worth it."

We stepped outside the tent, still in sight enough that we were "in attendance," and my sister wouldn't be able to complain.

I sighed. "I can't ask Tarryn to stay. When I think about my father and Izzie… I can't ask her to live in a pit of vipers. They want to have my mother committed to a group home, can you believe that?"

"What?" Cliff's eyeballs almost popped out of his head. "That's where they're going with this?"

I nodded. "I overheard them arguing about it earlier. I interrupted them, and they told me that they're worried my mother's drinking has gone off the deep end and that she'd be better off somewhere else. She probably didn't even know about the press conference until she saw it, saw the tale that they were spinning. It's disgusting, isn't it? How could I even think about bringing Tarryn into a situation like this?"

"So why did you say that?" Cliff asked. "About getting engaged? It doesn't make sense."

I sighed again. "I was trying to get some leverage with my father, which is the whole reason I brought her here in the first place. Big mistake. Because now I have feelings for her. And now I also need serious ammo against my father…"

I had another gulp of bourbon. "But I have to break things off with her—she's a prostitute, and someone will find out because someone *always* finds out. What have I done? I've probably ruined her life."

"Okay—I mean, it's not okay, but we need to slow down here for a minute. You're all over the place." Cliff squinted at the sun as it set. "First of all, the fact that she's a prostitute isn't the end of the world. I mean, Vivian's a prostitute. And I'm not shying away from it."

"It's different for you. You're a *Duke*. And there will be a scandal, of course. But it's not the same magnitude. You two will fade from the headlines soon enough, but if Tarryn and I were actually going to have a future together, they will never leave us alone. That's the truth."

"But they would never leave you alone anyway," Cliff reminded me. "There will just always be that angle."

"I can't ask her to put herself out there like that. Right now, no one knows what she does for work. It's *her* business. But if the press gets a hold of it, she'll be exposed for the rest of her life. It's not fair."

I had another necessary sip of bourbon. The way it burned at least distracted me from how I was feeling—my head was buzzing. I felt like I was spinning, a physical manifestation of my swirling mess of thoughts.

"So I never should have said what I said."

"But you *did* say it—there has to be a reason." The Duke stood protectively beside me, ready to ward off any interloping party-goers.

"Sure, there was a reason. A selfish one, like I said." I shook my head. "I realized this morning—at least, I finally admitted it to myself this morning—that I have feelings for her. Someone texted her, and I literally went off the deep end. Went to security, tried to read her file, the whole thing."

Cliff raised his eyebrows a fraction. "Instead of asking her about it?"

"Yes, bloody hell, instead of asking her about it! I was afraid, all right? Afraid she'd tell me there was someone else, and I wouldn't be able to hide my reaction." I winced. "And then she'd know the truth about how I felt about her. I was trying to save face. You're telling me you've never done that?"

"I've done it," the Duke admitted quickly. "We've all done it. Better safe than sorry, and all. I've spent a lot of time creeping ladies on the internet, trying to find out anything I could."

"Right. I wanted to take the roundabout route. Which was cowardly, but still." I frowned. "The Chief was no help—he told me to deal with her directly. So I did. And it was just a text from an ex-boyfriend, someone who must've seen her online or something. She said it was nothing."

"That's good." Cliff sounded hopeful.

I grimaced. "It *is* good, except that it made me realize that I was getting too attached. And that it wasn't fair to her."

"Meanwhile, have you told her how you feel?"

"Meanwhile, *no*, I mean a little, but I'm getting to that part. We had a great day together today—an *amazing* day. So before the press conference, I asked her if she'd stay with me after the wedding. Even though I know it's selfish. Even though I know that if we get caught, she's going to be the one to pay for it." I sucked in a deep breath. "And she said *we'll talk about it.*"

Cliff raised his eyebrows. "Oof, that's a tough one. You never know which way that one's going to go."

"Right? So at the press conference, my sister and father blindsided me with this story about my mother being sick. But I couldn't say anything because we were in front of the press corps, which is probably exactly why they did it." I clutched my glass. "They're plotting to get her out of the palace."

Cliff wrinkled his nose. "Isn't the timing a bit much? I mean, with the wedding and all? Are you sure your mother's not really ill?"

"She's fine. I stopped by her room after the conference. The lies they'd told shook her up, but other than that, she's in perfect health."

"So why now?" Cliff asked. "*Has* her drinking gotten worse?"

"I don't think so." I shook my head. "I think the wedding's just the perfect time to pull a stunt like this. The press is already in a frenzy—with the wedding, with me, with everything."

The Duke blew out a deep breath. "You have to give them credit. It's cruel, but it's brilliant."

I sighed. "I think that's why I said what I said at the conference. The press is already going nuts with speculation about Tarryn and me—I knew they would. The royals have never been more popular, never had more coverage. My sister owes me for that. So does my father. If I play along, maybe I can convince them to leave my mother alone…"

I scrubbed a hand over my face. "But I can't be *playing*. It's Tarryn's life, you know what I mean? I care about her too much to do this to her. Bloody hell."

"So what will you do?"

"I dunno." I had drained my bourbon. "That's the problem, isn't it?"

Tarryn was making her way toward us. "I think that's my cue to take my leave," Cliff said. "We'll *talk about it* more later—okay, mate?"

I gave him a dirty look. "Ha ha."

And then I took a deep breath as Tarryn approached. She was the most beautiful woman I'd ever seen, and even though everything around us was fucked, I had Real Feelings for her.

So why was I suddenly afraid?

TARRYN

I CLOSED the distance between us because I couldn't help myself. He was so handsome, it hurt to look at him. Clive in a tuxedo was a sight to behold. Tall with broad shoulders, power radiated off of him. But it was the beard that undid me, along with those eyes.

But he looked slightly off-kilter as I approached, as if he'd just woken up unexpectedly.

"Hey." I reached for him, linking my arm through his. As soon as we were connected again, I breathed a sigh of relief.

"Hey yourself. You look beautiful, as always." He bent and brushed his lips against my cheek. His scent overwhelmed me, and as if I was one of Pavlov's dogs, my mouth watered—and a hot, wet heat stretched between my legs. For fuck's sake, I could *not* get enough of him.

But that was the whole problem.

"What were you and Cliff talking about?" I asked softly. "The same thing me and Viv were discussing?"

"Probably." He gave me a weak smile. "I should've told him the truth—I feel like crap."

"That makes two of us."

He wrapped his arm around me as we watched the party. The mood had changed between us. The sun had set, and it'd taken the promise of our sexy afternoon with it. There was a new heaviness between us, something I didn't recognize.

He cleared his throat. "About what I said earlier, at the press conference…"

I waited for him to go on. How could I tell him the truth? That I wanted what he'd said to be true more than anything, but that it wasn't ever going to happen for us?

"I meant it." He pulled me closer and kissed the top of my head. "I know it's crazy because we barely know each other, but I love being with you. I don't want you to leave."

"Clive…" I took a deep breath, trying to steady the emotions I felt inside me. This was exactly what I wanted to hear. But it was also the thing that was going to undo me.

He leaned down and kissed me, and I felt his erection straining against his pants. "I need you," he whispered.

"Well, you can't have me right here," I whispered back. "And you can't exactly hide that thing! What're we going to do?"

"This way." He grabbed my hand and hustled me onto the lawn, where he stopped and kissed me again. His tongue roamed inside my mouth—claiming, persistent, while his hands roamed down my back.

I broke away, breathing hard. "We can't do it on the lawn, either."

"Fine." He clamped his hand around mine and practically dragged me into a garden surrounded by a massive hedge. We were alone, gloriously alone.

But even as I ached for him between my legs, my heart was aching in an altogether different way…

As soon as we were out of sight, he swept me into his arms. His mouth claimed mine again, and he wasn't playing. He stripped off his jacket, then his tie, his shirt, his pants around his ankles—suddenly he was naked, his glorious, massive cock springing out at me. The tip of it glistened.

I got down on my knees and took it in my mouth.

"Oh fuck, Tarryn, what are you doing to me?" But Clive knew. He thrust a little as I ran my tongue down his seam, taking him into my mouth.

"Oh…no. No." But he thrust gently, carefully, as I sucked him. I moaned, a deep, guttural sound, and pure female satisfaction bloomed in my chest. He was so hard, and he tasted amazing—clean, pure maleness. I was so wet I slid against myself, friction building, my need growing as I sucked his cock. I wanted to be close to him like this, to remember the taste of him, the way he smelled, the sounds he was making that made him seem so vulnerable, so mine.

Because I would never tell him, but I was in love with him.

"Tarryn, babe—I have to have you. I want to come inside you. This is amazing, but please." The vulnerability in his voice undid me. I gave his cock one last slow, long tug, and then sighing, I released it. I enjoyed being in control. It was pretty rare these days!

Clive was looking wildly around for somewhere for us to have sex. But that's exactly what his big muscular body was for! Laughing, I stepped out of my panties. Then I hoisted my dress up, threw my arms around his neck, and clamped my legs around his waist.

He caught me, surprised.

I didn't wait to explain things. I wrapped my fingers around the base of his cock and positioned him at my entrance. Then, enjoying the control for a few more precious moments, I lowered myself onto his massive, throbbing sheath.

"Babe." His eyes rolled back in his head as I slid back

and forth, squeezing him, taking him in. He was so deep this way. I felt so full, I cried out: I almost came right then.

He spread his legs a little to get his balance, muscular thighs tensing, and then he palmed my hips. Now he had control, and it made me feel all squiggly inside. I was about to lose it; I was going to give it all to him. Clive gripped my hips and maneuvered me up and down on his cock, finding a ruthless, brutal pace. It was a testament to his raw power that he could hold me like this and still fuck me senseless—but that's precisely what he was doing.

He grunted as he slammed into me, making me see stars. Then he did it again. And again. I cried out as the orgasm ripped through me. I ground myself against the base of his cock, wanting every inch of him, taking everything he had to give. He came in a torrent, shooting his seed into me. My body pulsed eagerly around him, greedily sucking him dry. I wanted to keep him inside me always, to never let go.

We were both breathing hard as he gently set me on the ground. Shaky and weak, I leaned against him. His clothes were strewn across the garden—my panties were tangled up with his tie. Clive's pants were still around his ankles. His seed leaked down my legs. We wanted each other so badly, we'd been careless. We'd made a mess.

I pressed my face against his sweaty chest and clung to him. I knew I had to say goodbye soon. This was too much. I couldn't afford to want something so badly, to be so out of control.

"Why do I feel like you're pulling away from me, huh?" His voice was gruff.

"I'm not." But now, the tears *really* threatened.

"Clive," called a voice from the other side of the hedge. "We need to talk to you, mate. There's an issue."

Clive immediately straightened. "What's the matter, Cliff?"

"It's your mother," he said, and I could hear it in his voice: something was wrong. Very wrong.

"Give me a minute—I'll meet you out front."

We hustled to get dressed. Again, I felt ashamed—something bad had happened, and we were sneaking around like horny teenagers.

"I'm sorry," I said as I wrestled my underwear back on. I didn't want to face anyone, to have the other guests see me like this—wild-eyed and freshly fucked.

Clive stopped buttoning his shirt and stared at me. "Sorry for what?"

"For this." I motioned between us. "Everyone knows what we were doing out here."

"So?"

Heat suffused my cheeks. I shook my head. "You better get going—I hope your mother's all right."

He wrapped his arms around me, then tilted my chin, so it forced me to look into his eyes. "We aren't doing anything wrong, babe. Let me bring you back to your room—it's on the way to my mother's suite. Okay?"

I nodded. "Okay." But I felt shaky, off-balance—as if I knew, deep down, that nothing at all was okay.

꙳

He'd kissed me again when he left me at my room. "I'll be back as soon as I can."

I wanted to offer to go with him, but I worried he'd say yes—and I had a feeling that his mother needed her son. "I hope she's okay." I hugged him fiercely.

"Me too." He kissed my hair and then disappeared down the hall.

I locked myself in my room, feeling shaky and unsettled. First of all, I realized I'd never eaten dinner. I'd had two glasses of champagne on an empty stomach; no wonder my head was buzzing. Second, I was shaky from the intense sex. The depths of the orgasms I'd been having with Clive were unlike anything I'd ever experienced before. I'd heard people rave about mind-blowing sex, but I'd never had it, not even close, until now. My body was jittery. My heartbeat seemed erratic.

I needed to calm down.

Taking a deep breath, I texted my mother. *Is everything okay? We need to talk.*

Three dots instantly appeared. God bless my mother; she always responded right away. *We're in a hotel room at the Four Seasons,* she wrote back. *It's amazing. But what the heck is going on?*

I called her. "I'm so sorry, Mom."

"Honey, what's wrong? We had a phone call from Chief Phillip—what a nice man. He said this was just a precaution, but two big guys showed up at our front door a minute later and said they were taking us here. They're in rooms on either side of us. What's happening, honey? Are you in danger?"

"No—I'm fine. But is Ellie okay? This must be confusing for her—"

"Honey, she's in *heaven*. The staff left animals shaped from towels and brand-new puzzles for her. She's already got Boo Boo tucked into the king-sized bed. Our suite overlooks the park. She's getting a grilled cheese and apple juice delivered from room service—trust me, she's great!"

My heart ached from missing my daughter. "Thank goodness. I know it's the Four Seasons, but I'm still sorry about this…."

I took a deep breath. "The thing is, Robbie texted me. I went to security because I just needed to be sure that you guys were safe. I hope that's okay."

"Of course it's okay. And *you* don't need to apologize for anything—unlike Robbie," she sniffed. "If he comes anywhere near you…" My mother was too nice a person to finish that sentence.

"He won't. I'm safe, you're safe, Ellie's safe. We're going to get through this. But I have to go—I'll call you first thing tomorrow, okay?"

"Of course. Are you ready for the big day?"

"Huh?"

"The royal wedding, honey. Are you excited?"

"Oh—yes. It's going to be fabulous." In all honesty, I'd forgotten all about it.

"Forget about everything else," Mom said. "Even though this happened, I want you to relax and have fun for once in your life, okay? Don't let him ruin it for you. He doesn't get to do that, honey."

I blew out a deep breath. "Thank you. You're the best, Mom."

"I love you, honey. I'll let you talk to Ellie."

She put my daughter on, and we said our I love you's and goodnights. It made my heart hurt.

After I hung up, I picked up the landline and asked for the kitchen. "Is there any way I could order a grilled cheese? And a bottle of white wine?" It seemed indulgent, but I needed food. And the wine was to numb me. I missed my mom and Ellie, my feelings were all tangled up about Clive, I was worried about his mother, and I had an unmistakable, irrational sense of dread descending on me, making my chest feel tight.

Grilled cheese and wine it was.

The staff delivered it soon, all smiles and politeness, and I longed to tell them the truth: I was one of them. I was the hired help, too, not some princess in training.

I poured myself a too-full glass of wine and scowled while I ate, even though the grilled cheese was delicious.

My phone pinged, and I reached for it—it was an incoming call. The screen read "Private Number." Was it the prince calling me with some emergency with his mother? Or Chief Phillip? Or…?

Hands shaking, I answered the phone. "Hello?"

"You fucking bitch," a white-hot angry, all-too-familiar voice said. "You think you can run away from me and then plaster yourself all over the internet? You fucking *slut*! Does the prince know that you're a fucking lying *whore* who runs away? Huh? Does he know what a cunt you are?"

My heart stopped. My throat closed up, but I gasped, "R-Robbie?"

"Oh, she *does* remember. The cunt that ruined my life—broke my heart and then ran away in the middle of the night like a fucking coward. Did you ever think about what you left behind, huh? I had to tell my parents, our friends, my co-workers—"

"How did you get this number?" It seemed like such a cliché question, but seriously. How *TF*. "Why are you calling me?"

"Are you fucking *kidding* me, Christine? I finally found out you're alive! I'd given up hope. But when I saw your picture—then I knew the truth. You always were a lying whore, Chris."

"Shut up."

"Oh, you've got an attitude now, huh? Good." He sounded as though he were gloating. "I'm going to enjoy smacking that out of you. I'm getting hard just thinking about it."

I felt like I might vomit. "You know what, Robbie? Fuck you. Fuck you for everything you ever did to me."

"Aw, Chris, you liked what I used to do to you, remember?"

"No, I don't remember." My voice was hoarse. "Don't ever call me again."

I threw my phone down—the screen shattered.

And then I promptly went into the bathroom and threw up.

CLIVE

Cliff met me at my mother's room. Three security guards, two women and one man were waiting outside. "What's the matter?" I asked them.

"There's been an…accident, of sorts," the shortest guard said. "The Queen is stable, but Dr. McManus is in there with her. We still might need to take her to the hospital; we're waiting to hear."

"Can we go inside?"

They nodded and stepped aside.

Before we entered, I addressed them in a quiet voice. "Listen, my mother has had a hard time of it lately. It's of the utmost importance that no one finds out about this —not even the other staff. Can I trust you to keep this to yourselves? If you do, I'll promote you. If you don't, you'll be dismissed at once. Are we clear?"

"Yes, Your Highness." The guards bowed as we swept past them.

"Who called you?" I asked Cliff.

"Dr. McManus—he was trying to reach you and when you didn't pick up, he tried me instead."

"Good on him." Dr. McManus was the royal physician; he'd been with our family since before I was born.

I took a deep breath as we headed through my mother's sitting room to her bedroom. "Mom? Dr. McManus?"

"In here," the doctor called.

"I'll wait out here for you, Cousin." Cliff patted me on the shoulder.

My mother was in bed, propped up, her skin ghostly pale. Her lips were chapped, and the skin around her mouth was dry. Dr. McManus was sitting at her desk, typing into his laptop.

"Mother?" I went and sat on the edge of the bed. "What happened?"

She cleared her throat and smiled at me wanly. "I watched the press conference again, dear. And when I heard that I'd taken ill, I figured I needed to do my part."

I took a deep breath. "Did you take something?"

"I took several somethings, dear. I'll spare you the details."

I turned to the doctor, who gave me a tight smile. "She'll be fine. I had to pump her stomach, though."

"Mom—"

"Shh honey, don't. My head hurts enough as it is." She sat up straighter and winced. "I know what it is your father is up to, you see."

I held still. With my mother, it was hard to know what to share and what to hide. She was so delicate, but sometimes, a glint of steel flashed through—probably the only way she'd survived at the palace all these years.

"And what is Father up to, exactly?"

She peered past me to Dr. McManus. "Will you excuse us, Arthur? And close the door."

He left without another word. Once we were alone, she said, "I don't imagine that you have any illusions about who your father is anymore."

"I don't."

She patted my hand. "That's good. Someday you'll make a great king, you know that? You've got your priorities straight. We can't say that about everyone in our family, now, can we?"

When I shook my head, she continued. "Your father wants me committed so that he has a valid excuse to seek an annulment."

"What?"

"That's right, dear. He wants to marry again without

violating royal custom. Divorce is still a scandal for the King of Astos. The only way he can be free of me is if I die or I'm declared to no longer have capacity. Then he can annul our marriage."

"He *can't*. You can't get an annulment when you've been married for forty years and have two children—that's bullshit."

"It might very well be, but he could still do it." She shrugged, her shoulders thin and frail beneath her pajamas. I hadn't seen my mother in pajamas since I was a child. "Honestly, I would even agree to it, but it doesn't work like that. I have to be legally declared to lack capacity. So it's death or a home for me, you see. That's why I took all those pills. Death's much simpler."

Her words crushed me. "Mother, you mustn't say such things."

"I'm old enough to speak the truth, and you're old enough to hear it, my son. I love you—and your sister, although she still acts like an impudent teenager most of the time. I love you both enough to want to spare you. Do you understand that?"

"No," I said, my voice hoarse. I'd known my mother was unhappy and in pain, but I'd no idea the extent of her private suffering.

She sighed. "Your father isn't happy with my performance as Queen. And he has every right to be disappointed—this isn't a role I was born for. I'm shy. I'm sensitive. I don't enjoy talking to people. I'm the worse possible choice for a queen there is, but he chose me. We were young and clueless, both of us. I can't blame him. I came here thinking it was going to be some fairytale. I didn't understand the work and the commitment to dealing with the public would be. Once I did, I wanted out. Trust me, this has been a long time coming."

"So why not separate?" I asked her. "Or get a divorce? Why has it come to this?" I sighed. There was so much fucking drama in my family. It seemed as though being a royal meant that there was no easy choice, no simple, ordinary answer for everyday problems.

"The King and Queen *can't* get a divorce. We're the heads of state. Our marriage is supposed to be sanctioned by God, the very highest authority."

"That's an old-fashioned notion, Mother. I think we can all agree with that."

"Of course it is, but royalty is all about pageantry. If we didn't adhere to the customs, what would happen? That's how we retain power. If we don't honor the old rules, the old rules die. And so do the old rulers. At least, that's how your father sees things. He's probably not wrong about that."

My mouth was dry, and my temples were pounding. "What about a separation?"

The corners of her mouth turned down. "Your father won't agree to it. He wants to remarry sooner rather than later. He wants to bring someone on board who's a better fit for the role. I can't exactly blame him for that."

"You can't hurt yourself to give Father what he wants," I said firmly. "You can't do that to me, or Izzie, or to yourself. I might be older, but I still need my mother, you know?"

"Clive." She put her hand on top of mine. "You haven't needed me in forever. You've always been a good boy. The very best."

I sighed. "That's not true. I didn't know you were hurting like this. What kind of son doesn't take care of his mum, huh?"

She shook her head, a rare, hard glint lighting her eyes. "Don't you dare put this on yourself. I'm the one who's in this position—no one put me here but myself. That's what I told your Tarryn. She needs to make sure she knows what she's signing up for. I'm sorry if I overstepped, but I just couldn't live with myself, otherwise."

"You spoke to Tarryn?"

The Queen blinked. "Yes…? I'm sorry, but I felt like I had to warn her. She seems like a lovely girl, Clive. But she also seems like she's come from a more traditional kind of life. Not everyone's cut out for this, you know? I had to talk to her. If I'm being honest, it wasn't even about her. It was to protect *you*."

"Protect me how?"

"I don't want you getting your heart broken again. I know what your father did with that other girl, the one from uni," my mother said. "You've never been able to have a normal life. I just wanted to warn Tarryn that if she thought this might not be for her, she should be honest with herself and you."

I sighed and looked at my mother.

She sighed and looked back at me.

"I'll let you get some rest," I said as I rose. "But you're not leaving the palace. I want you to get better and come to Izzie's wedding. Let's not let them run you off just yet, okay? It wouldn't be a wedding without the Queen Mother."

"Your father doesn't feel that way," she warned.

"My father is a prat." I grinned at her. "I love you, Mum."

"Oh honey." She sank back against her pillow. "I know."

∼

Dr. McManus assured me she wasn't in any physical danger. He planned to give her an IV to replenish her fluids and watch her like a hawk. "Nothing will happen to your mother on my watch. I promise you." I believed him.

I also believed him when he told me that the number of pills she'd taken had been dangerous but not deadly. He agreed she needed to start speaking with a therapist immediately and needed a full consultation to ascertain what would be best for her future. The possibilities included a change of environment, a detox program to help her reassess her alcohol consumption, and a top-notch divorce attorney. I told Dr. McManus that he worked for *me* now and that he was promptly getting a chateau and a raise. He was more than happy to agree to help me help my mother.

We were going to take things one step at a time.

Cliff and I decided we had to go back to the party to assuage any suspicions. The guards had sworn on their lives that they wouldn't say a word, even if Herbert came snooping around; having put them under fear of death, I believed them.

I stayed near Cliff at the party, nursing my bourbon and chatting to the best of my ability. Most of the questions centered around Tarryn. Where was she? She'd had a headache and gone to bed. Was it the same headache that my mother had? I certainly hoped not.

They also asked how I'd met her, were we serious,

was mine the next royal wedding? To my credit, I smiled. I answered without answering, with forced good humor. I had another bourbon.

Just as I felt it was safe to leave the party without inciting my sister's ire, I practically ran into the Duchess of Idrid. "Duchess—I'm sorry I bumped into you, but it's good to see you."

She leaned closer and kept her voice low as she asked, "What have they done to your mother?"

I sighed. "She's all right, Duchess. I'm taking care of it."

The Duchess stepped back and appraised me, eyes wide. "It's about time, Your Highness."

"You know, you're right. Will you go and see her tomorrow?"

The Duchess bowed. "I shall stay with her all day. You have my word."

It was my turn to bow. "Thank you."

With that, I left the party, grabbing a bottle of bourbon from the tent's bar on the way out.

I needed to see Tarryn, but I needed another drink first. There was a lot on my mind, and none of it was good. I went back to the garden where she and I had made love earlier, seeking solace in the high hedges. There was a lone stone bench; I sat on it, opened the bottle, and had a swig. The bourbon burned, which was fine with me. I looked up at the darkening sky, the stars shining through. It was a beautiful night, calm and mild, filled with the promise of early summer.

It only made me feel sad.

I felt terrible about my mother. I was still reeling from the fact that she'd taken such a drastic step. I'd known for years that my mother was deeply unhappy; still, that she'd considered ending her life had blindsided me. I had another sip of bourbon, feeling sick.

My mother had gone to see Tarryn. What was it she'd said? *This life isn't for everyone.* She'd done it to protect me, which needled my heart with guilt, but her words stung for another reason. She was right: being part of the royal family, your personal life on display for the whole world's public consumption was not for everyone. It wasn't for me, either, but I'd been born into this.

If it had just been about me, I'd leave the palace tomorrow with Tarryn and never look back. But the people of Astos had a large piece of my heart. My father was a tolerable leader, but I knew I could do better. There were so many things we could improve in the villages, so many positive steps we could take—there could be a brighter future for all the people of my country. I couldn't abandon them. It was my privilege to be able to help them, but it was also my duty. My crown felt very heavy at the moment, indeed.

You've never been able to have a normal life. My mother's words came back to me, hitting me hard.

No, I hadn't—and boo-fucking-hoo. I could live with it. I could survive.

But I couldn't—I *wouldn't*—live with myself if I ruined Tarryn. She was too good for my world. The public would judge her harshly for her choices. It wasn't fair. People didn't easily understand the financial disadvantage that so many women operated under, what an actual struggle to make ends meet sometimes ended up looking like.

Fuck those people. But Tarryn—*my* Tarryn, whom I was now certain I loved—should not have to be the subject of their scrutiny, scorn, and fascination.

I wouldn't do that to her. I couldn't.

I rose, bottle of bourbon in hand.

It was time to be honest with each other, even if it was going to break my fucking heart.

TARRYN

IT TOOK me a few minutes to get under control. Then I picked up my phone, cracked screen and all, and called the Chief. He calmly walked me through the conversation. He told me I didn't have to worry because security at the palace was airtight. He promised that my mother and Ellie were one-hundred percent safe. He said he would send a guard to collect my phone, and that he would find out where Robbie was, and that he would take care of it.

"I don't want him arrested," I said, hating myself for it. "I don't want to have to give a statement or be involved in any way."

The Chief said he understood but did he? Could anyone?

I paced the room after we hung up. Hearing Robbie's

voice was like talking to the devil himself. His spiteful words came back to me, making my skin crawl. How could he still hate me so much? Why had he called me such awful things? He blamed me for everything. He thought I was a bad person for leaving him like that. It made me feel crazy. Didn't he remember that he'd once beaten me so badly, I couldn't walk for days? Didn't he remember that I'd had to wear long sleeves and long pants in the summer, even when it was ninety degrees so that no one would ask about my bruises?

That fucker! He had me questioning my sanity once again.

The one thing I wasn't questioning was my decision to hide Ellie from him. The sheer ugliness of his words, the force with which he'd hurled them at me, left no trace of doubt. He was dangerous. He still hated me with a vigilance that took my breath away.

I went and stared out the window at the grounds and the glittering stars above. It was so beautiful in Astos; it was like another world.

It was a world I didn't belong in.

The thing about Robbie's call? It was a blow on so many levels. I knew he would be thinking about me as long as I stayed in the public eye. He would find a way to reach out. If I went back to America with the money I'd earned from this job, I could reinvent myself again. I could take Ellie and my mother away, to Canada, to the Caribbean, to anywhere in the world there were decent schools and good doctors. I would take care of my family. I would have enough money to keep us safe. He would never find us.

I had to leave Astos. I had to say goodbye to Clive. He didn't even know about Ellie! I could never bring her here, my daughter from an abusive past relationship. Everyone would know. Robbie would see her. We would never be free.

My gut twisted as the truth washed over me, cold and final. I could *never* have what I wanted: a happily ever after with the prince.

Forget tears—sobs threatened. But I swallowed them down, burying them with all the skeletons, all the better to make friends for eternity. That was the thing about being an adult. You had to face the facts and deal, and you had to do it fast. Because hesitating left room for feelings and regret, and you do not have time for that shit when you're a grown-up.

It was best just to move on.

There was a knock at my door. "Tarryn, it's me," Clive said. He sounded a little drunk, which was probably a good thing.

He was not going to like what I was about to tell him: the truth.

"Hey." He'd changed out of his tux and had put on sweats. Clive bent and kissed my cheek, the smell of bourbon wafting off him.

"Hey yourself."

He sank onto the edge of the bed. "Tonight's been shit, hasn't it?"

I nodded. "Since I left you, yes."

The prince smiled balefully. "The rest of the day was good, though."

"Yeah, it was." I smiled back, even though my heart was breaking. "Is your mom okay?"

"No." He scrubbed a hand across his face. "She took a bunch of pills. They had to pump her stomach."

"Oh my God!" I went and hugged him, holding him tight. "Did they bring her to the hospital?"

"She's here. The doctor is with her. She's going to be fine. That is if I can get her away from my father."

I blew out a deep breath as I pulled back. "I'm so sorry."

"Me too. It's been a long time coming, though. Those two are no good for each other." He squinted up at me. "She told me she had a talk with you."

I pursed my lips. It was yet another thing I hadn't told him.

"I'm sorry I didn't tell you about it. She just came to my room one day—"

A knock at my door interrupted me. "Who is it?"

"Security. The Chief sent me for your phone."

I raced to the door and opened it, keenly aware of Clive's curious stare following me. I handed my phone to the guard. "Thank you so much. I'll check in with Chief Phillip first thing in the morning."

"My pleasure, Ms. Clayton." The guard nodded.

"What was that all about?" Clive asked.

I wrung my hands together. I'd decided that I would tell the prince the truth—the whole truth—even though I didn't want to. Even though I felt certain that he would hate me for hiding it from him. But he deserved to know. He deserved to know why I could never get close to him, close to anyone.

"Remember that picture on my phone?" When he nodded, I continued, "The thing is, the man that sent that to me isn't just an ex-boyfriend. He's a bad guy, Clive. He's not someone I can have anywhere around me."

His brow furrowed. "What do you mean, a bad guy?"

"He…" I took a deep breath. "He was abusive. It was a toxic relationship. I left him when I was twenty-one—I literally packed my things and ran away in the middle of the night. My mother came with me. I started using my middle name as my first name, and I stayed off the internet as much as possible. So he never found me until now."

"Okay..." I noticed Clive's hands were clenched into fists. "D'you know where he is? Today? Because I'll take care of that fucker. It would be a fucking honor."

"Thank you. I—thank you. But I'm not really worried about him hurting me anymore. I mean, I guess he could, but that's not what I'm afraid of..."

Clive waited, watching me closely.

I wrung my hands together. I felt as though I might pass out. "The thing is? I have...I had... I was pregnant when I left him. That's finally the thing that got me to run. I thought he would kill me. I thought he would hit me so hard, he would kill my baby."

The prince's face was ashen.

"I have a daughter. Ellie. She's three." The tears spilled down my face. "I didn't tell you because I don't tell anyone about her—not even Vivian. I only told her tonight. She didn't even know. Elena doesn't know. I don't tell anyone because that's the only way I can keep her safe. Because if he finds out, if he finds *out*—he could come and try to take her from me. He could bring me to court. He's her father, and he has rights, no matter what he did to me. And I can't have that—I can't ever let him touch her or know about her. I swore to myself I would keep my daughter safe, do you understand?"

Suddenly I was sobbing, and Clive was holding me as I wept against his chest. The fear, the anxiety that Robbie's discovery had unleashed overwhelmed me. Deep, crushing sobs shuddered through me as the prince held me tight. His embrace made it better and worse all at the same time. Better because his powerful arms were around me. I knew as long as he held me, no one would ever hurt me.

Worse, because I knew I couldn't have him. That I could never have him. To feel what I wanted and know that it could never be mine was unbearable.

I made myself stop crying, and I pulled back. He handed me a box of tissues from the nightstand.

"I wish you'd told me." Clive's voice was gravelly.

I nodded as I blew my nose. "I wish I had, too. I wish a lot of things."

"Me too. C'mere." He pulled me against his chest, and we laid down. His arms stayed wrapped around me, holding me tight.

Once I finally calmed my breathing, I said, "I c-can't stay here. I can't be with you. It's not safe for me. It's not safe for Ellie."

He nodded, then sank his hands into my hair. "I can't ask you to put yourself at risk like that. It's too much."

So he agreed with me. My body convulsed as a dry sob wracked through me. Not that I'd expected anything different, but still, it hurt so bad. We could never be together. I felt like I might die.

"You know, I'm glad I met you, Tarryn Clayton." He kissed the top of my head.

"You are?"

"Course I am. Because I wasn't sure before, but now I know."

"Know what?"

His sad smile widened for a moment. "That I still have a heart. Because I'm pretty sure that it's broken."

I sniffled against his chest. "Well that makes two of us, Your Highness."

"I've said it from the beginning—we're quite a pair."

He kissed the top of my hair again. And we just stayed like that, together but knowing we would never be together, until sleep finally divided us.

CLIVE

I didn't move as Tarryn slept. I only held her, running through the conversation again. Her words were going to haunt me for the rest of my life.

I have a daughter, Ellie. She's an angel.

Before she'd drifted off, I'd asked to see a picture of the little girl. She was an exact replica of her mother, with long white-blond hair and big blue eyes. She *did* look like an angel; my heart twisted when I saw her beautiful, innocent little face. Tarryn had gone to work for AccommoDating to care for her daughter, who had a rare, genetic heart condition. She'd had to hide her child's existence because of an abusive relationship with the father—who I silently vowed to hunt down, punch in the face, and then maybe kill with my bare hands for good measure.

All of this, and I still couldn't protect her.

If we chose to be together, she'd be exposed. Her daughter would be exposed. How could I ever ask Tarryn to make that choice?

I couldn't. I cradled her against my chest as she slept, the truth washing over me. I was in love with her. Finally, after all this time, I'd met someone I could truly be myself with. And yet she'd held herself back from me, kept secret the thing that meant the most to her in her whole life…

I couldn't be angry that she hadn't told me about her daughter. But I was still hurt. Tarryn had a whole life that I hadn't known about; she didn't trust me enough to share the truth. And while I understood her reasoning, I still felt crushed. It made me feel as though the feelings I had for her couldn't be real because they were for someone who didn't exist.

Images from the past week raced through my mind, crushing me further. The first time I saw Tarryn when we picked her up from the airport. When she'd held my hand as we ascended the palace stairs. The way she moaned when she ate a cheeseburger. Our day by the lake, when I'd told her about playing pirates. Our outing on the boat, when I'd no longer been able to hide my feelings from her…

My phone's screen lit up from the nightstand. It was a text from my mother. *I am feeling much better,* she wrote. *Thank you for being my son.*

I stared at the message. Had I not intervened, my sister and father would've run my mother off without a second thought. They would have spun a fine tale about it, of course. Her drinking, her mental health, her best interests. And maybe they weren't wrong that living at the palace, with my father's constant disapproval and the unyielding pressure of the press, wasn't what was best for my mother. But it was her life—her choice. In the end, it was my father's disappointment with her performance as Queen Mother that had been her undoing.

He was always about the performance, wasn't he?

I gently slid out from underneath Tarryn, settling her on the bed. I watched her for a moment as her chest rose and fell. How was it possible, I wondered, for someone who I'd known for such a short time to have become so important to me? And how was it possible that I'd already failed her so intensely?

Thank you for being my son. My mother's words reverberated deep in my soul.

I was at a crossroads. On the one hand, I could leave all this behind. The pageantry, the burden of being a royal, the relentless pressure of the press, the constant scrutiny. My father's endless scheming, my sister's endless preening.

I could renounce my crown. I could leave, once and for all. Maybe I could even find a way to be with Tarryn, although I imagined the press would continue to hound me for a few years until they found someone better to badger…

On the other, I could stay and fight. Fight for my mother, fight for the people in our country who were struggling to make a better life for themselves and their families, fight for the press to back down—fight for a normal life, even though I was a royal.

But that meant I would have to let her go.

I watched her as she slept. She deserved more than this life, this world.

I silently dressed and crept out of the room. If nothing else, I could try to make things better for her.

It was the least I could do.

∼

"I'm not happy with you, Chief."

Chief Phillip scrubbed a hand across his face. We were sitting in his suite, and he was wearing a robe thrown over his pajamas.

"I'm not exactly happy with you at the moment, either, Your Highness. It's the middle of the night."

"You work for *me*. You should have notified me that there was a security threat against Tarryn. That's my business." I sat forward in my seat. "I want to know everything there is to know about the bastard. Tarryn told me a little, but it's not enough. I want to know where he sleeps, what he eats, what he searches for on the internet. I want to know how he found her—how the bloody hell am I supposed to send her home after the wedding, knowing that she and her family could be targeted?"

The Chief sighed. "I've already got her…family… with security. They're at a hotel."

"You mean her mother and her daughter," I spit out. "You knew, didn't you?"

He gave me a long look. "It's true that I work for you, Your Highness. My highest priority is to protect you. Legal wanted to keep as many details private as possible —it's safer for you that way. If the press finds out about Ms. Clayton, you'll be protected."

"Why is it," I rubbed my temples, "that the press is running my life? I don't give a *fuck* about them. And yet, that's all anyone thinks about."

"It's a difficult situation." The Chief nodded.

"And did you say that legal knows about Tarryn?" My

head was throbbing. The legal department was typically my father's attack dog, loyal to his every whim.

"Yes—they had to draw up the confidentiality agreement and also the…waivers."

"Waivers?" I stared at him blankly.

"Yes. She had to agree to accept liability if her past became public." He shrugged. "It's protocol in a situation like this—which is a fucked up situation, if you'll pardon my language."

I waved him off. "It's pardoned. Tell me about the ex—he's *not* pardoned. I want to know everything."

The Chief straightened his shoulders. "He's on our watch list. There's some speculation that he's on his way here, traveling under a different name."

"How has he managed that? And how did he get ahold of her cell phone number? Tarryn said they haven't spoken in years. She's been in hiding."

"He's a real piece of work." The Chief got up, grabbed his laptop, and opened it. He clicked through a few things before he continued, "Robert Egan, aged 28, single, no arrest record. He owns a modest home in Lanesboro, Minnesota. He has no debt. Works as a delivery driver—he's only been doing that for a few months. It looks like he's bounced around, a lot of different jobs. He's boring until you look at his internet searches—a lot of stuff about handguns, living off the grid, prepping, including maintaining your own food sources and home-medical treatments and remedies. He's bought a lot of chains, and handcuffs, and rope over the years."

My mouth was dry. "The fuck?"

Chief Phillip nodded. "There's a lot about security and technology—which might be where he learned to track down phone numbers. He also has a daily search habit that involves Tarryn, who he knew as Christine Clayton. He's been running searches on her for years. Do you want to know what I think?"

A sudden chill ran up my spine. "Yes." *No.*

"I think he's been looking for Tarryn ever since she left and that he was planning to kidnap her. My guess is that if we went to his little home in Lanesboro, we'd find a cell. Guys like these—he's a narcissist, Your Highness. It's been years, but he's only gotten more obsessed with her and more enmeshed in his belief that she did something unforgivable by leaving him. If you read the messages he's sent to her since he got her number or listened to the voicemails, you'd see what I mean."

"Give me her phone." My voice was hoarse.

"I'm not going to do that because it could implicate you if there's ever any criminal investigation."

"There's going to be one, right? He can't just get away with this—he beat her, and now he's threatening her."

The Chief gave me a long look. "Ms. Clayton doesn't want to press charges against him because of her daughter, which I understand. If Mr. Langford finds out that she's hidden his child from him, he has the makings of a strong custody case."

"He can't do that." I clenched my hands into fists. "After everything he's done?"

"Years have passed. There's no more physical evidence of his abuse." The Chief frowned. "It would be her word against his."

"Bloody hell." Where was the justice? "Do you really think he might be on his way to Astos?"

"He didn't show up for work yesterday. I checked all the incoming flights and didn't see him registered anywhere, but who's to say with a guy like that?" He shrugged. "He could've had documents ready to go for years. He's obsessed—I never underestimate someone obsessed."

I nodded. My head was swimming with everything that was happening, with everything that could happen.

"Chief, what about her family? Her little girl? Are they really safe?"

"I've got my best security with them. Of course, I'd feel better if they were here, but they're in good hands."

I stood up. "All right, about that…"

TARRYN

I woke up to pounding on my door. Clive was gone.

My heart leaped to my throat. *Ellie, my mother...*

"Ms. Clayton?" A guard asked from outside the door. "His Highness the King is here to see you. It's important."

I glanced at the clock—it wasn't even six a.m. "Just a minute."

What the hell did the King want with me? Whatever it was, it couldn't be good. I hustled to throw on something appropriate, settling on a baggy sweatshirt and leggings. It wasn't formal enough, but it covered me from head to toe, which seemed more important. I brushed my teeth, threw my hair up in a ponytail, and cautiously opened the door. "Yes?"

The closer of my two security guards bowed. "I'm so sorry to have woken you, Ms. Clayton. His Highness will be here in one minute."

Herbert, the King's steward, stood a few paces away. "Good morning, Miss. Shall I have the kitchen send up some coffee?"

I nodded. "That would be great, thank you."

Herbert immediately tapped something into his cell phone. "My pleasure. I'll make sure they know the King will be joining you; he prefers Italian Roast."

I turned to the guard. "What time did Prince Clive leave?" I asked in a low tone.

"Around three a.m., Ms. Clayton."

"Did he say where he was going?"

The guard's brow furrowed. "I'm sorry, he did not."

"Okay. Thank you." Crestfallen, I went back inside my room to wait for the King. Why did he want to see me, and why so early? Why in my room? It seemed inappropriate. I felt uncomfortable and miserable as I paced.

But His Highness didn't keep me waiting long. He arrived at the same time the coffee did. The kitchen had also sent up a large platter of croissants, bacon, and various scones with jams and jellies, but I couldn't even think about food.

"Ms. Clayton. Thank you for accepting an audience

with me so early." The King nodded at me. He looked as though he'd slept well and was already dressed for the day in a crisp suit, his pins neatly arranged on his lapel.

I'd underdressed, but I could still maintain custom. I dropped into a deep, flawless curtsy. The King's eyes sparkled with inappropriate appreciation when I rose; I was thankful for my shapeless sweatshirt.

"What can I do for you, Your Highness?" I regretted the question as soon as I asked it. I most certainly did not want to know the answer.

He poured me a coffee, then one for himself. I had an icky feeling as I accepted the mug from him.

"I understand you're in a spot of trouble," the King said smoothly.

I almost choked on my coffee. "Oh?" I didn't want to say anything, to give myself away. What did he know? How bad was it?

"You don't need to pretend anymore. I know who you are, I know what you are. And I know that palace security just had to change our levels to red because there's a threat against you."

Fuuuuck. Instead of answering him, I drank my coffee.

"Philip, our Chief of Security, is loyal to my son. But Elise, head of legal, reports directly to me. The prince is a fool if he thinks he can sneak a prostitute into the palace without me knowing about it. I have my own employees, you see—you aren't the first woman to sign those forms."

He waggled his eyebrows at me, and I wanted to throw up. I thought of his wife, the wan Queen, who'd warned me about joining the family. No wonder she was ill. Being married to a man like the King would make anyone sick!

"Why are you here, Your Highness?"

"Because I wanted to make you an offer." His smile was slick.

Having met men like the King before, my answer was swift. "I'm certain I'm not interested."

He seemed undeterred. "Do you care for my son?"

"Your son is a great man."

One of his groomed eyebrows rose a little. "I don't know about that, but I'll assume based on your tone that the answer is yes. Yes, you care for him. You care for him enough to leave him."

My breath hitched. "I think it's for the best."

"Of course it is, my dear." He circled me. "But what if I can offer you an alternative? What if I can offer you protection—and protection for your family, your little girl—all the security in the world? And you can remain here. You can even marry my son."

The fact that he knew about Ellie had me reeling. I

could barely process his words. "Why would you... What are you even saying?"

"You see, Tarryn, as a man of prestige I've become accustomed over the years to getting exactly what I want. But there's an unexpected downside to that! Now, things have to be...complicated...in order for me to extract pleasure from them."

I must've looked as confused as I felt because he explained, "When I was young, I used to take whatever I wanted. No beautiful woman was out of reach for me. As a young man, that was all that I needed to be satisfied. I feel like I can be honest with you and speak plainly, for this is your area of expertise, is it not?"

I considered throwing my coffee cup at his head, but instead, I was frozen by shame. *I can be honest with you. Your area of expertise.*

"When I married," His Highness continued, "the Queen and I had average relations for a few years. They beget us our heirs, for which I have no regrets. At first when I cheated on my wife, it was exciting. It was enough. But as the years have progressed, my tastes have...evolved."

He eyed me appraisingly. "What I am offering you is the opportunity to become part of our family. My son is enamored of you—I've never seen him like this before.

Of course, I've known the truth about you for some time, but yesterday during the press conference I saw my opportunity. He *wants* you. I shall let him have you, but I have a few conditions of my own, you see."

"N-No." My voice was hoarse. "It's never going to happen."

"Sharing you with my son, without his knowledge, is naughty, Tarryn. It's the *naughtiest*. The fact that you'd be complicit in it and forced to keep our secret? It gets me hard just thinking about it! You will be my plaything, my dirty secret, my whore. All while being my son's wife. My own wife will be long gone, and I'll replace her with someone much more socially acceptable—one who turns a blind eye to my many extracurricular activities. So what do you say, my lady?"

His eyes sparkled with excitement. "All your secrets will be safe with me. Your daughter will be raised in every luxury and security. No one will ever know about her. I can promise you this because no one has a better relationship with the press than me. I give them what they want, and therefore, I do what I please. And it pleases me to make you my mistress."

I felt ill. "Clive would never allow that. Why would you even consider doing something like that to your own son?"

"Because I am King. He, just like everyone else, needs to know that *I* am the one in power. It is my birthright, you see, to rule them all. Even my children." He smiled at me, and it wasn't a nice smile. "For too long, I've let my son do as he pleases, acting like a hero in the villages of Astos. To be fair, our subjects love him. He will be a ruler of the people, not above them. But he must learn that I am still the ruler of our great nation. No matter how independent he fancies himself, he's subject to my whims as much as anyone. He thinks he's better than me, you see."

He moved closer, and I could feel his breath on my cheek. I shuddered. "But once he shares his wife with me, and when he one day learns that she answers to *me*, he'll see the truth. He's not above me. I'm the one ruling in every way."

"He would never share me with you. He wouldn't do that to me, and he wouldn't do that to himself."

The King shrugged. "He doesn't have to know—not at first. I like to reveal myself in stages. And if you want to keep your daughter a secret, you'll agree to what I say. I have a lot of connections, as you know. They'd be more than happy to have the Daily Chat run a piece on my son's new girlfriend, who happens to be a hooker, whose daughter's existence she's kept secret from the child's father."

"You wouldn't." My stomach turned to lead. This couldn't be happening.

"Of course I would! That's why I'm here—as a *favor*. You don't have a choice, Ms. Clayton. I am the one holding all the cards."

He stepped closer, trailing his cool fingers down my cheek. "I would take you right now, but I rather think I'd like to wait until my son 'puts a ring on it,' as he said." He laughed, and I wanted to scream.

"Get out." I went and threw the door open so the guards would witness whatever he said next.

"It was a pleasure as always." He nodded, then had the audacity to wait for a curtsy.

Fuck you, Your Highness. But I was too chicken to say it. So instead, I slammed the door in his face.

What. The. Fuck. My first instinct was to cry, but I ignored it. I was so goddamned tired of men like the King, men who thought that because they had power, they could do whatever they wanted. He was trying to put me in a box from which there was no escape. Ellie, he knew about Ellie…

I paced the room. What had I done? Taking this job had been a terrible mistake. Yes, it was the one chance I would probably ever have to get ahead, avoid financial ruin, and build a life for my family. But at what cost? Robbie was back. I'd put myself in danger, and Ellie's future was at risk—the exact opposite of what I'd hoped for when I'd accepted the assignment.

And now the King was threatening to expose me because he wanted to make me his mistress. But, more than that, he wanted to show his son exactly how much power he wielded...

I swallowed hard. I didn't know what to do, where to turn. But the thing that was going to break me? It was the prince. The King wasn't the only reason that I felt ill. It was because of Clive.

I'd let myself get soft since I'd come to Astos. I'd let myself relax, and I'd been open to getting to know him. At first, I'd simply liked him. His laugh, the sparkle in his eye, his disregard for dressing gowns, his extreme love of the word 'freaking,' and how he enjoyed cheeseburgers just as much as I did. For someone in such extraordinary circumstances, he was probably the most normal guy I'd ever met. And I'd fallen for him hard. But, honestly, I didn't think I was *capable* of falling for someone—maybe that's why I'd let my guard down in the first place.

I'd believed that love wasn't ever going to happen for me. After what had happened with Robbie, I'd never been able to trust someone enough to get close.

But I hadn't chosen Clive precisely. It was more that he'd just *happened* to me.

So what on earth was I going to do now? I'd made my bed, but I still refused t climb into it if the King was waiting to pounce. *Ew.* I would never do that to myself; I would never do that to Clive.

But the last thing I wanted in the world was to have my background exposed—not because I was ashamed, but because of Ellie. She didn't deserve to grow up with a black mark against her like that. Even worse was the King's threat to make her identity public. That was the one thing I couldn't bear: to have Robbie come into her life and acquire legal standing or *to take her away from me.* That was my worst nightmare.

If I didn't do what the King asked, he threatened to make all of my fears come true.

I poured myself another coffee and resumed pacing.

What the King had planned for his wife was wrong, although maybe Her Highness was better off somewhere else, far away from this madness. I couldn't believe that Izzie would be a part of such a plan. Perhaps she'd tired of her mother's frailty, too, or maybe she was beholden to her father's whims for other reasons.

Pacing, I ran through the facts as I knew them.

The King had demands.

Robbie had found out where I was.

Ellie and my mother were safe and anonymous —for now.

Clive and I had agreed to call things off; I didn't know where that left us.

And I had no idea what would happen next.

CLIVE

The sun had just crested the horizon, and yet it had already been a long day. I'd left the Chief's office with his promise to keep me updated at every moment. He'd given me a new cell phone for Tarryn. He held her previous one in case The Douche Who Would Not Be Named texted her again.

I almost hoped the fucker did. Every move he made added fuel to my fire. I couldn't undo the hurt he'd caused in the past, but I could sure as hell do something about the future.

Tarryn's future. Everything hung in the balance…

I hustled through the palace halls, surprised when I found myself outside my sister's chambers. Her guards bowed. "Is she awake?" I asked.

"She's busy at the moment," the taller guard said. "Shall we give her a message?"

"No need." I unceremoniously pushed past them and opened the door.

Izzie was inside, wrapped in a silk dressing gown, in what appeared to be a heated discussion with none other than Herbert, my father's dreaded attendant. My sister's cheeks were flushed; she looked angry. For his part, Herbert looked pleased with himself. He had a smile on his face, as if he'd just done his favorite thing— my father's dirty work—with his enormous belly tucked snugly into his trousers.

"Oh! Clive!" Izzie shot out of her seat. "What on earth are you doing here so early?"

"It's your wedding day." I smiled at her. "I thought we might have a word." I turned to Herbert, the smile sliding from my face. "In private, of course. No pests allowed."

"Ha, Your Highness, your sense of humor improves with age." Herbert bowed to us. "I've got what I need, anyway. You two enjoy yourselves. Many blessings, Princess Isabelle. I hope you have a wonderful day."

"I'm sure," she sniffed as the steward's stubby little legs carried him out the door.

"Why is he here at the crack of dawn?" I dropped into an overstuffed chair without being asked to sit.

"Why are *you* here?" Izzie asked me coldly. "It's my wedding day—I'd appreciate the chance to relax so that I don't show up at the ceremony frazzled!"

"Herbert's rather frazzling, I think." I put my feet up on the nearby ottoman, a clear indication that I wasn't going anywhere soon. "So why was the little tick here, anyway? You might as well tell me the truth. George is making you an honest woman this afternoon. No time like the present to start living up to that, I daresay."

Izzie's nostrils flared. "I disagree with Herbert—your sense of humor has not improved one iota. But if you must know, Father wanted to check on some last-minute things for the wedding. So he sent Herbert."

"As he does." I grinned and sat back a little.

"What do you want, Clive?" The redness in her cheeks had subsided a little, but her scowl was intact. "Don't you have an American to go feel up or something?"

"Ah, I love it when you don't bother to be classy. It must be exhausting, being so perfect all the time." I waited until she was fidgeting to say, "I want to know why it is you would turn on mother so easily. What's the angle, Iz? What's the benefit to you?"

She straightened her shoulders. "Who says there's a benefit?"

"I do. You don't do anything without a benefit."

"I beg your pardon." She pouted for a second. "Is it *so* difficult for you to believe that I honestly think Mother would be better off somewhere else? Away from Father? Because I honestly think she *would* be. She can't handle it here. She hasn't been able to handle it for years. Why wait until something terrible happens?"

Izzie hopped up and poured herself a coffee, decidedly not offering me one. "It's already happening. She's already drunk every night by six. It's only going to get worse over time. She doesn't want to live like this—so why should we force her to? I see it as a kindness. You might be on your high horse, but you're not here most of the time. You're off digging ditches in the settlements while the rest of us have to live with each other. Then you swoop in and act like the hero, here to save mom from the rest of us."

"That's a pretty speech." Still, it stung. My sister wasn't one-hundred percent wrong. "I understand what you're saying, Iz. I *am* gone most of the time. I can't stand to be here—I feel like I'm a rat in a cage."

"We're all in the same cage. It's rather nice, all things considered."

I sighed. "Some of us are better at it than others. But Mom…mom doesn't deserve to be run off like this. You humiliated her last night. I want to know why. I can't imagine what's so pressing that this has to happen at the same time as your wedding. Is this really what you want?"

She hesitated for just one second, but I saw it. "What's he got over you, huh?"

Izzie groaned. "Nothing—my reputation is spotless, as you know."

"Then *why*? Why are you letting him strong-arm you into this? I can't imagine that you want bloody Herbert in here at the crack of dawn on your wedding day, buzzing about. Tell me what it is."

My sister opened her mouth and then closed it.

"If I have to go find Herbert and beat it out of him, I will." I climbed out of my seat. "It's been a long time coming."

"Stop…just stop." She wrung her hands together. "Father said he'd give me something that I want if I helped him with Mother. He wants to move her out now, you see, because of the wedding. He feels like it'll be such a whirlwind, it won't get as much coverage as it otherwise would. And by the time the dust settles on my honeymoon, he'll already have the annulment in place."

"He can't be serious about that—"

"He's very serious about it," Izzie interrupted, "even though we both know it's a farce. He wants to be able to marry again. In some respects, I don't blame him for that. We're not in a normal position, you see. You can't just haul off and get a divorce if you feel like it, even if you're terribly disappointed."

I waited for her to continue. When she stared into her coffee cup instead, I asked, "So what is it? What is he giving you in exchange for the sacrifice of your wedding? We both know it's not nothing. You've been waiting for this day for forever, and you've always wanted it to be a huge celebration. Moving Mom out in the middle of the night is a much more precarious PR move than my hot American girlfriend and me."

She took a deep breath. "You aren't going to like it."

I laughed. "There was never any chance I was going to like it."

She lifted her chin defiantly. "He said he'd let me develop the series I've wanted to do for years."

"The reality-tv one?" I stared at her, incredulous. How could my sister want *more* attention?

"Yes." She drew herself up to her full height as if daring me to chastise her. "It's going to be like that American television show, the one with all the sisters. It's a lifestyle program. There will be lots of tie-ins and branding opportunities. Mindy Fitz has assured me that it'll be an enormous hit."

Mindy Fitz. An enormous hit. "Why do you want that, Iz? You're already on the cover of every magazine. Not a day goes by that the internet isn't buzzing with a story or a picture of you. Why do you want more? And how is it worth trading your own mother for?"

She narrowed her eyes at me. "I would like to have something of my own, dammit."

"You already have a crown. And a title. And a country."

She frowned. "Well it's easy for you to say, isn't it? You've got the world at your feet. You can come and go as you like, and no matter what, you will someday be king. But not me. And it's just because I was born a woman! I would be one hundred times the ruler that you'll make—no one loves our country and its traditions more than me. But it will never be. It's been yours since the moment you were born—I've always known that. So it's up to me to find my way in the world, to make money from my station, to protect my family. One day my children will stand by and watch their cousins on the fast-track to the throne. But they'll have a legacy of their own because I am fighting for it."

My sister was right. She wanted the crown more than I did. "You could do something else—anything else," I said gently. "Why this?"

She raised her chin. "Because I get to control the message, and because it's going to make me a bloody fortune. And then my children will have an empire all their own."

"Let me get this straight—Dad arranged this deal for you if you cooperated about Mom?"

She nodded once. "I know you think I'm a monster, but he's been planning this all along. It's just been a matter of time. I used the circumstances to my advantage, true. We'll be announcing the show just as soon as the wedding wraps."

"Do you hear yourself? 'As soon as the wedding wraps'—it's your life, not some production!"

"And you have so much room to talk?" Izzie asked me. "Mr. 'Put a Ring on It?'"

"I meant it," I admitted, "although it was a mistake to say it at the press conference. I thought if I stirred up more excitement, it would give me more bargaining power with Father. But I see now that was futile. He's made up his mind."

"I think the most we can do now is make Mother as comfortable with the idea as possible."

"Actually, I had another idea." I smiled at my sister with genuine warmth for the first time in years. "I need to make a few things right. You're correct when you say that it isn't fair—I *have* come and gone as I pleased over the years. It wasn't fair to you, and it wasn't fair to Mother. It wasn't fair to our people either, although in my defense, a lot of the time I spent away was working in the villages. Even so, I've been distant."

I crossed my arms against my chest. "I also agree it isn't equitable that I'll rule because I'm a man. Maybe we can do something, Iz. Maybe we can make some changes together."

She gaped at me.

"But I'm going to need to know—are you a team player? Because I'm looking to add to my roster."

∽

IT TOOK LONGER with my sister than I'd anticipated, but then again, we had a lot of ground to cover. I didn't share the details about Tarryn's past with her—I needed to talk to Tarryn before I shared her secrets.

And yet, when I'd left her, it had seemed like we'd both agreed it had to be over between us.

I'd felt like ending things was the only path for us. But as I left Izzie's suite, I found myself thinking, When had I become such a fucking coward?

It came down to how much she would risk—how much I could *ask* her to risk. It was easy for me: I was a man, a prince. I would never be judged as harshly as she would, even if the truth came out about her background.

But there might be a few things that I could do to secure her future.

There were several openings on my roster. It was time to see who was willing to play for a new team.

TARRYN

I PACED MY ROOM, my heart in my throat. What was I going to do? If I told Clive about the King, what would happen? I wouldn't put it past the King to expose me even at the expense of his son. If he was willing to solicit me as his mistress, he was capable of anything.

I longed to call my mother to see if everything was still okay, but it was the middle of the night back in the states. I went and stared out the window as the sun crested the horizon. I'd forgotten: it was Princess Isabelle's wedding day. Her wedding was the whole reason I'd come to Astos, and yet, I'd forgotten all about it. I thought of the pale lavender dress I'd be wearing. It seemed like a million years ago that I'd held it up against myself at the agency, in awe of its elegance…

One thing was for sure. No matter what—no matter

how gross the King was, no matter that fucking Robbie had come back like a zombie, no matter that my mother and Ellie were ensconced at the Four Seasons, watched over by security guards—I was going to this wedding. I would stand by the prince's side, smile for the cameras, and finish the assignment. It was the least I could do.

Still, I wished there was some way to be better than that. To do better than *the least*.

What about fucking *triumph*? What about kicking some ass, huh?

It was a truth rarely acknowledged that people—women, especially—on the lower rungs of society rarely thought about such things as triumph and kicking ass. We thought about scraping by. We thought about feeding our families. What would it be like to have a mindset like the King's? He acted as though the world was his for the taking, and so it was. He wasn't being held back by fears about what was right or wrong. He was doing exactly what he wanted, everyone and everything else be damned. And here I was, running scared—which was precisely what he wanted.

But who was I to fight the King? What could I do?

I watched the sun as it rose, and the inkling of an idea came to me.

People wanted things from me. That gave me power.

Not as much as the King's, but it was something. It was a start.

I hustled into the shower, the beginning of an idea itching at me.

∼

"Tarryn?" Clive called from the room as I finished drying my hair.

My heart leaped into my throat, but I tried to calm down. "I'll be out in one minute." Things might not ever be the same between us—they might never be what I wanted—but I could still give him my best. I could fight for him.

I swiped on some lip gloss, took a deep breath, and went out to meet him.

Clive looked handsome as ever, somehow even more so because of the deep lines etched into his face. He'd changed into a blue suit, which surprised me at this hour. I wanted to blurt out what had happened with his father and what I thought we might do about it, but I should probably say 'hi' first.

"Hi." I didn't go to him, even though it hurt to keep my distance. "You left early."

He nodded, then scraped a hand through his hair,

which was still damp around the edges. "I had some business to attend to—I met with the Chief."

My heart immediately started pounding. "Is everything okay—Ellie, my mother?"

"It's fine—they're fine, I promise you." He took a step toward me, then stopped himself. "I made sure of it."

"I feel guilty that I'm not there with them—"

"They're being taken care of. I swear on my life. It's safer for everyone to be doing what they're doing right now. The thing is, the Chief told me something—about Robbie. I don't want you to be upset."

"Okay…" I said, even though at the mention of his name, nothing was okay. "What is it?"

"They've been watching him, and they think he might have left the country."

My mind whirled. If he'd left the country, that meant he couldn't get to my mother and Ellie. That was great news. Except… I gaped at him. "To come *here*?"

"We don't know. I almost hope so, I'll tell you that. He doesn't stand a chance with security. And then I could bash his face in." My face must've twisted because his shoulders slumped. "I'm sorry to say that. It's just… the thought of him makes my blood boil."

"That's okay." I was happy Clive wanted to beat him up. Still, I was reeling from the news. Robbie might be coming for me after all these years. You had to give it to him: he had some fucking nerve.

"The wedding's today. It's almost over, Tarryn." Clive's voice was soft.

My heart twisted. What if I didn't want it to be over?

I put on a brave face, nodding. "I know. And no matter what happens, I won't disappoint you."

He gave me a long look. "Since when have you ever disappointed me?"

"Yeah, well. There's just a lot going on." I twisted my hands together.

"None of it's your fault." His voice was firm, final.

"Listen, I had an idea—"

"I've been thinking—" Clive said at the same time.

"Ha. Go ahead—you first." I wasn't eager to tell him about the King's inappropriate behavior. Hadn't we already reached the asshole quota for the week?

Clive took a deep breath. "Like I said, I've been thinking. A lot. About my mother, about a lot of things. I'm sad to say, I'm partly responsible for what's happened to her. I haven't been here to protect her and to keep my father in line. That ends now. Things are going to be changing around here."

I took a deep breath. "About keeping your father in line... I have something to tell you. But I don't want to."

His hands clenched into fists. "What is it?"

I felt sick as the memories from this morning washed over me. "First, you have to promise me something. You have to swear."

"What did he do?"

I raised my right hand. "Swear it, Clive. Otherwise, I can't tell you."

"What am I swearing to?" he bit out.

"That you won't do anything—say anything, hit anyone—unless I expressly give you permission."

The muscle in his jaw bulged. "I am going to kill that fu—"

"Clive." I went full-on Mom voice on him. "Swear it."

He reluctantly raised his right hand. "I swear." His voice was gruff.

"Your father came here this morning. He knows about me."

He looked visibly startled. "How…?"

"Legal. I met an attorney when I first came here, and she had me sign some documents. She told him everything. He's known all along." Clive cursed, and I continued, "He also knows about Ellie. And Robbie—all of it. He wants something in exchange for keeping my secrets. Otherwise, he said he'd expose me."

Clive shook his head, a confused expression on his face.

"He wants to make me his mistress."

Clive opened his mouth and then closed it. Then he started for the door.

"Clive, no." I threw myself in front of it, barring his exit.

He didn't look at me—he looked at the floor as his shoulders rose and fell. He was taking deep, heaving breaths. "Get out of my way."

"Remember you swore?" My voice was pleading. "I made you do that for a reason. This is the reason, Clive. No patricide allowed." I'd learned the word patricide while studying Shakespeare in the twelfth grade. Who knew it would come in so handy?

Clive turned his face toward mine. It had gone white, save for two red blotches on his cheeks. "Of course I'm going to kill that fucker! Did he come here to ask you to *sleep* with him? Behind my bloody back? Well, Christ, it's not like he'd do it in front of my face!"

I nodded. "But you still can't kill him. There's got to be another way. He told me what he wants—he wants you to know that he's the one in charge, that he's got all the power."

The string of expletives that issued from Clive's mouth would have been impressive under different circumstances.

"Listen, that's what I was thinking…what if we show him he's wrong? You're the prince. That's not for nothing. And I'm..." I cleared my throat. "It occurs to me that I'm not for nothing, either. He can't get away with this. Acting like you're a child, that I'm just a pawn because I'm an escort, and that your mother's not worthy of her title because she doesn't act the way he wants—it's not fair. He's *bad*. He shouldn't get away with it."

Looking a fraction less pissed, Clive raised his eyebrows. "You're right."

I nodded. "I know."

"So, what were you thinking?" he asked. "You said you had an idea."

I swallowed hard, my courage faltering. I did have an idea, but it was risky, so risky... "What was yours? You said you had one, too."

Clive held out his hands toward me. "I do. But it's asking a lot. I'm asking a lot."

I nodded. I was willing to give it to him. Him and only him.

I took his hands. "Okay..."

∽

I NERVOUSLY ADJUSTED my dress for the seventh time. I should call my mother before I did this, but it wasn't even four a.m. in Boston. She should get some rest while she could.

"You look great," Clive said for the seventh time. "Don't be nervous." But that was a dumb thing to say, wasn't it?

The executive came out again with another clipboard. "I spoke with the owner of the agency. She's asking for the business to be mentioned by name. She said it would be great for business. So if you're comfortable with that, can you sign here? That was I have proof that this was discussed with you, and she can't come back and accuse me of forgetting it."

Clive looked at me. "Tarryn?"

I sighed. In for a penny, in for a pound.

I skimmed the paper and then signed it. Clive scrawled his initials next to mine.

"She'll see you, now." The executive motioned for us to follow him through the double doors to the conference room. They set it up with microphones, ring lights, and pale-cream chairs in front of a gray wall adorned with neutral-toned modern art. The background was tasteful, perfect for the event.

Heels clacked in behind us, and a cloud of perfume billowed into the room. My eyes immediately watered. "Hi, Mindy."

She clapped her hands together. "Hiya yourself! I knew it all along, Tarryn! You were going to do great things—Astos will never be the same!"

"I guess you could say that."

Mindy Fitz laughed her honking laugh. "God love you. You're just as down-to-earth as ever! I'll be able to say I knew you when. Lending me your magazine! Ah, you helped me then, you're helping me now." She waggled her eyebrows at Clive. "And you, Your Highness. Can I tell you what a pleasure this is? In my business, we don't often get an opportunity to do something like this."

"Like what, Ms. Fitz?"

"The right thing." Her bright-pink mouth broke into a huge grin. "If Americans love anything, it's the good guy winning. Amiright?"

CLIVE

I CHECKED MY WATCH. The timing had to be perfect. First the wedding, then the delivery, then the special. Then by all means, all hell could go ahead and break loose.

I still didn't know what was going to happen with me. With us. If I'd learned anything this past week, it was that I couldn't control everything. Not my feelings. Not Tarryn's feelings. Still, I wished she'd tell me what she wanted after all the drama finally died down…

But she and Vivian were getting ready for the wedding, and Cliff and I were waiting like two sad pups yearning for their humans to take them for a walk.

My cousin and I stood on the terrace outside the palace, waiting for our dates. The weather was perfect for Isabelle and George's wedding; the gods were indeed shining down on them. My sister had promised to help me. Maybe that's why I was suddenly feeling sentimental about her wedding.

"You're a wreck," Cliff teased.

"And you're one handsome ginger," I teased back. "Did you really convince Vivian to stay on?"

"I did." He grinned at me. "Did you really scare Tarryn off?"

"Probably. Maybe. We'll see."

He arched a reddish eyebrow. "So you're saying there's a chance?"

I shrugged. "I dunno, Cliffie. Women are a mystery, aren't they?"

"They sure are."

We watched the limos coming and going, bringing guests staying at the palace over to the wedding venue. Everyone was dressed in their best—tuxedos for the men, gowns, and fascinators, those strange little hats broken out for such events, for the ladies.

"Is your mother going to make it to the ceremony?" Cliff asked.

I nodded. "She's going after my father departs, just to make things simple."

Now my cousin raised both his eyebrows. "Simple, eh? That's not how I would describe any of this. I've got to hand it to you, mate. You're putting up a rather nice fight."

I cracked my knuckles. "Just wait."

"Hoo boy."

"I mean, I don't know if I'll get to actually *hit* anyone, but a man can dream, can't he?"

"What? Er, sure. But I wasn't hoo-boy-ing about you and your ugly knuckles. I was talking about the ladies!"

"What? Where?" But as I turned and saw them, my heart stopped. Tarryn looked absofuckinglutely gorgeous. She wore a floor-length lavender gown. She'd pulled her hair back into a low, elegant chignon. Her fascinator was small, modern, and as good as a bloody fascinator could be. *She looks like a princess,* I thought.

"She looks like a Duchess," Cliff said.

I glanced at my cousin. He was staring at Vivian like she was the only woman in the world, the most beautiful woman on earth. Old Cliffie wasn't waiting for an answer, for a sign. He was going for it.

The ginger was, of all things, giving me courage. "Thank you, Cliff."

"For what?" he asked absently. He couldn't stop staring at his hot new American girlfriend.

"For everything. Ah, here they are."

I bowed to Tarryn when she reached me. "My Lady. You always look stunning, but tonight especially so."

"Thank you, Your Highness. You're looking dashing,

as well." She curtsied to me, and when she rose, she smiled.

It made my heart stop.

I held out my hand to her, vowing to not let her go all night. Or maybe longer…

The four of us made our way to the waiting Town Car. To my surprise, Stellan hopped out to open the door for us. "Aren't you coming to the wedding?"

He motioned to his tux. "I'm meeting Mindy there. But I didn't want to leave my favorite passengers behind. It just wouldn't be the same." We climbed inside, and I put my hand on Tarryn's thigh. Vivian and Cliff sat next to us, laughing about something. Stellan put the car in drive and, flanked by security vehicles, we headed to the wedding.

Something felt funny inside my chest. Despite all the crap that had happened over the past few days, I felt…happy.

"Tarryn, I have to tell you something."

She immediately looked panicked. "What happened? Was it my mother? I still couldn't get in touch with her—"

"No, shh, it's okay." I reached for her hand and squeezed it. "I didn't mean to alarm you. It's nothing like that."

"Phew, because really, it's been that kind of day. Or

week." She sighed in relief. "So if it's nothing bad, I'm all ears."

"It's just..." I glanced around the car, which had gone quiet. Were they all bloody eavesdropping? I tugged at the collar of my tuxedo. "I'll tell you later."

"Okay." She looked out the window while Vivian and Cliff started whispering to each other again, and Stellan turned on the scanner. The Chief was reporting that although there was a vast crowd of onlookers, everything was peaceful and security was confident that there were no issues.

Tarryn kept looking out the window. "It makes me feel sad, you know? I really haven't seen much of the city."

I nodded. "I'll need to give you a proper tour at some point."

She glanced back over her shoulder. There was a somber look in her eyes. "That would be lovely." She sounded as though she didn't believe it was ever going to happen.

My heart was in my throat. *Steady, mate.* We were almost there.

The Town Car snaked through the traffic. As we got closer to the chapel, the crowds increased. Thousands of Izzie's loyal followers had lined the streets to cheer her on.

"We should wave to them." I rolled down my window. "Cliff, Vivian, is that all right with you?"

Vivian grinned at me from beneath her navy fascinator. "I'd love it!"

"Then here we go, darling," Cliff cooed as he opened the window. "Let's give them a smile!"

Tarryn got into the spirit of things, waving and smiling at everyone we passed. People yelped with excitement when they saw us; one little girl jumped up and down, pointing at her favorite blond American. "Aw, she's so cute." Tarryn grinned and waved.

The Town Car snaked through the traffic, but we'd caught up to the entourage. My father would arrive first —there would be a massive buzz of speculation about the Queen, of course. Little did my father know that my mother was dressed in her finest and would arrive at the ceremony only moments before my sister.

I continued to smile and wave at the people lining the streets. They tossed flowers at our car. There were too many smiles to count, and my heart warmed at the public outpouring for my sister. This was her triumph.

The car slowed more, coming to a rolling stop.

That was when I saw him.

A flash of a dark buzz cut was the first thing that caught my eye—but then it was the angry glare, so out of place with the other expressions, that had me staring.

He turned and was gone before I could be sure. But I knew it in my gut.

Robbie was here.

Tarryn was still smiling and waving. "I'm getting a bit hot," I said quickly, "can we put the windows up for a minute? Don't want to be sweating on arrival."

Our windows were bulletproof. Still, if we weren't two minutes from the venue and surrounded by cars on both sides, I'd forced Stellan to turn around. My mind raced as I grabbed my phone.

I just saw Robbie on the corner of Gennata, I texted the Chief. *In the crowd—we r 2 minutes out.*

Tarryn didn't look at my phone; she was too busy staring at my face. "What's wrong?" That little line was back in between her eyes.

"Nothing." I would tell her as soon as I could, but I didn't want her to panic.

Stellan's scanner started squawking. "Team A-4, Team A-4. Possible person of interest reported near the intersection of Gennata and Main. Team A-4, please report to the Chief."

"What's going on?" Tarryn asked.

"Is everything all right?" Vivian turned to Cliff.

"It's probably just someone who's had a bit too much liquor, camped out here in the sun all morning," he said. "Not to worry—that's why we have security. Did you know that Astos has the lowest crime rate in Europe for the past eleven years straight? We pride ourselves on that."

Vivian nodded, but Tarryn still looked troubled.

I took her hand and gripped it in mine.

She didn't say anything, but her posture spoke volumes. It was rigid. *She knows.*

We reached the chapel, and Stellan pulled into the queue. The crowd was larger here, swelling to thousands. They had erected shrines on the sidewalk. There were hundreds of flowers, posters featuring the happy couple, and candles burning.

Barracks separated the ceremony from the spectators. Astos police and royal security were in full force, standing between the public and the wedding guests. The Chief himself was out there, dressed in a dark suit, a walkie-talkie gripped in his hand.

Vivian took a deep breath and peered out at the crowd. "I can't believe we're here. This is amazing! I can feel the love."

"Me too." Cliff put his arm around her and pulled her close.

I leaned closer to Tarryn. "We'll get out on the left-hand side, away from the crowd. Let me go first—I'll tell you when to come out."

For a moment, her eyes shone with tears. But then she took a deep breath and nodded.

"Your Highness—we're next." Stellan turned to me. "I'll see you inside?"

"See you inside."

He parked the car, and our door was opened by a security guard, who ducked his head down to speak to us. "Everything looks fine. One at a time, please. I'll deposit you in the press queue for photos." He held out his hand, and Vivian accepted it. She turned around and winked at Tarryn. "See you out there, T."

Tarryn forced a smile back. "See you—you look perfect, Viv."

The guard escorted Vivian out, the Duke close on her heels. I was next. I took a deep breath and rechecked my phone: no update from the Chief. *Steady, mate.*

"Tarryn?"

She'd gone pale, her eyes wide.

"I'm not going to let anything happen to you. You have my word. You're safe."

She nodded. "T-Thank you."

The guard appeared at the door again. "Your Highness?"

"I'm ready." I squeezed her hand one last time and left the cool interior of the SUV for the bright, disorienting outdoors. The sun momentarily blinded me. The spectators cheered and chanted; the press was taking pictures and filming; it seemed my name was being called from a hundred different directions. Cliff and Vivian were beside me, smiling and waving at the crowd.

It was so much louder than I'd expected. So much more confusing. I blinked out at the spectators: how the bloody hell was I supposed to find Robbie in a mob of thousands?

"Ms. Clayton." The guard bowed as he deposited Tarryn at my side. For a moment, she looked exactly as I'd felt—disoriented and frightened.

But then the crowd began chanting her name, and she straightened her shoulders, a determined look briefly settling over her features before she flashed a dazzling smile. She waved at the crowd, and they went wild.

I took her hand in mine. That was when I saw it: the streak of a buzz cut, an angry face in the crowd.

Everything happened at once. The Chief shouted something, then hurtled toward the spectators. Robbie hurdled over the barriers—a pistol raised in his hand. I shoved Tarryn into the security guard's arms and took off running.

I didn't even realize I was screaming until I heard

myself: "DON'T SHOOT HIM. DON'T SHOOT THAT FUCKER UNTIL I GET MY HANDS ON HIM!"

Robbie leveled the gun at me, and I don't know what the fuck I was thinking, except that I was so *mad* as I launched myself at him. His expression was shocked, almost comical, his mouth forming a little round "o" as I flew through the air and tackled him.

The crowd screamed as we landed in a heap. Robbie's gun skittered out of his grasp as I pummeled his face with my fists. God, it felt good. "You like to hit women, huh? You sorry *fuck*? Does that make you a big man, you fucking coward?" His face was getting mushy beneath my blows, A-fucking-right, but then the Chief and three other guards pulled me off him—

"Let me go! I'm just getting started!" I struggled against them as Robbie covered himself, writhing on the ground.

"Is that him?" A female voice shrieked behind me. "Is that the fucker who hit Tarryn? Let me at him!"

Vivian barreled past us in a streak of navy satin and kicked Robbie in the stomach. Then she jammed her high heel into his thigh, digging in it like a dagger. *Ouch.*

"You piece of shit!" she screamed. "No one hurts my best friend and gets away with it!"

"Okay, okay." Chief Phillip pulled her off, and she looked as though she would go after him next. "We've got him, Ms. Park. He's going to be punished. I can promise you that."

Sirens wailed in the distance, and the Chief looked at me and sighed. "Go to the wedding. This show *has* to go on—I can't handle a crowd like this again. I'm ready to retire."

"No problem." I straightened my jacket and held my hand out for Vivian. "My Lady?"

She accepted it, but not before she gave Robbie the evil eye once more. "You ever come near her again, my spiked heel's going to hit a lot worse than your thigh. Got it?"

Robbie squinted at us through swelling eyes; that seemed to be answer enough.

We hustled back to Tarryn and Cliff as the press went wild with questions. Guests from inside the church came back out to see what the hell was going on.

"Are you all right?" Tarryn rushed us.

"Yes." I scrubbed a hand across my face. "No."

"Are you hurt?"

"Not exactly. But it's been freaking killing me, Tarryn." I put my hand over my heart. "I *love* you. I haven't told you that I freaking *love* you."

She threw herself against my chest. "I freaking love you, too."

And the crowd went wild.

TARRYN

Understandably, the press was going bananas. They were closer to the chapel and had missed most of the action.

"Your Highness, what happened?"

"Who on earth was that?"

"Was there a gun? Someone said there was a gun!"

"Are you all right, Your Highness?"

"Is the wedding still on?"

Clive turned to face them. He looked remarkably unscathed and handsome after such a fight. "Everything is fine—and of course, the wedding is still on. You think a minor altercation will keep my sister the Princess from marrying her dear George?"

He grinned at them, and they went berserk.

The King came out of the chapel, a confused expression on his face. He looked from the press, who were going mad asking the prince questions, to Clive, who was answering them calmly and smiling.

The King came even with us. "What's going on? I heard there was some sort of security breach—"

"Everything's fine, Father." Clive's grin remained intact. "In fact, everything's perfect. Izzie's wedding is going to be the event of the century."

A limousine pulled up, and Clive turned toward it. "Ah, here we are."

Security opened the door, and the Duchess of Idrid climbed out, resplendent in a pale-yellow gown. She waited, smiling and waving to both the crowd and the press, as her companion climbed out.

The Queen Mother was radiant in her mint-colored gown, a large, feathered fascinator adorning her head. She gave her husband a long, hard look and then turned and waved to the crowd. They went wild.

"Your Highness—Your Highness!" Mina Mays from the Daily Chat wailed. "We thought you'd taken ill? Are you better?"

The Queen glanced over her shoulder. "Much better, thank you. I believe I'm quite cured."

A thundercloud descended over the King's face. He stared in shock as Clive offered one arm to his mother, one arm to me—and we swept past him without a word.

"Was there some sort of altercation?" the Queen asked her son. "My driver mentioned something about a person of interest."

"He's not particularly interesting, and it's handled." Clive pulled me closer as he said, "The man will be going to prison. Brandishing a handgun at a public event with the intent to do harm is punished by a lifetime sentence under Astos law. We have all the evidence we need against him. He won't be bothering anyone ever again."

The world spun for a moment. I stopped walking. "Really?"

"Really." Clive's voice was gentle but assured.

"Well good riddance to bad rubbish," the Queen said. "No one should have to fear for their safety at a happy event like this—or ever!"

I blinked at the Queen, then at Clive. And then I almost burst into tears—but that would be a waste of high-end mascara! Robbie was *so* not worth it.

Reporters were elbowing each other out of the way to photograph us when the crowd erupted in cheers. "The Princess is here! It's Izzie, Princess Izzie!"

We stopped in time to see the Princess arrive. She climbed down from her carriage, a vision in a swirl of white tulle. In a surprise twist, she'd worn her hair down, curls cascading over her creamy shoulders. The smile she gave her fans was breathtaking.

"Doesn't your sister look beautiful?" The Queen's eyes filled with tears. "She was born for this moment."

Princess Isabelle waved enthusiastically to the crowd, accepting the outpouring of love and emotion with evident gratitude. It meant something to her that her people had come to celebrate and wish her well. She blew them kisses. George emerged from the chapel. He looked very handsome in his ceremonial uniform. He reached her side and took her hand, then they raised their hands together in a show of unity.

The crowd went wild. Some of the spectators had tears streaming down their faces.

"It's quite moving, isn't it?" The Queen fanned her face. "Thank you for helping me be here, son."

Clive grinned at his mother. "I wouldn't have it any other way."

With that, we headed inside, to the wedding of the century.

MINDY FITZ and Stellan were slow-dancing most inappropriately. His tall body loomed over hers, hands roaming down her backside, as she rested her face against his broad chest. Both of them were smiling.

"I'm not doing it," I told Clive again. "*You* interrupt them! He's your driver."

Clive clutched his bourbon. "And he's got his hands all over your friend's American arse!"

I sighed, and then I decided to be manipulative. I batted my eyelashes at Clive and stuck my chest out. "Please?" I begged. "I'll rally and stay awake long enough to…you know…after the reception if you interrupt them. But we need to get going! It's been a long day!" I yawned for effect.

"Bloody hell—like I'm going to say no to that. Hold my bourbon." He handed me his glass and marched onto the dance floor.

I laughed as he hesitated, trying to find a time to tap Stellan on the shoulder while he was so occupied grabbing Mindy's ass.

"What're you laughing at?" A familiar, cold voice suddenly asked me.

I turned to find the King standing close. His face was pinched and angry. I'd kept an eye on him—during the ceremony, he seemed unsettled that his wife was in attendance. She'd gone home early to rest, avoiding him at the reception. He must've heard about what happened with Robbie at some point because I overheard him questioning a guard about it.

At dinner, he seemed baffled that Mindy and Stellan had chosen to sit at our table, completely blowing him off. Izzie and George had been mixing with the other guests all night; I hadn't seen the Princess speak with her father once.

Now he just looked angry and more than a little drunk. "I asked you a question."

I stared straight ahead. "I know you did—I just chose not to answer it."

"How dare you," he seethed, "speak to your King in that tone of voice?"

"You are not *my* King." I allowed myself the pleasure of a small smile. "I'm American, remember? We vote for our leaders. And I most certainly did not vote for you."

"I'll tell the whole world that you're a whore." His voice was low, but it was shaking. "We had a deal, Ms. Clayton."

"I never agreed to your deal." I raised my chin. "And as for me being a whore, what do you know about someone like me? Someone who wasn't born into a position of power and privilege? All you know is your own gratification, which has gotten twisted from no one ever saying no to you. But I am saying no. No, we don't have a deal. You want to tell the world I'm a whore? You go right ahead."

Clive had finally extricated Mindy and Stellan from the dance floor. I went and joined them without giving the King a backward glance.

Clive's expression was fiery. "What did he say?"

"Nothing important." I linked my arm through his. "And no, you can't hit him yet."

◈

I TOOK A DEEP BREATH. I couldn't believe I was about to do this, but I was about to do this. I quickly crossed myself. *Dear God,* I prayed, *please let Ellie understand this someday. Please let her forgive me for the choices I've made.*

I'd done it out of love. Which was precisely the reason I was doing this, now.

If I didn't tell my story, in my own words, someone else would. I decided to be brave.

"Good evening, everyone! This is a special edition of Entertainment Hour coming to you live from Astos." The attractive reporter grinned at the camera—and she should be smiling; it was the scoop of a lifetime. "I'm Mina Mays, reporter for the Daily Chat, with an exclusive interview with Prince Clive of Astos and his girlfriend, American Tarryn Clayton. Welcome, Prince Clive and Ms. Clayton!"

Clive gripped my hand, and we stepped into the conference room, which was the same place we'd taped the earlier interview.

"Good evening, Your Highness. How was the wedding?" Mina Mays asked.

"Perfect." Clive still looked impossibly pulled together and handsome after a fight and such a long day. He smiled at Mina; he smiled at the camera crew; we were all putty in his big, strong hands. "It was everything that my sister and George could have hoped for and more. I hope everyone will join us in wishing them every happiness."

"Of course, of course—it was an honor to have been there," Mina Mays gushed, "I will never forget seeing Princess Isabelle in her wedding gown! Such a gorgeous bride."

She smiled at turned to me. "You've had quite a day, haven't you?"

"Ha. Yes, I have." I nodded, trying to calm my nerves. A royal wedding, Robbie's ambush, and a television appearance all in the same day—*oh my*. "I've never been to such a beautiful wedding. The Princess was the most gorgeous bride in the whole world."

"Absolutely. Well, thank you for being here. I'm

incredibly grateful to both of you—thank you for sharing your story. With that," Mina turned back to the cameras, "we have a special program for you this evening. What you're about to see is an interview that Prince Clive and Tarryn Clayton taped earlier today. In it, they talk candidly about their relationship. Ms. Clayton also exclusively shares details about her past, things she's never discussed before. Please be advised that some of what you are about to watch contains details that may be upsetting to some viewers."

Mina Mays positioned herself between us. "After the taped interview, I'll be back live with the prince and Ms. Clayton to discuss the details, the incident at the wedding today, and also, what the future holds. Don't miss a moment of this ground-breaking, exclusive interview!"

The cameras stopped rolling, but it did nothing for my nerves. The segment that we'd taped earlier appeared on a screen in front of us. I crossed myself, thanking God that Boston was in a different time zone and that my mother and Ellie wouldn't be able to watch the program air live.

With the wedding and all the craziness, I still hadn't been able to talk to my mother. Chief Phillip had texted Clive religiously throughout the day, assuring us that Robbie was in custody and that my mother and Ellie were safe with security. You'd think that would help me feel less guilty—but show me a mother without guilt, and I'll introduce you to a llama that can tap dance!

The screen lit up, and I held onto Clive's hand for dear life.

From behind the camera crew, Mindy Fitz gave me a thumbs-up. I smiled at her shakily and then took deep, calming breaths as I watched the screen.

Mindy, Clive, and I sat at the conference room table. "Hello, world!" Mindy said. "My name is Mindy Fitz, and I am the President of Unscripted Programming at World News. My father Herman started the company—and oh boy, is he proud of how it's doing today! If you're wondering, *yes*, it's unusual that the President of Unscripted Programming is doing an interview like this." She let out a honking laugh. "But I happen to be the most qualified person for the job! Let me introduce you to my two great friends, Prince Clive of Astos and Tarryn Clayton of America. Your Highness, Tarryn, thank you so much for being here and for granting World News your exclusive interview."

"It's my pleasure, Mindy." Clive bowed his head.

"Thank you for having us," I added in a shaky voice.

"We're here today because there have been some issues, as I understand it, with the King?"

Clive and I both nodded. Mindy lowered her voice

and asked, "And were these issues directed at you, Tarryn?"

I nodded again.

"Why don't you tell us what happened, in your own words?"

Mindy was really very good at her job.

I cleared my throat. "Well, the thing is... The King found out some information about me. About my past." My face was pale, my eyes enormous in my face. "I didn't meet the prince at a bar on Commonwealth Avenue, you see. I met him through an agency. An agency I...work for."

Mindy nodded and leaned forward. "Tell us more, honey. You're among friends here. What type of agency? What's its name?"

"AccomoDating." Elena had wanted it in the interview. "It's a dating agency. People come to us and are matched. With a date."

"And is there a fee for this service?" Mindy asked, her tone all business.

"Yes," I croaked.

"So the prince went to the agency, looking for a wedding date, and was matched with you. Is that right?"

I nodded. Clive gripped my hand as he said, "It was the luckiest day of my life."

"Aw." Mindy fanned her face. "You're the sweetest,

Your Highness. But you're right—Tarryn is quite the find. I knew it the moment I first met her."

He grinned at Mindy. "Me too."

"This is giving me all the feels!" She laughed her honking laugh. "So let me get this straight, Your Highness—you hired her as your date, and as soon as you met her, there were sparks."

"I'd say so." Clive glanced at me. He seemed almost shy. "At least, for me."

I laughed. "There were definitely sparks for me too."

"Aw, I love it." Mindy's expression turned serious. "But there was a problem, wasn't there, Tarryn? After you got to the palace, you started receiving threatening texts. Someone from your past came back."

I nodded. "My ex-boyfriend. I still don't know how he found my number. Security's still trying to figure that out."

"But I understand he tracked you down and started harassing you. What happened?" Mindy asked.

"At first, he just sent me a picture. But then he called me. He said some terrible things."

"Did he threaten you?" Mindy asked. When I nodded, Mindy said, "Now, this may be hard to talk about. But I think it's important. This man, your ex—why did you leave him? Why did you break up with him in the first place?"

My shoulders rose and fell as I took a deep breath. "He was…abusive. I left him because he… He…"

Clive looked at me, anguish etched onto his face. "You don't have to do this, Tarryn."

I nodded. "Y-Yes, I do. People need to know that this happens. This sort of thing happens every day to people all over the world. People need to know that there's hope. You can get out. You can get help. You don't have to be ashamed and suffer for the rest of your life."

I swallowed. "He…beat me—many times. I had internal bleeding. A shattered collarbone. I lived in fear that he was going to kill me one day. But then, I found out I was pregnant."

I raised my chin. "And I refused to bring a child into that kind of environment. So I left him—I ran away in the middle of the night. I never listed him on my daughter's birth certificate. I lied. I lied, and I hid her from him, and I don't regret it for a single second."

Mindy reached out and gripped my hand. "I think you're courageous for coming here and telling the truth. People must be wondering why, though. Why tell your story now?"

"It wasn't something I was planning on doing," I said, my voice soft. "I didn't ever want to expose my family. But King Wesley found out about my past, and he threatened to go to the press about it if I didn't do what he wanted. He was trying to control me—to control his family. But after what I've been through, I can't accept that kind of treatment. I made a promise to myself that I'd always look out for myself, and for my daughter, after what happened to me."

Mindy squeezed my hand and released it. "I think you're an amazing role model for your daughter, Tarryn."

I glanced up at her, then back down at my lap. "I don't know about that."

"Well, I do."

"I agree with Mindy," Clive said, "you're brave. You Americans are really something, aren't you?"

The tape faded to black, and before I was ready, the cameras were rolling once again. "Well," Mina Mays said, "*that* was really something. I'm so glad you came back tonight to give us an update. Because something happened today at the wedding, didn't it?"

Clive said, "Yes, it did."

Mina looked directly at me. "What happened? Was he there—your ex-boyfriend?"

"Yes. He was in the crowd outside the chapel. Thank goodness for the amazing palace security team and for this hero right here." I patted Clive's big shoulder. "He saw him in the crowd and threw himself on him. He knocked the gun out of his hand. He saved us—he saved *me*."

"Do you hear that, Your Highness? You're a hero." Mina beamed at him.

"Tarryn's *my* hero," Clive said easily. "And I have a surprise for her."

"You—you do?" I asked.

"Yes." He gripped my hands in his. "I wanted to announce a new global initiative we're spearheading with the help of World News. It's a charitable outreach foundation to help domestic abuse survivors. World News has committed a *billion* dollars to it, Tarryn. And my family is matching that contribution."

I gaped at him.

He grinned at me.

"That's a wrap," Mindy called.

∼

"I HAVE another surprise for you," he said once we got back to the palace.

My heart-rate kicked up again. What could it be? I followed him and his big shoulders down the hallway toward my room. But instead, he stopped at the door next to mine. Two guards waited outside. "I want to show you something."

With a nod to the guards, he slowly and quietly opened the door. The room inside was dim—whoever was in there was sleeping. Clive grabbed my hand and we took two steps closer. I peered at the bed.

On it were my mother and Ellie, both in a deep sleep.

"We had them flown in as soon as possible, but of course they're exhausted," he said softly. "Your mother agreed to us looking in on them—otherwise I wouldn't have snuck you in here."

I gripped his hand fiercely.

My mom was on her back, her chest rising and falling peacefully. As usual, Ellie was on her side, blonde curls tumbling over the pillow. The little line in between her eyes creased her forehead even in sleep.

I promptly burst into tears.

CLIVE

ONE YEAR LATER

ALL IN ALL, things had worked out better than I'd ever expected.

Tarryn had decided to stay on in Astos. Her mother and Ellie now lived at the palace.

Robbie was in prison for the rest of his life. We never gave him a second thought.

Chief Philip had retired. To his chateau on the coast, which I'd promptly bought him as a retirement gift.

After the wedding and our news special, things changed at the palace. My father was no longer the one who was sought-after by the press and gratified by the staff.

It was me. And Tarryn. And my mother and sister, because I told everyone that was how it was going to be. And so it was.

My father was disgraced when my mother openly admitted—in an exclusive interview with Mindy Fitz—that she'd suffered from depression for years and was checking herself into rehabilitation for alcohol addiction. She also revealed that she would promptly be divorcing my father because he was, in her words, "an insensitive prat."

As soon as she was feeling better, she moved back into the palace. The Queen began wearing pants. She'd made friends with Tarryn's mother, who was reportedly teaching her how to cook. She took long walks with the Duchess of Idrid every day and even sometimes ventured outside the palace grounds to lunch with Izzie. All in all, her life had improved vastly since she kicked the King to the curb.

The same could not be said for His Highness. Izzie had decided to take matters into her own hands. She gave an exclusive interview to Mindy Fitz—that aired during prime time, over the course of four evenings—in which she detailed her father's controlling behavior over the years. She talked of how she often felt like a prisoner at the palace and how he rewarded her for good behavior and punished her for being "bad," even once she was a grown woman.

King Wesley and Herbert now lived in a small

section of the palace, most likely plotting their revenge against us. But no one seemed to ever listen to them, so I wasn't too worried…

My father was still the King, but I realized something: people didn't like him very much. So when I stayed on at the palace and started involving myself in the day-to-day operations, our staff was relieved.

I hadn't punched my father out. I didn't need to. Actually, every time I saw him I felt a little bit *sorry* for him. Only Herbert remained loyal to him. I realized that was punishment enough!

It surprised me that I realized, over time, I *liked* the work of running the country. It was different from visiting the villages, which we still did regularly. But it was interesting, and I found that I could help our citizens by doing a good job. I found it quite rewarding.

Izzie and I had decided to split the sovereign duties equally. We had *also* decided that wouldn't change once my father passed, and I inherited his title. We were still working out the legalities of it all—with our brand new legal team—but they assured us that we would be able to pass our respective wealth down equally among all our heirs.

Izzie had decided she didn't want the reality-television show, after all. Mindy Fitz often sent her to

America to guest-anchor the popular morning show *Good Morning Daily*. Izzie's celebrity had earned her lucrative endorsement deals, and she and George were pregnant with their first child and *deliriously* happy. Old George had proven to be reliable, constant, and loyal, precisely what my sister needed.

I did believe they were going to end up living happily ever after.

In other breaking news, The Duke of Clifton had proposed to Ms. Vivian Park, his long-time American girlfriend, and they were getting married that summer.

Mindy Fitz and Stellan were *also* engaged. Stellan had retired. He and Mindy split their time between her home in America and Astos, where they stayed at the palace as our most welcome guests. They'd invited us to spend a month with them on their yacht that summer.

Chef made us spectacular dinners every night, including *banging* cheeseburgers and twice-baked potatoes with chives whenever we asked.

All in all, life was pretty damn good.

～

"You know what, mate? I'm tired of hearing you gloat."

"I just think that you ought to give some credit where credit is due," Chase Layne said. The American quarterback was quite pleased with himself for introducing me to AccommoDating—and of course, to Tarryn.

"I give you credit." I sat back on the blanket, sun on my face, my cellphone pressed against my ear. "I just don't feel like I need to give it to you every five seconds."

"But the pictures of you two are so *cute*," Chase teased. "Who knew the bad-boy prince could be so *cute*?"

"Shut it, Chase." My words were gruff, but my friend knew me well enough to understand that I didn't mean them harshly. "I'll talk to you later, okay?"

"See you at the ceremony."

"Yes, see you." I was smiling as I hung up.

Chase was going to be one of my attendants.

For my wedding.

To Tarryn.

Speaking of my hot American girlfriend—*fiancé*—she was busy with Ellie and Matthew over at the stable. We'd come for a picnic, but also for a surprise. I was full of surprises these days!

"Matthew—buddy, may I have a word?"

The little boy hustled over to me, his eyes wide. "Is it time?"

"It is. Are you ready?"

He nodded solemnly.

"Is *she* ready?"

He nodded again. "She's wearing the pink bow, just like you asked."

"Excellent, mate." I grinned at him. "I'm going to get you one, too."

"A *bow*?"

"No, a pony." I laughed.

He frowned. "I don't want a pony, Your Highness. I want a *horse*."

"Matthew!" His father hollered.

"Fine, then you shall have a horse." I winked at him. "Would you tell Ellie to come here? And go and get the *you-know-what*?"

Matthew, who played with Ellie almost every day, hollered for the younger girl. "Ellie, your dad wants to see you!"

Tarryn gave me a quick look, and I smiled at her. After the wedding, I was legally adopting Ellie. I was more than happy for her to start calling me Dad because I already loved the little girl so much it almost broke my heart.

Ellie ran over to me, hair flying out behind her. Like her mother, she loved to play outside. Like her mother, we often had to clean the twigs and nettles out of her hair at the end of the day. She threw herself down onto the picnic blanket and sat there, waiting.

"I have a surprise for you."

Her eyes widened.

"Matty's bringing it."

She nodded. Ellie was pretty quiet, except when she told her grandmother about Boo Boo's adventures in the palace or was playing pirates with Matthew. But her mother said that she loved books about horses and ponies, so I'd decided to buy her a pony. Because I was the prince, and I could!

Matthew emerged from the stable towing the little pony, a caramel-colored Shetland wearing a large, pink bow. Ellie jumped to her feet.

"Ellie, this is Toffee," Matthew said solemnly, "your new pony. She's American, too!"

Matthew's father came over and handed Ellie a carrot, instructing her in low tones about feeding the pony and petting her.

Tarryn hustled over to me, that little line evident in between her beautiful blue eyes. "Clive Harrison Wesley Richard Thomas," she said in a scolding voice, "*what* did you do?"

"Daddy bought me a pony, Mommy!" Ellie grinned at her.

Tarryn stopped dead in her tracks and stared at her daughter. And then she promptly burst into tears.

"Mommy?" Ellie ran to her, and Tarryn scooped her up into a hug. She kissed her daughter's hair, her cheeks and hugged her with a fierce intensity.

"Mommy's not sad," Tarryn explained, "Mommy's *happy*. It's so nice that D-Daddy got you Toffee. You've always wanted a pony."

Ellie hugged her mother back. And then, to my surprise, she raced over to me and hugged me, too. Our first hug. "Thank you!" She ran back to Toffee with a massive grin on her face, and then *I* almost burst into tears.

Tarryn sat down next to me, still wiping at her face and sniffling. I threw my arm around her. "Sorry I didn't tell you."

"No, you're not." She sniffled again.

"You're right. I'm not." I grinned at her, my wife-to-be, and then I grinned at Ellie. "We're going to live happily ever after, you know that?"

She leaned against me, then started laughing even though she was crying. "I *do* know that, Your Clive. I sure do."

∼

I HOPE you enjoyed the story! Please sign up for my mailing list at www.leighjamesauthor.com and never miss a new release.

Thank you for reading, love to all of you!

xoxo

Leigh

AFTERWORD

If you or someone you love is struggling with domestic violence, help is available. Here are some resources:

https://www.thehotline.org
https://ncadv.org/resources
https://www.onlinemswprograms.com/resources/supporting-survivors-domestic-violence-resources/

ABOUT THE AUTHOR

Sign up for Leigh's new release notifications at www.leighjamesauthor.com!

USA Today Bestselling author Leigh James is currently sitting on a white-sand beach, sipping a mojito, and dreaming up her next billionaire.

Get ready—he's going to be a hot one!!!

Full disclosure: Leigh is actually freezing her butt off in New Hampshire, driving her kids to baseball practice and going grocery shopping because her three boys eat non-stop. But she promises that billionaire is REALLY going to be something!

Leigh loves to hear from readers! You can reach her at leigh@leighjamesauthor.com.

Thank you for reading. Lots of love to all of you!

www.leighjamesauthor.com

ALSO BY LEIGH JAMES

The Escort Collection

Escorting the Player

Escorting the Billionaire

Escorting the Groom

Escorting the Actress

Escorting the Royal

Midnight Royals

Traded

Chosen

Claimed

Silicon Valley Billionaires

Book 1

Book 2

Book 3

The Liberty Series

My Super-Hot Fake Wedding Date